More advance praise for Kim Michele Richardson
and *Liar's Bench*!

"Century-old lies, murder, and racial injustice propel a feisty teen heroine to dig into the past in this richly imagined Southern gothic tale."—Beth Hoffman, *New York Times* bestselling author of *Saving CeeCee Honeycutt*

"With magical writing and a strong sense of time and place, Kim Michele Richardson introduces us to an engaging and unforgettable protagonist in Muddy Summers. We meet seventeen-year-old Muddy at a moment of tremendous personal loss complicated by unanswered questions. Muddy's courage and passion drive the story and I didn't stop cheering for her until the riveting end." —Diane Chamberlain, USA Today bestselling author of *The Silent Sister*

"You'll hear echoes of *To Kill a Mockingbird* in this haunting coming-of-age story, in which old and more recent tragedies collide. Beautifully written, atmospheric and intricately plotted, Kim Michele Richardson's debut novel will stay with you long after the last page is turned."—Susan Wiggs, *# 1 New York Times* bestselling author

"Mudas Summers, the seventeen-year-old protagonist of Kim Michele Richardson's atmospheric first mystery, grabs your hand and takes you along as she navigates the twists and turns of her life and in the process unearths the dark secrets of Peckinpaw, which have kept the townsfolk chained to their destructive past, dooming them to repeat the same sins over and over. That is, until the headstrong Mudas unleashes her own fury against those who would hurt her and ironically—through yet another act of violence in Peckinpaw's long, brutal history—discovers the truth that will clear her mother's name. In this way, Richardson boldly probes behind the facade of place to unmask the damaged psyches of its inhabitants." —Gwyn Hyman Rubio, author of *Love & Ordinary Creatures* and *Icy Sparks*

Please turn the page for more advance praise!

LIAR'S
BENCH

Kim Michele Richardson

KENSINGTON BOOKS
www.kensingtonbooks.com

KENSINGTON BOOKS are published by

Kensington Publishing Corp.
119 West 40th Street
New York, NY 10018

All Kensington titles, imprints, and distributed lines are available at special quantity discounts for bulk purchases for sales promotion, premiums, fund-raising, educational, or institutional use.

Special book excerpts or customized printings can also be created to fit specific needs. For details, write or phone the office of the Kensington Sales Manager: Kensington Publishing Corp., 119 West 40th Street, New York, NY 10018. Attn. Sales Department. Phone: 1-800-221-2647.

Kensington and the K logo Reg. U.S. Pat. & TM Off.

eISBN-13: 978-1-61773-734-3
eISBN-10: 1-61773-734-8
First Kensington Electronic Edition: May 2015

ISBN-13: 978-1-61773-733-6
ISBN-10: 1-61773-733-X
First Kensington Trade Paperback Printing: May 2015

10 9 8 7 6 5 4 3 2 1

Printed in the United States of America

For Joe,
who anchored a certainty in my words,
and believed they could soar on eagle wings

Acknowledgments

I owe much thanks and love to a generous community of kind helpers and supporters along the way: Alissa, Angie, Linda, Liz, Thomma Lyn, Sheri, and the always supportive purglet gang, and to all those who have given feedback or advice.

Thank you to Vietnam veteran Mike Schellenberger for talking with me about this important war, answering my many questions, and for your service and sacrifice for our country.

I am deeply indebted to very dear friends and writers, G. J. Berger, Alice Loweecey, and Jamie Mason: for reading more times than I can count, for their superb second eyes, and constant commitment to me and this novel over the last six years. *Also, for not taking away my comma key.*

A "Shakin' Your Tree" salute to my old friend Billy Gibbons for great thoughts that begin on an airline cocktail napkin.

A promised mention and thank-you to my wonderfully crazy and talented hairdresser Cathy Nuss for support and the lovely, big hair days.

I am forever grateful to my editor, John Scognamiglio, for missing his subway stop. Thank you for loving this book and for warmly welcoming me into the Kensington family.

Endless gratitude to my very wise and tireless agents, Stacy Testa and Susan Ginsburg, for your hard work, dedication, and for giving *Liar's Bench* the very best seat in the house.

To my forever family: My son, Jeremiah, who gave me Peckinpaw and his take on Southernisms. My daughter, Sierra, for inspiring the always-important theme in this work. My husband and superhero, Joe, for your unfailing love and support. I love you all most dearly.

To you, Cherished Reader, my deepest gratitude for allowing me into your home.

Southern trees bear a strange fruit.

—Abel Meeropol

A Cornerstone

August 1860

When a lie seeps into the very heartwood of a town, soaks the beams and posts that hold it up from the earth, the rot sets to its work. The ruin that cruelty brings is always just a matter of time. And ruin had fully taken hold in August of 1860, when Mrs. Evelyn Anderson, mistress of Hark Hill Plantation of Peckinpaw, Kentucky, reported that she had been poisoned by her house slave, Frannie Crow.

The plantation's overseer had soiled Frannie on the dirt of the kitchen floor in the big house. Bruised and bloodied, Frannie was unable to perform her house chores the next day. When Frannie failed to serve the morning meal, Mrs. Anderson called her into the dining room and demanded an explanation.

Unable to control her tears, Frannie confessed the rape and the loss of two brass buttons during the assault—buttons given as marks of gratitude for twelve years of faithful service.

The mistress immediately sent for the overseer, then ordered him to bring Frannie outside. He gladly dragged Frannie out to the Osage tree, the one that shaded the side yard, bent her over a whiskey barrel, and flogged her until her dress was in shreds and the blood spidered down the length of her legs, pooling at her feet. Then Hark Hill's mistress said to all the Negroes watching, "Since Frannie meant to cheat me out of a day's labor, let it be widely known she has now done it."

Two weeks later, and in delicate condition, Mrs. Anderson summoned Frannie to her bedside complaining of stomach cramps and fretting the safety of her unborn child. Frannie went outside to the old Osage orange tree, picked two of its fruits, and went about making a warm, milky tea concoction for her mistress, a remedy her mammy had taught her.

Just hours later, Mrs. Anderson miscarried. She called to her husband, Bartholomew Anderson. Weeping, she exclaimed, "Frannie poisoned me." Mr. Anderson reported the poisoning to the town marshal, saying, "Our house slave did it. Frannie Crow."

Four days later, a trial was conducted at the courthouse. At the end of Frannie's fifteen-minute trial, the jury of white men found her guilty of poisoning. And, as an addendum, thievery was added to her charges: two brass buttons: value—two cents.

Over the course of the next five days, the good townsfolk of Peckinpaw built a gallows in front of their courthouse. On the sixth day, Town Square filled up with people from as far away as Bowling Green, Lexington, and even Louisville. Many spread quilts on the courthouse grounds, eating picnic lunches and catching up on news and gossip as the children played games of marbles, Graces, and hide-and-seek around the gallows.

At noon, black slave Frannie Crow, Poisoner and Thief, was led up to the gallows, where she was afforded a brief allowance of words.

"Let it be widely known," Frannie said, "since Mistress Anderson meant to cheat me out of my honesty, she has now done it."

The hangman placed a seed sack over Frannie's head and cinched it with rope.

Below, Mrs. Anderson, dressed in a silk taffeta day dress with a matching spoon bonnet and fine kidskin gloves, steadied herself against the gallows post. She watched in silence as the trap door opened and Frannie's body dropped through. The rope jerked tight, snapping her neck. A stain spread quickly across the crotch of her burlap dress. Frannie's body released a final death tremor and then went limp. A faint stench wafted across the crowd.

A parasol's long fringe tassels hid the mistress's expression, just as her string of lies hid the truth.

Frannie's body swayed back and forth. A thin, white, holey sock slipped slowly down and off her foot. The wind kicked up, blowing it away from the gallows just like a page ripped out of history.

Frannie's kin was ordered to dismantle the gallows and store it on Hark Hill Plantation, out in one of the wood sheds near the slaves' quarters. In 1862, Amos Crow, yellow slave and son of Frannie, was given the pieces of his mama's gallows and two healthy hogs, along with his Freedom Papers.

Mr. Anderson instructed Amos to use most of the wood, bolts, and square nails to build a pen for Amos's hogs, but to save the finer pieces of oak and hardware to fashion a bench for Town Square—a gift to the town to commemorate the benevolence of one of their most honorable sons.

The name, "Anderson's Bench," faded with his memory to "Square's Bench." But its legacy of misfortune drawn from lies, false promises, and tall tales earned the name it kept for good—Liar's Bench.

Somewhere, whether in Heaven or Hell or in between, the ghost of Frannie Crow smiled.

1

The Scars of Others

It could've easily been left unnamed, but like most small towns carved out from the back roads of Anywhere, USA, Peckinpaw, Kentucky, had its staple—its Liar's Bench. Used for both the telling of tales and for courting, the bench sat on the curb, nestled between two geranium-filled copper pots positioned in front of a Dolly Parton and Porter Wagoner dream-themed leather goods store: the Parton & Porter. Next door, the scents of peach cobbler and chicken fried steak wafted out from the Top Hat Café and onto the bench. And in western Kentucky, a good cornerstone was the strength of any town, tale, or courtship just as sure as the bench's weathered planks of oak and wrought-iron arms and legs cradling it were the support for its tale spinners and sinners.

Now, you didn't necessarily have to be a liar or a courter to sit on Liar's Bench, just maybe the *better* liar or courter at the time. My daddy, Adam Persis Summers, was a good one. Liar, that is, when he sat on this bench and swore to my mama that he hadn't betrayed her.

But Mama's next husband, Tommy Dale Whitlock, had proved to be the better courter and liar three times over.

On this very bench, he'd promised my mama, Ella Mudas Tilley, that he would always love her—but he cheated. He swore to protect her—but he beat her. He vowed to honor her—but he buried her under six feet of rich Kentucky soil.

Mama only lied once. She promised Tommy she'd never leave him—but she did.

Today, on my seventeenth birthday.

The legacy of the old bench—what it had heard, what it had borne witness to—sat like a deep scar covering broken bones, bones that hadn't healed right and never would. I'd known as much from the first time my grammy Essie warned me of its taint, to the day I'd sat on it and accepted a friendship ring from my ex-boyfriend, Tripp Seacat, not so long ago. But the very worst was way back when: the day I'd spied Tommy Whitlock holding my mama's hand here on this bench, snugged up tight as a tick, and telling tall tales.

There'd been plenty of talk about Liar's Bench being cursed—whispers of how it had soaked in the wrong of Frannie Crow's death. Of how those lies would splinter into anyone who sat upon its weather-beaten wood. And on more than one occasion over the years, a God-fearing citizen of Peckinpaw would even go so far as to take up a petition to burn it. But the elders wouldn't hear of it. When I'd asked Grammy Essie, who was also the town librarian, *why not,* she'd quoted St. Jerome, saying, "Muddy, the scars of others should teach us caution."

And so the elders would quiet the naysayers, insisting that the bench served up a dish of "cautious reminder" to others.

But everyone knows that liars and their willing sponges don't heed warnings. That's why I have been, on occasion, firmly in the camp that would like to see it burn.

Today, this bench seemed like the only place that could soak up my grief. I sat down on Liar's Bench, lit a match to my gasoline-soaked thoughts, and wept red-hot tears.

Moments later, Daddy walked up behind me, put his hands on my shoulders, and squeezed. "Thanks for waiting," he said, circling around the bench to take a seat. Closing up his law office always took a while since he had lots of important legal papers that had to be locked up. I ran my thumb across each finger of my right hand, picking up speed. Continuously gliding, ticking off my rattled thoughts.

"Muddy, everything's going to be okay." Daddy noted my longtime habit, and lifted my hand and squeezed.

He grew quiet for a spell.

"Sheriff wants me to meet with him as soon as possible."

I turned and looked up at him. He paused, drawing his lips back to his teeth. "I'm so sorry, lil birdie, real sorry. I don't know what to say. It isn't right losing your mama like this . . . and on your birthday, too." His eyes filled up same as mine. "Ella was a good mother, a good woman. . . . There's not a day that goes by that I haven't wished it had turned out differently between us. I'm sorry, Muddy. I'm so sorry." A breeze stirred as the silence lengthened around us.

Normally, I'd light into him for calling me Muddy. Instead, I shuttered my grief-soaked eyes, leaned into his shoulder, and inhaled the comforting blends of his woodsy aftershave. For this moment, I let his mistakes with Mama slip away. My thoughts became mercifully numb, suspended somewhere between calm and pandemonium.

"Before I forget, baby, Pastor Dugin called and asked to drop by this evening. I told him that would be fine." I nodded my consent. "Muddy, there's something else. . . ."

I met his eyes and saw the flatness that meant bad news was coming; like the time he'd told me my dog Charlie had been hit by a pickup. Then, again when Grammy Essie crossed over, and soon after, when Papaw had followed. Now, my mama was dead, too. What more could there possibly be?

"Nothing's official yet, but they're strongly leaning toward ruling this a suicide."

I stiffened. "Suicide? No. No way! Everything was just fine when I visited her Thursday. . . ." I ran my hand over my face to swab off the sorrow left trailing down my cheeks. "I don't believe for one minute Mama took her life!"

Daddy shook his head and studied his secretary as she crossed the street toward his courthouse office. "Me neither, baby." Weary, he pulled himself up. "I'm so glad you got to see her yesterday. . . . Right now I'm fixin' to head on over to Ella's to talk with the sheriff and the coroner. I'll take you on home first."

I stood to face him. "No, I have to see her. I'm going with you." I planted my feet firmly in front of his.

He cleared his throat, ready to lend argument and put his foot down with me.

I crossed my arms. "I'm old enough to go with you. I'm seventeen now—an adult."

Daddy cocked his head and shoved his hands deep inside his pockets. "You sure 'bout this?"

My throat locked up, forcing out a croaked, "Yes." With a shaky hand, I grabbed the back of Liar's Bench, leaving one more lie to soak in and feed.

2

The Better Liar

By the time we reached Mama's, I was having second thoughts. Despite it being one of the hottest days of the year in Kentucky, a cold shiver slid over my body. I peered upward to distance myself from the crime scene before me and watched the choreographed movements of a flock of birds veer, then turn in an unpredictable fashion, erratically stippling the summer skies. Their puzzling flight was punctuated by the intermittent cries coming from inside my mama's house, those of my seven-month-old baby half sister, Genevieve.

Daddy flexed his jaw and I saw his soft gray eyes darken to cavern-cold. "Daddy . . . Mama wouldn't kill herself. And that one trooper said she did it in front of baby Genevieve. . . ."

"Shush, baby." He squinted his eyes to keep out the broiling sun, intent on the exchange of conversation nearby.

We watched Sheriff Allen, aptly nicknamed "Jingles." It was a well-known Peckinpaw fact that you could hear him coming long before you saw the glint of his spit-polished gold badge.

Jingles unsnapped his official oversized jail key ring from his utility belt and pulled off another ring that held his rabbit's foot, a metal horse-head bottle opener from the Dixie Brewing company, and his lucky Indian head penny, then ducked into his car to place a set of keys in the ignition. He grabbed his clipboard and jingled his way back and forth across my mama's front yard, pausing to talk to the different officials scattered around.

He stopped a few feet from us and tapped his clipboard's pages with a pen.

The sheriff sneaked a peek at me, then shuffled a little farther away so that he was partially hidden behind a police cruiser. But not far enough away that I couldn't hear.

I listened in horror as Jingles explained to the state trooper standing beside him. "I'm not gonna call it yet, Herb. . . . And nobody's gonna put much stock in the neighbor's statement, him being touched and all. . . . Hell, it does look suspicious, what with how many times Ella showed up for her shift wearing sunglasses to hide Whitlock's marks."

"And with him stoned out of his mind on LSD and God-knows-what-else, he could've done this," the state trooper chimed in. "And then there's her suitcase—out and half-filled. Looks to me like she had enough of living with him, not just in simply living."

Suitcase? I tried to remember if I'd seen one when I was visiting her yesterday.

Jingles shook his head. As his voice softened, his words slowed and slid easily away. "Some days that gal would jus' sit at that desk of hers an' refuse to take off those sunglasses, all the whiles, she's busy fussin' about them florescent lights hurting her eyes an' making her head pound. . . ." He clucked his tongue and sighed. "Lil Ella couldn't have weighed more than ninety pounds soaked, him, damn near two hundred. Damn pillhead!" Jingles turned and spat. He handed the clipboard to the trooper.

"Your desk clerk talked to Whitlock at about ten this morning?" The trooper looked over the notes.

"Yeah, 'bout an hour ago. Hettie had called to see why Ella'd missed her shift," Jingles said, and pointed to the house. "If ya need to talk to her, she's in there taking care of the baby until Child Welfare gets here."

I looked at Mama's home—the bare windows curtained with nothing more than bird droppings splattered down the panes. It was hard to believe that a banker's daughter and a once-prominent member of the Peckinpaw community lived in this rundown old clapboard, held together by peeling paint and thick moss layered over shadowed boards. That she'd been living her life just pennies shy from collecting a government draw check.

I silently prayed that she'd walk out arms wide, ready to cradle me and make this nightmare go away. I'd sent up the same prayer the day she went off to the big city with Tommy and left me here in Peckinpaw with Daddy. That bright summer day right before my ninth birthday, when I'd felt my childhood halved like an onion, leaving me trapped between the tear-stained slices of Before and After. That split, that cold gloom cast across my heart, always dogged me, forever measured into my past and present.

My legs wobbled, a darkness threatened. Then rage filled my core, swelled and bruised, bringing back function. I was shocked by my sudden anger toward Mama and her death, and at everyone I felt was responsible.

Daddy must have sensed it, too. He grasped my elbow and urged me to sit down on the grass. Intent on unlatching my hurt and finding a target, I jerked away. "You! It's your fault! You drove her away with all your lying, your cheatin'. You. You and this Podunk town!" I waved my arm. "The founding fathers got it right when they named it Peckinpaw. No wonder Mama couldn't stand living here. Nothing more than a place where chickens peck and horses paw!"

Wounded, Daddy took a step back. "Muddy, you're . . . you're having a nervous spell. You go wait in the car and I'll be along after—"

Before I could collect myself, clanging bells and cheerful music toppled his words and my regret. We both turned and watched a Mister Softee ice-cream truck—painted with candy-colored cartoons and treats—grind its gears and come to a halt alongside the police cruisers.

For a moment, a glint of my long-ago summers, chocolate-kissed smiles and cotton-candy scents, crowded out the dark. I'd loved Mister Softee's jaunty carnival song even more than his confections: It had lassoed the nights, matching my delighted squeals and proving a balm for the bruises of childhood, both the kind you could see and the sort you could only feel deep underneath your skin.

The Mister Softee driver, Joey Sims, a boy from my biology class, slid back the large square window of the truck. His dark eyes popped out like buckeyes in buttermilk as he craned his head out to study the scene.

Baby Genevieve's screams drifted outside again, jolting me back to the present. Sims turned his head, and his neck stretched toward the house like a snapping turtle targeting a minnow. I took a step back, trying to hide behind Daddy before Sims's eyes could grab hold of me.

Jingles hollered across the road, "Move along, Sims." He waved his arms in the air. "This here is a police investigation. That truck ain't due to sell treats 'til after supper, son."

Sims ducked back in, slammed the window shut, and took off. I knew that in less than an hour, he'd have told everyone about *the something horrible going on* out at the Whitlock place. By nightfall, the town would be buzzing with gossip and speculation. I worried about my boyfriend, Bobby Marshall. Well, not exactly my boyfriend . . . but getting close. Still, I wished I could reach him before Joey found him first.

I drew in a weary breath. It didn't matter, nothing mattered except Mama.

Jingles leaned over to Herb and flipped through the pages of his preliminary report. The trooper pointed. "See this? The coroner said if that damn living room rafter would've been drywalled over instead of partially exposed, this wouldn't have happened. But, then again, she went out to Whitlock's truck and got his rope to throw over the beam. So if she was that determined, who knows? Her keys *were* found in the cab of the truck. . . ."

Rope . . . the rafter? I turned to her truck. Oh, dear God, had Mama gone and done that. . . . A protest lay strangled in my throat. *No*. It couldn't be.

Mr. Harper from Harper's Filling Station pulled up behind it. He backed his wrecker up to the rear of Mama's truck, then climbed out and unwound the metal cable from the winch, drowning out everyone's conversation. After he had Mama's vehicle hooked up to his, Mr. Harper smoothed back his oily brown hair and grabbed my mama's pocketbook from inside her truck. I'd bought it for her this past Mother's Day. Now, old man Harper was soiling it with his dirty paws, speckling the white leather with dollops of black oil grease and tobacco juice. I lurched forward to snatch it from his fat hand, but Daddy latched on to my arm and cut me a warning look. Mr. Harper startled and pinched his catfish mouth shut.

He strolled past, clutching the purse to his smelly union suit. Jingles took the purse and thanked him for retrieving it; then he asked Mr. Harper to tow the truck on down to the jail lot. "We'll have it searched later for possible evidence," Jingles told the state trooper.

My half sister screamed yet again, chilling the air, wounding like a knife. I pulled to the cry, but Daddy sidestepped me. "No, Muddy. That's a crime scene they're working. The baby will be fine."

My insides knotted.

Jingles adjusted the brim of his uniform hat. "Poor lil baby Genevieve." He sighed heavily. "That sorry piece of pig shit Whitlock always whopping up on Ella. The missus and I tried to talk her into going to Louisville or Nashville to get some counseling help. . . . Damn, I'd hoped when I gave her that dispatching job down at the station, it would help some." He turned to the side, spat out a wad of tobacco.

"Hell's bells. It's all a coin toss," Jingles went on. "I still think Whitlock's too much of a coward for the likes of that in there. A crazy dopehead, a drunkard, and always good for a petty slap or sucker punch, but I have my doubts about him bein' a murderer."

I took a step closer to Jingles.

Jingles dug into his back pocket, pulled out his Boker knife, then reached into his shirt pocket and pulled out his Warren County Twist. He slowly cut himself a generous fresh plug and stuffed his jaw. Wagging the knife at the state trooper, he said,

"Doc Lawrence examined her body and it shows Ella's bruises are fresh. All I can do is wait 'til the bastard sobers up, question him, and hope I can make some sense out of it all before he lawyers up. Meantime, I'm bookin' him for abuse of a corpse and illegal possession of drugs. Most I can do right now." He tucked the Boker back into his pocket and pulled a handkerchief from another, wiped his mouth, then brought it up to his nose and gave a loud honk.

Jingles looked our way and took a few steps toward us, stopping to curl his fingers under the large flab of flesh overhanging his utility belt. With a quick tug upward, Jingles readjusted the waist of his britches and hooked his thumbs into his waistband. "Adam, mind if I have a few words with you?" he asked, stealing a glance at me. He hesitated, then added, "Without Muddy, if that'd be okay."

"Sheriff Jingles, I'm seventeen now. And"—I stuck my chin out and tried to make my quivering voice strong—"I . . . I'm not stupid. That's my mama and I ain't budging until someone tells me what's going on."

"Not disputin' that, Muddy. Everyone knows you've got the smarts, but there's some things best not said in the company of females." Jingles dropped his gaze to the ground and rocked on his heels, waiting.

"Never mind that. Muddy can handle herself," Daddy said. "You're booking him on murder, right?" I nodded, grateful for his support.

Doc Lawrence, Smitt County's coroner, walked up and handed the sheriff a paper. "Jingles, right now I'm calling the time of death at nine a.m., Friday, eleventh day of August 1972. I need to confirm Ella's age?" He gave me a sidelong glance before turning to Daddy.

Daddy looked down at his shoes. "She should've got out sooner," he mumbled. "She was so close. . . ."

"So close to what, Daddy?"

Doc Lawrence softly cleared his throat. "Adam?"

"Thirty-seven," Daddy snapped. "She was thirty-seven and too damn young to be robbed of the rest of her life from that ne'er-do-well hayseed!" He jerked his thumb toward the sheriff's car, then shoved his hands into his trousers and kicked the dirt, a film of brown air settling on his finely pressed khakis.

I looked away as a silence descended on us, thick as dust and just as cloudy. Finally, Doc Lawrence asked, "Jingles, anything else from the neighbor . . . Higgy Flynn?"

"Check with him before you leave. Higgy doesn't have a phone." Jingles nodded a dismissal to Doc and turned back to Daddy. "Adam, you know we can't do anything till we've processed the scene, collected all the evidence, and—"

"I don't give a dried apple damn, Jingles." There was a razored edge to Daddy's voice that I'd never heard before. "As the Prosecuting Attorney of Smitt County, I say that bastard's guilty of murder. And I want the highest bail set."

"You're putting the cart before the horse," Jingles huffed. "Case hasn't even been ruled a homicide."

Daddy balled a fist. "You best charge him with murder before you end up doubling your paperwork."

Instinctively, I put a protective hand on Daddy's arm.

"Now, Adam"—Jingles raised his palm—"settle down. You're gonna have to argue this one to an empty room. You know good an' damn well we'll have to call the Attorney General's office and have them send over a relief prosecutor if it's ruled murder. Being she's your ex and the mother of your child, ain't no judge gonna allow you to set the trial." Jingles shot me a glance and moved in front of me, blocking. "Sorry, son." He put his hand on Daddy's shoulder. "Ya know I want to help you out here, but from what I've pieced together from the neighbor's statement, Hettie's, and everybody and everything else, it's pointing to sui—"

Wails of indignation erupted from baby Genevieve as the state trooper struggled to open the ratty screen door while trying to straitjacket the baby's flailing arms with his own. The trooper whispered to the infant as he left the house and hotfooted it across the lawn.

"Genevieve," I said, running to her. "Please," I begged the official. "Please let me hold my baby sister." The exasperated trooper handed her to me. Genevieve buried her face in the crook of my shoulder, muffling her cries. I turned away from him and bounced her gently in my arms, cooing softly until her sobs faded into a string of hiccups.

After a few minutes, the trooper said, "Ma'am, we need to take her now." He opened his arms.

"Please," I backed up, "I'm all she has."

Daddy gripped my shoulder. "It's okay, Muddy. The law needs to move her to safety. She'll be fine."

"I don't understand. Why can't we take her?"

Genevieve cried out as the trooper lifted her from my arms.

"Them's the rules, baby," Daddy said. "Don't worry, they'll take good care of her."

When I kissed Genevieve good-bye, she twisted and tried to wriggle out of the trooper's grip. Her tear-soaked face reddened as she stretched out her arms to me.

The trooper handed the squalling baby off to another official who was waiting to place her inside the cruiser.

I turned away to bury my own face on Daddy's shoulder.

Tommy, securely handcuffed with his hands behind his back in the rear of Jingles's car, began to yell and bang his head against the side door window. "Let me out, I didn't do anything. . . . I done tol' ya, Jingles, I was 'relaxin' in the bedroom. Why'd ya go an' bust my jaw like that, huh?" Tommy rubbed his chin against his shoulder, nursing. "Hey, let me out, Jingles. . . . How many times did I tell ya already, Ella climbed up on that chair and done her own deed! Just as sure as Frannie Crow had sealed her own gallows fate, way back when! An' you can bet Summers is behind all this," he snarled, butting his head toward Daddy. "Summers . . . you jackleg liar. Nothin' but goddamn lies. You an' Ella! I saw y'all squeezed together on Liar's Bench! Liars! Nothin' but lies, Summers . . . Hey! Wait a goddamn minute! Where are you bastards takin' my baby?"

Tommy turned sideways, leaned back on the car seat, and gave two powerful kicks, shattering the car door's window. "That's my baby!"

"Sumbitch!" Jingles fumbled for his mace, dropped his clipboard, and darted to the car. Trooper Herb followed, with Daddy trailing right behind them. "Stay back, Adam." Jingles pointed him a warning finger as they approached the cruiser.

Opening the car's opposite door, Herb aimed his own canister of mace and shot three bursts straight into Tommy's face.

"Ahh, my eyes, my eyes! Bastard! Ya blinded me—I can't see!" he raged between violent coughs.

Jingles leaned across his steering wheel and grabbed the keys out of the ignition. Moving quickly, he yanked open the damaged door, then yelled at Herb, "He's drooling. Don't want the sumbitch to die of asphyxiation." He tossed his keys to Herb. "Grab my jumper cables from the trunk. Aw, damn you, Whitlock! You've busted up my cruiser. Ah, shit, shit! Sit up! You're slobbering all over my automobile!"

The trooper dashed to the trunk and pulled out the battery jumper cables, then sped back to Jingles.

"Move him upright, Herb, and fasten his lap belt while I secure these cables!" Jingles wrapped Tommy's feet and ankles with the cables, then pulled the ends tight underneath the door and slammed it shut.

Everything seemed to weigh me down inside, sift into corner edges. *What the hell is going on here? Why is Tommy blaming Daddy? And why doesn't Jingles just let that son of a bitch die!*

I felt myself torn between kinging myself a Kentucky hill to hurl my anger from, to digging a cave where I could crown my heartache.

My stomach landed at my feet. Nausea got the best of me and I turned quickly away from the chaos to quietly escape behind a tree. After a moment, I moved away from my mess and spotted Jingles's clipboard not two feet away. Shaky, I picked up the preliminary report and skimmed the pages. Tommy, Daddy, and the officials' shouts and curses faded and bowed to respite as I soaked up the words.

As I read the testaments to Mama's death—how the neighbor went from window to window, how Hettie kept on calling and calling, and the unspeakable thing Tommy had done with the ribbons—anger shattered what grief had not yet claimed of my senses, leaving them strewn like pickup sticks around my thoughts.

A knob rattled, pulling me out. I watched as the door to Mama's house creaked open and the coroner's assistants slowly made their way outside with a heavy stretcher. My mama. *Mama* . . . Genevieve . . . *Poor baby Genevieve* . . . Jingles's report . . . The ribbons, and what he'd done after . . . *Murder isn't enough?* Two of the coroner's assistants adjusted the top of the white tarp, tucking it securely around Mama's body, but not before I saw her exposed ankles.

I dropped the report. "Mommy, my mommy . . ." My heart cartwheeled up into my throat, stealing my breath. I took off at full speed toward the stretcher. My mouth dropped, twisted, and my every inch of life slid rabbit hole down.

I don't know how long I stood there screaming at the metal gurney, my hands clamped tight to my ears, trying to drown out my own frightening voice and the visions in my head.

Daddy rushed over to me. I reached for one of the pink ribbons fastened around her swollen ankle. *Ribbons. How? She never has ribbons in the house.* I jabbed a finger toward Tommy. "He always made her use ugly rubber bands, cheap bastard."

"Muddy, c'mon, let me take you home," Daddy said in a commanding whisper. I gripped the ribbon harder. "You need to get some rest, let the police do their job now. Let's go, baby. C'mon."

One of Doc Lawrence's helpers clamped his hand over my wrist and twisted, forcing me to release the ribbon. It felt like he was taking another piece of Mama along with it. I shot out my hand, reaching for everything I'd lost. An official took hold of my arm and whipped it behind my back.

"Let go of me. I said, *let go!*" I lifted my heel and back-kicked hard, breaking the man's grip, then took off toward Jingles's cruiser.

I pulled on the door latch.

Jammed.

Tommy's dilated eyes popped, his sweaty face reddening even more. Fresh spittle coated the glaze of dried beer on his whiskers.

He rocked himself away from the door. "You . . ." I banged my fist on the roof. "You took away *everything.*"

A state trooper locked his arms around my waist, lifting me away from the car.

I wriggled out of his grip and dropped to my knees. Grabbing fistfuls of bluegrass, I rocked in the dirt, and howled, "MURDERER, MURDERER."

Daddy knelt down behind me and wrapped my sorrow in his embrace.

Weak, I lowered my head to the ground, letting my heartbreak choke the earth.

3

A Lie Riding
on Another's Truth

Before he drove us away from Mama's house, Daddy pulled out his handkerchief and gave it to me. I clutched it and sat stone-faced. From the car window, I watched the mailman gawk before stuffing Friday's mail into Mama's old cast-iron mailbox hanging off the siding under her porch. I turned away as Peckinpaw's undertaker pulled slowly out of the driveway.

The ride back to our farmhouse was silent. When we reached home, I hurried out, leaving Daddy sitting in my Ford Mustang—the birthday gift he'd surprised me with on the day that would now mark my final visit with Mama.

I stood on the porch stoop, the memory of our last time together replaying, flickering back and forth and over and over, like a grainy scene on a reel of film, projected onto a worn screen. It had been a perfect, sunny Thursday. Hard to believe it was only yesterday.

"Silver blue," Daddy announced, holding up a car key. "And it complements your gray eyes, too, Muddy. It's fast. And 'bout as powerful as those runner legs of yours, grown two city blocks long this year." He raised a finger. "You be careful now, ya hear?"

I kicked up my long, awkward legs, squealed, and ran my hands over the Pony's hood and compared the shine of my 1965 to his 1970 Mustang Boss, his "Goober-Grabber-Green" as he called it, and the one I'd been testing my driving skills in for over a year.

"I can't believe it! It's perfect! Can I drive it now?"

"You act like it's your birthday or something," he teased.

"Tomorrow . . . just hours away!" I laughed. On cue, I did a little pushing and pleading and some fine pouting until, laughingly, he agreed to let me drive. "It's sharp, Daddy."

"You'll see," he pointed out, "it's a clutch, like mine. Not one of those automatics. That way you'll never be stuck. And you're more likely to keep your hands on the wheel, instead of that tube of lipstick."

"I love it! Thank you, thank you!" I pecked him on the cheek. "I need to go get some stuff for it. For her," I corrected. "I'm going to call her Peggy! 'Peggy Sue . . . I love you . . .' " I sang Buddy Holly's song.

"One of your grammy's favorite songs." He smiled.

"I still have the record she gave me." I bent over the hood, arms wide in a sweeping hug. I'd waited so long for this—worked so hard. Counting last night's shift at Ruby's Dog 'n' Suds and the six hours of babysitting before that, and Nettie's Nest four hours from the week before, I'd tallied up 1,224 hours and 45 minutes of "hard" during these past three years. At last! "Wait here, it'll only take a minute to get my things."

Daddy chuckled. "Not going anywhere. And you deserve it, gal. I told you three years ago that if you worked after school and did summer jobs and saved, I'd match your earnings. He nodded at me, pride shining in his eyes.

I met him a few minutes later in the driveway with a large hatbox.

Daddy dangled the key in front of me. "You sure you can't wait 'til Friday . . . ? Oh, never mind, on second thought, you'll have me worn down to a frazzle, with not a minute's peace." He tossed me the keys.

Laughing, I jumped into the car. I inhaled the scent of vinyl and traced circles on the eye shadow blue and white bucket seats. After I emptied the contents of the box onto the passenger side, I tossed my compact, tissues, and a lipstick tube into the glove compartment. Then I carefully arranged some of my favorite 8-track tapes of music—Johnny Cash's *Man in Black,* Neil Young's *Harvest,* and The Who's *Who's Next*—inside the cartridge box on the passenger floorboard. I fastened the seat belt across my lap. Satisfied, I flung the box to the backseat.

My feet found the pedals and I pumped the brake, the clutch, and gas. I ran my thumb over the silver pony emblem in the center of the steering wheel. Taking a whiff of the interior, I noticed a faint smell of cigarette smoke. Not my style, but it fit the muscle car.

"Lasso that pony, gal," Daddy called out.

"Okay!" I fumbled for the ignition. The key slid in. Taking a deep breath, I gripped the skinny wheel, pressed my foot heavy on the clutch, pushed the stick in neutral, and cranked. The engine caught on the first turn and purred.

"Can we pick up ThommaLyn?" I asked.

"Not until you've gotten the feel of the car. Plenty of time for driving your friends later." Daddy chomped on his unlit cigar, studying. "Let's see that shoulder-check."

"Got it!" I stretched my neck over my right shoulder, then back over my left, and then over to my right again. "Satisfied?"

He wiggled the cigar clenched between his teeth.

I adjusted the rearview mirror. Peering into it, I inspected my light pink lipstick, ran my fingers through my hair, and tousled, hoping I would pass every senior at Peckinpaw High. Every senior boy, that is.

"Oh"—Daddy raised a finger—"'fore I forget, the radio has a short. It comes and goes, and it's missing the on/off button. Mike said to bring it by next week and he'd have the mechanic fix it. Okay, hands at ten and two."

I nodded and placed my hands over the wheel in clock position.

He slid his lanky body into his own car. Leaning his head out the window, he called out, "Wear that lap belt."

"Buckled!"

I pushed the stick into first gear and eased up on the clutch while I pushed down on the gas pedal, all in one magnificent sequence of commands and response. Relieved, I released a burst of air and pulled out carefully ahead of him.

The radio blared out a few lines of ZZ Top's bluesy "(Somebody Else Been) Shakin' Your Tree," giving my fingers an itch to snap along, then just as quickly, and for my own good, it went dead when I hit a mud hole.

I drove a few miles down country roads with a knuckle-white grip, nervous and thrilled, watching out for crossing critters and other cars, keeping Peggy straight and steady, and away from the shoulder. Doing it all with Daddy following close behind in his car.

When I made it safely back to our house, Daddy gave a thumbs-up.

I ran upstairs to use the old rotary dial phone. After waiting for what seemed like forever for the party line to be free, I called Mama.

"Mama, is Tommy around? I finally got my car! Yes, yessum . . . He gave it to me today! I just drove it!" I laughed. "Yes, ma'am, today, Thursday! Yes, I do know tomorrow's my birthday! Guess what I named her? I named her Peggy. She's so pretty, Mama. When can I come over and take you and Genevieve for a ride?"

She whispered into the phone receiver, "Tommy will be down for his afternoon 'nap' soon. Come in about two hours, sugar. We'll celebrate."

I smiled, knowing that Tommy's afternoon naps were a sure guarantee for us to have a peaceful visit. I looked forward to them.

Tommy hadn't made his intense dislike of me a secret when he married Mama eight years before. I saw it in his eyes when I first spied them cozying up on Liar's Bench after Mama divorced Daddy. The feeling was mutual. At first she took me to Nashville and a short spell later, Tommy was there, too. He'd grown up with a mix of relatives, straddling the borders of two home states.

I knew right off that I was in for a fight; I just didn't know what type. Within a month, Tommy had wormed his way into her heart with his startling good looks, the promise of a better-paying job, and a sophisticated city apartment, leaving no room for me. The very next month, they'd married, and the month after that, she'd dumped me back at Daddy's.

I'd sung Tommy's good riddance when Mama dropped me back home from Nashville. But I was baptized with a new hurt when she'd left Daddy and me to go back to Tommy.

I thought for sure she'd stay with us and leave Tommy's broken promises and half-baked brain behind. Especially after the eviction man came knocking at our Nashville apartment, and then when we'd walked in and found the empty place along the wall where the three-seater Chesterfield had been. I'd heard her and Tommy's arguments with the repo man, and talk of late bills. Tommy had hit bottom, she'd said, and she didn't like his new set of pals.

I recall how I could hardly sit still on the drive from Nashville to Peckinpaw. Mama'd kept a nervous smile glued to her lips all the way there. I'd rolled down the window and stuck my head out, lapping at the breezes, hungry for home. More than once, Mama gently pulled me back inside the car. We hit the final stretch of road with my bones bursting sweet hallelujahs. I couldn't remember the last time I'd felt safe, and no Tommy around to snatch me up by my hair. When we pulled into Peckinpaw, I was so excited to be home, I barely heard Mama when she said, "A lot of kids live with their daddies." For a second I tried to think of someone who did, but I didn't know of anyone. She opened the car door, and said, "I won't be able to stay, but you'll be safe with Adam."

"But—"

"I'll be back before you know it. No time at all, Mudas. Lickety-split."

I felt the color leave my face, and I had a fear creep hold and worry my insides. "Today?" I needled, trying to measure lickety-split. "Are you coming back today, Mama?" I reached out for her. She didn't answer, just rushed me out of the car and busied herself with the wrinkles in her dress.

Back in Peckinpaw, I attached myself to Grammy Essie, who

settled me carefully into her bosom, keeping me busy with homestead chores, school, and having me sign up for the track team.

Still, I sorely missed having a mama even before Tommy'd barged in and especially after. Folks looked at me peculiar, too, like I'd lost an arm or something. I guess I had. I still moped around for her. I wanted to Band-Aid our little family, and I knew if I could apply the right amount of ointment, I'd have them all back.

So when Mama moved back to Peckinpaw last year, I'd been hopeful, and excited about having a baby sister. I pushed aside my feelings about Tommy and met Mama on the front porch of her house, anxious and bursting for her to show me where my new room would be. I handed her a jar full of wildflowers that I'd carefully picked. But instead of welcoming me, she'd guided me off the porch and out to the crepe myrtle, making sure we were out of earshot from Tommy. "Sugar," she'd said, "there's not enough room for you and the new baby."

"I can sleep on the couch," I'd said. "Or, I could even make a pallet beside the baby's crib. And I can help with chores, and I'll babysit anytime you want."

She'd peeked over her shoulder at Tommy. "Not enough room. You have to understand, sugar."

I didn't.

Tommy's smug face showed he did. Mama had smoothed down her dress and linked her nervous hands behind her back. "You can come visit, Mudas. It'll be just like living together. You'll see."

I wouldn't.

I'd had a fine sense of abandonment. Of loss. All over again. It wasn't fair. To have her back only to have her sealed off from me so quickly. Here she was so close. I'd stood there staring hard at Tommy, who sat on the porch all cocky—leg perched on the railing, arms crossed. His glare felt like sleet stinging my face. Big droplets weighed down my lashes, forcing me to run away before he could have the satisfaction of seeing.

But I couldn't stay away long. What with Grammy Essie's

passing and Daddy's job busier than ever, I'd gravitated back to Mama.

For so long, Grammy Essie had given me her uninterrupted presence that at first I tormented myself when Mama returned home, afraid to go visit her—refusing to doormat my heart for another interruption. Daddy tried to push me to see Mama, too, offering to give me rides. I ticked off exactly six calendar days waiting for her to pack up and split again. When I saw she might be around for a bit, I found myself slowly gathering up female questions about hair and makeup lessons, boys, first dates, and fading friends. And I couldn't help but seek the answers in maternal arms.

It wasn't no time until we took solace in the mostly sneaked visits with each other. They were our little secrets: the one thing that Tommy hadn't stolen from me.

Yesterday, I'd sat on my porch stoop waiting for Tommy to go down for his nap so I could visit with Mama. Cursing Tommy with each and every tick of the clock, I felt the two hours inch by. Finally, Daddy opened the screen door and shooed me on my way, saying I was wearing out the porch boards.

4

And Many More . . .

I rested my head against the porch beam with a pound of regrets slowly monkey-wrenching my brain—wishing I hadn't left Mama at Tommy's doorstep yesterday and wishing I'd let Daddy drop me off at the homestead this afternoon instead of insisting on going to the crime scene with him.

Daddy was still in the car, his head stuck to the steering wheel with his arms cradling his head. I watched from the porch, worrying for him, wanting him to be strong. I felt panic claw at my throat. "Hey," I finally managed to blurt out, "it's hot out here. Coming?"

"Give me a minute," he croaked.

I studied him sitting there in my birthday present, hugging the Mustang's steering wheel, and was reminded of another birthday, my sixth. I'd fallen asleep on the porch swing, watching and waiting for him to come home from work to celebrate. Mama's face had soured a bit more with each tick of the clock. My small birthday cake sat unsliced, the lard icing cementing around the six unlit purple candles. When Daddy came dragging in after midnight, his fine clothes rumpled like morning pajamas, she'd screamed at him about his "floozy." The same floozy I'd tattled to her about a year before: the judge's pretty daughter, the one I'd caught kissing Daddy on the lips when I'd charged into his office after school to show off my latest drawing. Daddy'd shooed me out, but the very next day I'd told Mama that "the pretty lady loved Daddy, too." I'll never forget the look in her eyes: a strange blend of grief, anger, and then the vindication that came after she'd poured herself a refreshment.

Maybe if I'd kept my big five-year-old mouth shut about what I'd seen, they would still be together. Maybe Mama would still be alive.

Again, I hollered from the porch, "C'mon, Daddy." I saw a flash of something metal in his hands and I squinted and craned my neck, suddenly nervous that he was sneaking a drink in the car. It had been years since I'd hidden his flask, and I wasn't eager to revisit the last time. Four years ago, Daddy'd bumbled a case after spending most of the weekend glued to a bottle. When the main witness Daddy was supposed to meet after Sunday church fled on account of Daddy was hung over and forgot to show up, I heard Daddy curse loud enough to shake the dirt off a field crow. It wasn't that Daddy had missed a witness meeting, it was without that witness and the telltale ball cap the witness had seen the rapist wearing, Daddy had no case.

The rapist walked, and it wasn't a week later when he found another ten-year-old over in Mallardsburg and had his way with her, leaving her broken-boned and laid up in the hospital. Word got around about Daddy missing his meeting, and folks did some sideway talking when he was out of earshot.

When Daddy went to visit the Mallardsburg girl in the hospital, he took along a big cutting of Grammy Essie's blue hydrangeas and a fistful of field daisies. That night after he got home, I watched him bust all his whiskey bottles against the side of the barn. I took the silver flask from inside his jacket and ran and buried it under the front porch. He hadn't tried to claim it or buy another bottle since.

"Daddy, come in and have some tea. Too hot out here to be sitting in a car."

He straightened and I saw it was only the car keys in his hand. "Coming," he called back. Relieved, a ragged breath whisked past my lips. The rage I'd unloaded at the crime scene had left me drained and I didn't have the energy to fight any more battles. I grabbed the doorjamb for support and shot one final glance over my shoulder.

When I saw his foot hit the gravel drive, I slipped into the house, letting the screen door bang behind me, and made my way up the narrow stairs. I was suddenly desperate for my bed. My flip-flops smacked against hundred-year-old hardwoods as I hurried down the hall to my room and flung myself onto the mattress. Balling up Grammy Essie's old chenille coverlet in my fist, I pressed it to my forehead and kneaded my thoughts. After a while, I turned over on my side and studied the small picture frame on the nightstand. It was a Polaroid snapshot of me, four years old and sitting on Mama's lap in the middle of Daddy's big ol' sunflower field. Our eternal smiles, bright as the huge golden flowers that seemed to have tilted to blow petal-kisses down upon us. I fell asleep, drawn into a maze of sunflower fields, both beautiful and terrifying.

Sometime later, I managed to pull myself out of my deep sleep and answer the knocks at my door. "Baby," Daddy said softly, "come on down and let me fix you supper."

I bolted up and checked the alarm clock. "Why didn't you wake me? It's after five." I slipped on my flip-flops. "Not hungry, but I'll start your supper."

He held his hand up and slowly shifted his weight to the other leg. "I can fire the grill. You take a break."

I knew he had an old knee injury from his school days. It'd been acting up more in the last years, though he never talked about it, just let his fingers worry it a lot when sitting.

"I don't mind," I said, patting his shoulder as I moved past him. "I thawed out chops this morning. It won't take long to fry 'em up for you." I hurried down the steps, needing to do something routine to feel normal.

I went into the kitchen and put on the apron that was hanging on the tack beside the back door. I fumbled with the apron strings. For a second my head felt weighted as I tried to complete the simple task of tying the knot. Then I realized my footsteps had mimicked Mama's yesterday. My grip weakened, my fingers stopped working, and the apron slipped to the floor.

* * *

Thrilled to show Mama the birthday present, and my superb driving skills, I rushed over to her house yesterday (probably a little faster than Daddy would've liked) and was surprised to find a silver Mercedes sitting in her drive.

After knocking softly on the door so I wouldn't wake up a passed-out Tommy, I waited. When I didn't get a response, I edged open the door and peeked inside.

Genevieve was asleep in her playpen. Careful to not let the screen door clap, I stepped in and crossed the living room to go check on my baby half sister. She lay sprawled out with a faded pink blanket snugged under her chin. I couldn't help feeling a little resentment that she had Mama all to herself and whenever she wanted. That she'd never have to call to make an appointment, or sneak around to see her. But, again, at the price of Tommy . . . I sighed and placed a fold of blanket over her little chubby leg and smiled down at her face. Then I heard a sharp smack in the kitchen. I stood abruptly, frozen. Surely Mama would've called if Tommy was awake.

Genevieve rolled over on her stomach, snoring softly. I took off my flip-flops, my wide bell-bottom jeans swish-swashing as I padded over to the kitchen's wooden French door.

I placed my hands lightly on the door and leaned in to listen. A man spoke in an angry whisper, his words flying fast. "Ella," he hissed, "as a banker's daughter, you damn well know your numbers. I'm tired of waiting for that Rooster Run ledger."

A murmur leaked past the door.

"Ella, no more excuses! You best get my ledger tidied and back to me real quick," the man said. "And, if I find out you're lying, stashing away one red cent of Rooster Run's money, my money, you'll have more to worry about than a couple of little red marks—"

Muffled exchanges. Then, another sharp slap.

The man said, "I've been putting up with you moonlighting over at that clown sheriff's office, but don't you go forgetting who butters your bread. And if you're wondering who has the biggest—"

"Put that gun away, Roy, please," Mama whispered.

"I do," he growled.

My legs jellied.

Heated whispers.

The kitchen door flew open; the hard smack of wood against my forehead, watering my eyes. I stumbled back, surprised to see Roy McGee standing inches from me. He was a handsome man dressed in fine clothes, not the dirtbag I'd been expecting from what I'd just heard.

"Mr. McGee," I sputtered, lowering my gaze to the floor, "I . . . uh, I came to call on Mama." I raised my head and met cold blue eyes. "I didn't mean . . ."

McGee glared like an old barn cat, disturbed from its catch. I tried to look away, but he hooked his thumb under my chin and squeezed hard. "Better put some ice on that noggin, looks like you've got yourself a snooper-scrape, and a goose egg popping up. You know what happens to snoops, don't you, gal?"

"Let her go, Roy!" Mama begged, close on McGee's heels.

McGee's eyes never left mine. "Get my numbers, Ella."

"Roy, please go."

He turned to Mama, lifted a lock of hair that clung to her breast, and stroked. Mama grimaced and looked away. He gave a sharp tug, before slipping out the door.

We stood there in the living room staring at each other for what seemed like forever, the baby's soft breath the only sound.

The wind blew the door shut and the baby let out a cord of hiccupped snorts. I carefully touched my forehead and, sure enough, felt the tenderness of a bump.

Mama moved in quick, leading me by the arm into the kitchen. She set me down at the Formica table. Digging into the side pocket of her floral sundress, she pulled out a rubber band and swept her long chestnut curls up into a tight bun. She wouldn't meet my eyes, but I could see that hers were damp, troubled, as if a storm had pulled up the ocean's depth.

"Here, Mudas, before we get started"—she shifted her eyes and quickly patted her side for another rubber band—"let's ponytail your hair. It's such a hot day. My, it's grown at least two inches this summer, and, oh, look at those honey highlights the sun's brought out. Beautiful!"

I took the band and twirled it between my fingers. "Mama?"

Silence.

Somewhere near Knobmole Hill the whistle of an afternoon train broke the stillness, its steady *click-clack* echoing over wooden cross ties.

"Mama, what's going on with—"

"Sugar, let me get you an ice pack." She opened the freezer and got out a dented aluminum ice tray, dumping its contents into an empty bread bag and handing it to me.

"Mama?"

"Oh, aspirin! I should get you some aspirin. And a Band-Aid. There's a tiny cut on your head." She rummaged through a kitchen drawer and pulled out a packet of Goody's Powder.

"Mama, I don't need aspirin powders or bandages. I'm worried about you. And where's Tommy?"

"Let me get the water—"

"No, Mama, talk to me." I glanced over my shoulder. "Is Tommy here?"

She lowered herself into the chair next to mine. "Tommy woke up earlier than usual and took a ride over to his cousin's in Dayre County. We have all day to visit, sweetheart." I grinned a little, and for a moment pushed aside the worry that had settled deep in me. "And, sugar, before I forget, we need to get your back-to-school shopping done. Are you going to need a track uniform this year?"

"No, I don't think so." I sighed. "Mama, why was Mr. McGee—"

"Why not? Is it because of that coach?" she back-burnered Mr. McGee.

"Sort of. Coach Grider says us girls embarrass him and it ain't right for females to play sports. He's angry about that new law being passed."

"I'm not surprised. I expected him to fight the Title Nine.

Your daddy and me can come to school and have a talk with the principal."

"No, don't. It's fine."

"Somebody needs to set that coach straight!"

"Mama, don't go to Coach. Please don't."

"Okay, okay," she said, shaking her head. "But, remember, you're letting him win. It's your right! You can best that coach's boys any day. . . . Be happy to talk to Coach Grider—"

"No, Mama. Please. The last thing I need is you or Daddy going over there and making a fuss and—"

She held up a hand. "All right, Mudas. Just keep up your good grades. You can practice track on your own, sugar. Once you girls get into college there'll be a lot more opportunities, you'll see. By the way, are you and your girlfriends planning on going to the State Fair?"

Friend. Singular. "ThommaLyn's mama said she'd drive us. We're supposed to meet up soon and make plans."

"Will Mrs. Green be taking a carload?"

I brushed my toe over the curling linoleum and shrugged, embarrassed. I couldn't even imagine what it'd be like having more than one friend, a carload of girls to share in all the fun. I'd come close to something like that in my freshman year when Charlotte Moss had told me to join her during lunch at her popular table when school started up again. For over two weeks, I'd lie in bed each night worrying up the most fidgetiness of Freddie Fidgets. Getting my clothes ready for my first day. Practicing things to say—and how I'd act at that table. I'd fretted one year of shine off my pine boards and at least an inch of glaze from my mirror. It didn't work. I quickly found out that she was one of those friends who'd accept you and reject you between a screen door's closing clap.

The second week of school, Charlotte invited me to her house for supper. After we finished washing the dishes, I excused myself to call home for my ride. That's when I overhead her parents whispering about "bottle, divorce, and Daddy."

Mrs. Moss had hissed to her husband, "He drinks. And I

won't have Charlotte hanging around someone from an unstable home."

Mr. Moss weakly defended, "But she's Essie's granddaughter."

Then Mrs. Moss said, "Ella's daughter."

Shame burned holes in my cheeks so badly that when I got home, Daddy feared I had caught a cold, and dug out the thermometer.

The next day at school I showed up at Charlotte's popular table, but she waved me away and called someone else over to take my spot.

"Mudas, are those kids still calling you 'narc'? Making fun 'cause your daddy's the town prosecutor? I can call their parents and have a word with them. I'll stop by school and talk to your teachers in September."

"No, no, Mama, it's really no big deal. Really, it's my last year . . . I'm used to it." I was. Twelve years used to it.

"You can get used to hanging if you hang long enough. I can talk with the principal—"

"Mama, it's okay. . . . Please don't." I looked at her worn, dated dress, stained with sour milk and baby food. "You can't just waltz into my classes. I told you, conferences are for after school."

"I haven't been to any." Mama pressed down the folds of her dress. "You keep forgetting to give me the dates. You know, Jingles wouldn't mind letting me off work to meet with your teachers. Tommy will never know. Most evenings he's at work."

"Well, we don't have many and, 'sides, Daddy always does school business by phone. And school's fine, Mama. Just fine." I reached over and pressed the lie neatly over her hand.

She squeezed back. "Are you seeing a boy?"

"No, not really . . . Well, 'cept for Bobby Marshall. He's been hanging with me a bit. We're just friends." I wasn't quite ready to share yet. But, a very cute friend, I thought, and more polished than some of the western Kentucky boys who seemed to have been fished up from mud-bottomed ponds. He was different, more like the freshwater rainbow trout I used to catch out at Tuckspit Creek when Papaw took me fishing. Born three counties over in Chetburg, Bobby and his family had moved up north to New York City when he was seven and then finally settled back in Kentucky for the last semester of his junior year. In those nine years of citying-up, he'd scraped off most of the rural rust, but had somehow managed to hold on to his country soul.

I'd visited Mama enough when she lived in Nashville and Chicago to grab a bit of the worldly shine that came with city living. But, mostly, I'd clung to Grammy Essie's handmade apron strings and held on to my Kentucky rural. It was something Bobby and I seemed to share—the pull of both worlds.

Two months ago, he'd bumped into me in front of Town Square. We'd spent the day talking and people-watching on Liar's Bench. Before we parted, he'd asked if I wanted to go swimming in Darby's pond sometime. Maybe fish a little, too. We'd been hanging ever since. ThommaLyn and I used to be attached at the hip, but things had changed since she'd started seeing Paul Jameson. It was nice to have a new friend.

"Bobby Marshall, hmm?" Mama pulled me out of my thoughts. "I don't think I've ever talked with Mrs. Marshall."

"They moved here about four months ago. His daddy got a job transfer of sorts. And they don't live in town. Their house is way out past Dark Branch Bridge, near the county line."

"Your eyes are grinning."

I closed them and smiled. "Mama, stop it."

"You like him? Is he smitten with you? Has he asked you to be his girl?"

"Mama, no! He's a friend. For Pete's sake, he's never even kissed me." My cheeks burned. Eager to change the subject, I dusted imaginary breadcrumbs off the table, glanced around, and finally lit upon Mama's fresh bruises. I reached out to touch the reddish handprint on her face. She flinched and pulled away. "Mama, what happened? What was Mr. McGee doing here? I heard y'all arguing. And look, there's an old bruise on your neck. . . . Has Tommy been whooping up on you again?"

"I'm fine, Mudas, now don't you go prying into adult business. Roy's one of Tommy's bosses."

"Is he your boss, too?"

"Don't be silly, sugar. Tommy's working part-time out at McGee's farm, along with his bartending job in Braggs Fork. I try to help out when he needs me to look over Mr. McGee's books, that's all."

"Did you lose his ledger? Is that why he hurt you?"

She waved her arm in the air dismissively. "It was an accident."

"The kids at school say Mr. McGee is a bad man. Daddy says so, too." I set the ice bag on the table. "I heard he runs a fancy-pants compound out there on his horse farm 'bout once a month for Kentucky big shots to gamble on cockfights and pick up whores. And—"

Mama clamped her hands over my shoulders and gave a stern shake. "Language, little Miss Mouth of the South! And don't be spreading gossip." She wagged her finger. "It doesn't do anyone any good to pluck their chickens in the wind," she admonished.

A blaze of shame leaped up to lick my ears. "I didn't mean—"

"Some things are best left alone." She stood and pressed down the wrinkles of her dress, her warning that the discussion was over. "C'mon," she coaxed, her face softening, "let's get that bump down and celebrate your birthday. I'll be working tomorrow and today is my only day off this week."

She walked over to the stove. "I'm making your favorite dinner." She smiled as she pulled out a casserole dish from the cabinet. "And after the baby wakes up, maybe we can take a ride in that fancy car of yours."

She poured us each a glass of tea, and I couldn't help but notice it wasn't her usual refreshment. Still, she smiled just the same as when she'd drink the vodka, only a little more jittery, but a lot brighter. And she wasn't running to her medicine cabinet, pulling out the codeine bottle. . . . Something had changed.

She winked and reached for her apron that was hanging on the back of the pantry door. I watched her carefully knot the matching family apron we'd sewn together right before the divorce. She smoothed down the ruffles and patted down the heart pocket I'd insisted on sewing onto hers. She'd done the same for mine.

5

Closet Monsters

We reached for the apron at the same time. Daddy picked it up off the floor and dusted it off before handing it back to me. Our fingers linked together for a second, our eyes, too. I knew he remembered. After me and Mama had sewn those matching aprons, we'd chased him through the house with the one we'd made for him. Daddy'd escaped into the bedroom and we'd all fallen across the bed in a tangle of scarlet ruffles and red cloth and hoots, trying to pin him down. Laughing, he'd finally modeled the apron saying that when he'd grill out he'd wear it, but if he heard the neighbor's bull snorting, he'd have to take it off.

Daddy quietly cleared his throat and moved over to the sink. "Muddy, go on upstairs and rest. I can throw the chops on the charcoal."

"Thanks. Not feeling too good. I think I will." I hung up my apron.

I sat on my window seat and looked out below as Daddy lit the grill. He slipped back inside and after a few minutes came back out carrying a plate of chops. Then I watched him slide his big ol' hand inside the delicate sweetheart pocket me and Mama'd sewn onto his apron. He pulled out a handkerchief and slowly wiped his eyes.

I dabbed at my own tears and curled up in my bed. I got lost in my thoughts, until I heard him outside the door again.

"Pastor's here," Daddy called. He opened the door. "His missus sent over a pretty sunflower bouquet." He held up the vase.

"Why don't you come on down? He wants to say a prayer with us."

"I'm still not feeling so good."

"Okay, I'll tell Pastor to come back another time, then."

I studied the flowers.

"Daddy, wait."

"Yes?"

"What about Genevieve? Do you know where they took her?"

"I called the state police. The trooper said they took Genevieve to her next of kin."

"But I'm her next of kin."

Daddy shook his head. "You're a minor. Law says it's her grandmother, baby."

"Mrs. Whitlock?"

"Muddy, folks say she's a real nice lady, keeps a clean house, and attends the First Baptist church over in Dayre. Your mama always spoke highly of Mrs. Whitlock."

I nodded, sleepily. "Hard to believe Tommy was her son." Worry set in. Did she have her favorite teddy, Chitterboo? Her ratty pink blanket that cradled her to sleep? Did Mrs. Whitlock know that she was quirky with mashed potatoes, but always fancied sweet potatoes? And what about her favorite lullaby I'd made up for her . . . ? Would she sing to her?

"I've already called Mrs. Whitlock. Genevieve is doing fine. We'll run over there soon," he said, pricking through my silent worries. "You sure you don't feel up to seeing Pastor, for a few minutes? Maybe try an' eat something?"

"No, thanks, I need to sleep."

"All right, then, Muddy. . . . Oh, by the way, a boy named Bobby called. Is this one of your school friends?"

"Huh? When did he call?" I straightened up.

"Fifteen minutes ago. Told him you were resting and he said he'd try back tomorrow. You get some rest." He shut the door.

I hope he will call back.

I took an old gown of Mama's from my dresser drawer and managed to slip into her thread-worn flannel and climb into bed, pressing the folds of the nightgown close.

When I was five years old and feeling scared, Mama'd let me choose from her many gowns to chase away the nightmares. I'd always reach for the one with the hyacinth blooms, trimmed with cotton lace. It was so huge on my body way back then that Mama would have me sweep up the bottom and knot it so I wouldn't trip when walking. Once in bed, it had felt like I was wrapped in Mama's soft hug, sheltered and safe. When she left us for Tommy, she'd left the flannel gown in Daddy's dresser.

I lay in bed watching the silhouettes of branches flicker across my walls, their shadows growing larger as the sun set. I closed my eyes and drifted off. Soon, images of lemons filled my dreams. I found myself surrounded by them. Smothering. I kept knocking them off onto the floor, but they kept piling back on, only to have me knock them off again, and again. The thumps of fruit echoed and grew louder.

I awoke with a start, thinking about Mama fixing my birthday dinner, yesterday. She'd accidentally knocked a bowl of lemons off the counter and the fruit had scattered everywhere. I'd jumped up to help her gather them, but she'd shooed me away and pointed to my ice pack.

I put the ice pack back to my forehead. The smell of stale yeast from the bread bag assaulted my nostrils. I winced. The bump that McGee had given me was starting to swell. "You knew about the birthday pony, didn't you, Mama?" I tried to smile.

Mama placed the last fallen lemon back into the bowl and set it down on the table. "Uh-huh, Adam told me about it as soon as he bought it. You got yourself a powerful pony there. Just be careful not to let it get away from you. And always wear your lap belt, sugar." She lit the pilot light on the stove. "Hey, Mudas, do you remember the day you helped with the red cabbage casserole?"

I did indeed, and answered with a giggle. The last time I tried to make the dish, we'd waited hours for the casserole to cook only to pull it out and find raw cabbage. I'd forgotten to put in the apples and to turn on the oven.

"Well, how 'bout today you just watch me cook and then I'll write the recipe down for you after?"

Red cabbage casserole really was my favorite dish. Daddy's too.

"And, oh my," Mama chatted on, "remember the Thanksgiving dinner when I asked you to wash the turkey before I stuffed it? I stepped out for a minute, only to come back and find the sink overflowing with bubbles! Joy dishwashing soap bubbled up from that turkey's cavity like *The Lawrence Welk Show*!" She chuckled, wiping away a happy tear.

Caught up in Mama's mood, I leaned in close. "Without a doubt, that year the Summers had the cleanest and most joyous Thanksgiving in all of Peckinpaw!"

Mama laughed, but her eyes took on a distance.

I studied my sneakers.

I'm sure she was remembering, just like me, that it was the Summers' last Thanksgiving dinner. The last one before Daddy cheated, the last one before she hooked up with Tommy. And the last one before she started sporting Tommy's bruises.

"Listen, Mudas, I don't want you to tell your daddy, or anyone, about what happened today, okay? It's complicated. And there's no sense in riling up Adam's temper with this, do you understand? My hands are full enough with my job and taking care of Tommy and the baby. I don't need to be worrying about Adam going off half-cocked. Okay, sugar? Promise me?"

"But—"

"I know you're worried, but I'll handle it. I am handling it, Mudas. I promise. Your mama's not all out of tricks just yet. You'll see. Now, let's have that promise." She raised two fingers.

Reluctantly, I brought two fingers up to my mouth, kissed, then raised them in the air, like she'd taught me long ago, knowing she wouldn't be pleased and the promise wouldn't be sealed until I did. "Promise."

Mama kissed her fingers, pressed them to mine, and nodded. "Now, wait till I show you what I found!"

"What?"

"Go get the box that's sitting on my bed."

I found a medium cardboard box on her sagging mattress

and lugged it to the kitchen table. Mama plucked off the blue tissue paper that had been stuffed inside and pulled out my toddler blanket (or, the shreds that were left of it), a dog-eared copy of *Heidi,* and my junior chemistry set.

I laughed. "I haven't seen this stuff in ages."

"I found these in your memory trunk last week and thought it would be a good time to show you. It's not every day you turn seventeen, sugar. This age is special. It's the twilight between youth and adulthood. Sometimes a bit gray, sometimes a prism full of colors. You'll want to savor it."

I pocketed her words.

"Look here, Mudas," she said, holding up the wad of faded yarn that was the remains of my baby blanket. "Nothing but strings left here! Lawd, you sucked on that blanket so much when you were falling asleep, I feared you'd end up with a ball of yarn in your belly big enough to knit a new one."

I picked up the old chemistry set and unfolded the metal accordion-style box. "I remember how bad I wanted this thing and how excited I was when I got it." I ran my fingers over the test tubes.

"Yes, and you drove us all crazy with your experiments! Especially that invisible ink—marking up everything you could get your mitts on!"

"Uh-huh." I chuckled. "And do you remember me mixing up those smoke bombs? I still remember how: Take sulfur, charcoal, and potassium nitrate, and voilà!"

"I'm not likely to forget your famous stink bombs, Mudas. I do believe a couple of them found their way onto Jingles's porch, and that a certain young lady"—she sly-eyed me—"ended up doing time with a month of prayer study over at the pastor's house."

I snorted with laughter at the memory.

"Your granddaddy Tilley gave me a chemistry set a lot like this when I was your age. Oh, I wished you had met your grandparents. You would've loved your granddaddy Tilley."

"We hardly ever talk about your mama and daddy. Or any of the Tilleys. I do wish I could've met them."

"Me too, sugar. God, that was so long ago, but to me it feels like yesterday. It was more than I could bear, losing them to that crash. And then losing Adam so soon after that . . ." She placed her hands in her lap and folded them prayer-like.

Unsure of what to say, I looked down at my own.

"You know," she said, clearing her throat and plastering on a stiff smile. "Your granddaddy Tilley used codes and invisible ink in World War I, just like you did with your chemistry set. He sure did love showing me all of his old war stuff. And, before you came along, Adam and I had our own secret notes we'd pass back and forth. I taught him what my daddy taught me." She smiled wistfully. "Your daddy even wrote me a poem once, and it was the sweetest thing."

"He did? What did it say?"

"I can't remember now. It was silly," Mama said, a spot of red heating her cheeks. She turned abruptly. "I think I hear Genevieve squirming around. Why don't you go get her up and put a change of clothes on her?"

We spent the afternoon playing with Genevieve and eating. Inviting scents of simmering red cabbage, onions, and apples filled the room, helping our happy chatter along.

Mama sang "Happy Birthday" to me, and the baby cooed and clapped. Afterward, we went outside to the car. I wanted to show off Peggy, but instead I nervously chewed on a fingernail, worrying it was too much, me getting this cool car and all. I would be riding in style while she drove a fifteen-year-old rusted pickup truck, trailed by streams of blue smoke as it coughed and sputtered around Town Square. Snooty townsfolk would wrinkle their noses, and some even shouted out rude remarks. But Mama was never curt to those folks, forgiving to a fault. She'd always feign indifference or offer an explanation for their insults: "Mrs. Kern's been having tough family problems," she'd say, or "Who cares what Doris thinks?" or "James lost his job last month."

"Really sharp ride, Mudas," Mama said sincerely.

I stammered, "Mama . . . I've been thinking. I can drive Peggy over here in the mornings and walk to school, so you can use her during the day."

"Thanks, sugar, but the truck runs just fine," she responded, tamping the offer.

I nodded even though I knew ol' Blue had stranded her twice last week.

She let me drive her and baby Genevieve down the road, first to Harper's Filling Station, the only gasoline pump in town, for my first official fill-up. Old man Harper took his time filling up the Mustang, wiping off the windows, shooting wolfish glances at me when he thought Mama wasn't looking, and letting his sweaty hand linger on mine when he gave me back my change. His three little boys played over by the air pump, spraying each other with bursts of air, giggling. Mr. Harper cut them a look; then he leaned in close to my ear, his breath soured with beer, and whispered, "Now that you're old 'nough to drive, maybe you're old enough for some other grown-up things, hmm?"

I expected Mama to ream him out with a good tongue-lashing, but when I looked over for help, I saw that she had turned her attention to the baby, trying to calm her fussing. I tucked my chin under, wondering how to best blunt Mr. Harper's advances. Harper followed my gaze and shot Mama a nasty smirk before running his tongue over brown teeth. Then Roy McGee pulled into the lot. Harper gave two raps to my roof, before strutting over to McGee's car. I breathed a sigh of relief. Harper leaned into McGee's window, with his elbows resting on the door, and turned back once to eye me. He set to wiping down McGee's windows.

"Time to go," Mama said when she saw McGee's car, waggling her hand at the windshield urgently.

We decided to head to town to share an ice cream. I pulled in front of the Top Hat Café, showing off my parallel-parking skills by squeezing the Mustang perfectly in between two other parked cars.

I waited beside Liar's Bench with Genevieve hitched to my hip while Mama went inside the diner and bought us a strawberry cone. Genevieve grinned up at me. Her sweetness was irresistible. I kissed her soft cheek and blew raspberries on her chubby arms and neck. She squeezed her eyes in joy and beamed up at me. I couldn't help but worry about the kind of life she was going to have with Tommy. I hugged her close. A good-natured baby, she hugged me back real tight, lapping up all the attention.

When Mama returned, we sat down on the bench, tucking Genevieve in between us. We laughed as we watched her lick the cone, then clap her sticky hands and grace us with strawberry-kissed smiles.

Afterward, Mama sat Genevieve on the patch of grass below Liar's Bench and gave her the house keys to play with. Rummaging inside her pocketbook, Mama pulled out a pen and an index card containing her cabbage casserole recipe. Using the plank of wood between us, she wrote: *RED CABBAGE—HEAT. Don't forget the oven.* She tapped the words and laughed. "And be sure to share this with your daddy. I bet it's been a while since he's had this dish. Oh, and make sure you use the River Wolf apples, not those Granny Smiths."

She swept up Genevieve, who was rolling Osage balls toward the street, and placed her on her lap. "And don't forget your promise. Our promise." She raised two fingers.

More like our lie, I wanted to say, a lie riding on the back of another's truth. But I stopped myself when I caught the woe in her eyes. Instead, I raised two fingers and pressed them to hers, then returned my hand to its rightful place on Liar's Bench.

She looked across the road to the town clock. Mama said, "I better get back. Be sure and let me know how the casserole turns out."

"I will," I said, fanning the recipe in the air. The paper smelled lemony, like her. I folded the card and tucked it carefully inside my jean pocket.

When I pulled into the driveway, Mama reached into her pocket and pulled out a ten-dollar bill. "Happy Early Birthday! I thought maybe you could use some money for gasoline an' ice cream. And here, take this, too, just in case." She pressed a Band-Aid into my hand.

I didn't want to take her money, knowing she couldn't afford it, and knowing it would take from Genevieve's milk and diaper money. But I didn't want to insult her either. I murmured my thanks, and said, "You know, I'm getting too old to be carrying around Snoopy Band-Aids, Mama." I couldn't remember the last time we'd parted ways without Mama giving me a Band-Aid. "Just in case," she'd always say. I knew it was her small way of showing her love and mothering me from a distance. It had become tradition since she'd married Tommy.

"Thanks again, Mama, it was a great day." I looked up at the house and frowned. Normally, if I saw him, I'd go inside. Make it seem like it was all my doing to see her about some urgent school business.

"I can come in . . . maybe help you put down Genevieve?" I offered halfheartedly, when the last thing I wanted to do was to lock horns with Tommy. Always scary. Once, he broke my wrist, and he said that if I told, he'd break both of hers. So, I had to tell Daddy I'd tripped over a log while running laps around our backfield. What I really wanted right now was to cruise a little, pick up ThommaLyn, and see if I could find Bobby before I went home.

Mama twisted around to follow my stare. "Well, I s'pose it wouldn't be a bad idea. . . ." She turned back, and I knew she'd caught the fret in my eyes.

"Nah, sugar. You go ahead. Don't forget our call on Sunday," she reminded. Relieved, I didn't push it this time. She kissed my forehead, hoisted Genevieve onto her hip, and headed across the lawn, leaving her citrusy scent lingering behind.

Tommy leaned over the porch railing, plastered and pouting.

I came fully awake to Daddy knocking on the door once again. "ThommaLyn's here." He cracked open the door. I rubbed the sleep from my eyes.

My friend poked her head in, her lake-blue eyes filled with grief, robbed of their usual sunshine. She sniffled. "I ran across the field as soon as I heard about Ella. Oh, Muddy . . ."

I wanted to run to her, but my grieving head weighed me down and I couldn't lift myself from the forgiving warmth of my bed. ThommaLyn set down her overnight bag and knelt beside me, gently cupping my face in her hands. I closed my eyes, grateful.

The door clicked gently behind us and my words trickled out. I let the day's tragedy spill forth, repeating some of the horrors I'd read in the officials' report, and the words I'd heard at the crime scene, carefully leaving the ribbons out. I didn't think I could ever bring myself to utter that . . . not even to ThommaLyn.

ThommaLyn rubbed my back and did her best to comfort, but I could see her lip quivering and her head shaking. Each shake waggled the quilting thread that dangled from her puffy red earlobes. I'd pierced her ears myself just last week with an ice cube and one of Grammy Essie's darning needles. It had turned out to be messier and more dramatic than either of us had imagined. I'd won the coin toss, leaving ThommaLyn to go first. This weekend was supposed to be my turn.

After a bit, ThommaLyn asked quietly, "Have you heard from Bobby Marshall?"

"No, well, yes . . . he called, but Daddy answered and told him I was resting."

"What'd your Daddy say about you seeing him?"

"I haven't told him yet. And, as far as I know, he's only seen us once on Liar's Bench, and he thought it was just another guy hanging 'round for a ride out to Ruby's. . . . I was waiting to tell him about Bobby on my birthday, figuring that'd be a good time. . . . But now, all this . . ." I trailed.

"I bet he lets you date him," ThommaLyn predicted. "He won't care about color. Everyone knows your daddy doesn't have an ounce of prejudice in his bones."

He didn't. Still, I worried about it more and more. Bobby had a different heritage of sort, something that reached into other lands, in a different time, maybe. I wasn't quite sure what. Bobby didn't talk about it. And I hadn't been too concerned at first. But this past month that we'd been hanging out more, I'd started to notice the occasional whispered slurs from elders huddled on Town Square sidewalks, whose words trailed just a hairbreadth behind us when we'd pass by. Just loud enough for us to hear. "Mutt," they'd call him, telling him to "stick to his own kind." "T'aint right," they'd mutter, or "Nigger Injun ain't got no business with a white girl." The very worst kind of ugliness. Bobby would talk over them and we'd hurry past, both moon-eyed over around-the-corner possibilities like cuddling, kissing—us.

"I'll worry about this later, ThommaLyn. My mind's stretched as is."

" 'Course, hon. I just want what you want . . . Just want you to be safe, too."

I nodded, understanding. We rested our heads together a bit, and ThommaLyn sighed heavily, stitching her worries into mine.

After we'd talked everything out, and our pauses fattened with silt, ThommaLyn changed into her pajamas and crawled into bed beside me. Most times, I would make her a fluffy pallet atop the rug beside the bed, to save her from my long, restless legs. But tonight, the idea of a pallet so far away frightened both of us.

Reluctantly, I turned off the bedside lamp. About an hour later, panic clawed at me in the dark and I cried out for Mama. ThommaLyn rolled over and reached her shadowy hand toward mine like we used to when we were little and scared of closet monsters. I grabbed hold and tucked it tight between my pillow and my cheek, locking my fingers with hers.

I awoke close to midnight, feeling shaky and disoriented. I switched on the lamp. ThommaLyn was snoring softly, mouth parted, with her cat-black hair draped across her eyes. She was usually a heavy sleeper. Quietly, I sat up and opened the drawer of my nightstand, pulling out my old diary.

I thumbed through the pages, moving over to the window seat to study my spidery ink marks on the pale blue pages— mostly notes I'd jotted down after track meets about the points I had earned. Then I read the last entry, one of several ink-smeared and tear-stained pages about my cheating ex-boyfriend, Tripp. I traced the sketch I'd made of the pearl ring he'd given me, then scratched my nail across it, ripping the page. I couldn't help but wonder why Bobby Marshall hadn't called back yet. I'd come to depend on his company.

I finally turned to the page I'd been looking for, dated 1964, the year I'd gone to Nashville to live with Mama and Tommy. I looked closely at my scrawl: a big old frowny face filled with raindrop tears above the words: *Tommy whooped me VERY hard today when I got lost.* Tommy, the under-the-bed boogey-man of childhood dreams, had finally crawled out to blacken the day. Wasn't it bad enough that he had destroyed her spirit? But to do that unspeakable thing with the ribbons . . . ?

Still, a tiny part of me caved to denial. I studied on the sher-iff's preliminary report. What if he hadn't killed her? What if her *refreshments* had caught up with her? What if she had done this to herself? I pressed the page to my lips. And doing it on my birthday, well, she must not have loved me very much. . . .

Finding nary a speck of comfort in denials, I tucked my grief into the night and hummed a birthday ditty.

My song drifted through Grammy Essie's homespun curtains, out my open window, and melded with the distant rail hymn of a midnight train.

6

Burial of the Fourth Sister

Early Tuesday morning, four days after Mama passed, Daddy called softly from the bottom of the stairs, "Muddy, you 'bout ready? Your mama's service starts soon, baby."

I pressed the hem of Mama's nightgown to my cheek one more time and slowly took it off. I spread it out across my bed, careful to smooth out the wrinkles so it looked perfect.

"Muddy—"

"Coming . . ."

I slid on a boxy dress—the only black clothing I had—and examined the snug fit, which left me tugging at the cap sleeves to cover my bare shoulders. God forbid Pastor Dugin, a huge, balding man with a voice like nails across chalkboard, should take note of my immodesty and condemn me to eternal Hell. "I'm going there anyway," I sighed to my empty room, "just as sure as I killed my mama by leaving her on Tommy's doorstep."

Daddy called again, "Muddy, breakfast. C'mon down and try to eat."

"Coming," I shouted, as I slipped into heels and then hurried down the steps.

Daddy stood at the kitchen table reading over Mama's will for what seemed like the hundredth time. The day Mama died, he'd spent hours turning the house upside down looking for her Last Will and Testament, the one they'd had drawn up together the year I was born.

"I am so relieved that she never changed it," he said. "It's all written up just how she wanted things. And where she wanted them. Ella will be buried in Summers Cemetery."

Yesterday, Sheriff Jingles had dropped by and told Daddy that after he'd gone to the jail cell and told Whitlock about Ella's burial plans, you could hear the ruckus bounce around Town Square like a possessed rubber ball. Rattling the cell bars, Tommy had screamed, "It's my right to bury my wife in Pauper Field next to my family, where she belongs!"

Sheriff said that the judge had set Tommy's bail, and that Roy McGee had phoned to say he'd be by sometime this week to post it. But when he told Tommy the good news, Tommy went berserk, said he'd come up with his own bail—that he didn't want nothing from McGee.

Daddy turned away to wipe his eyes, then folded the document and tucked it carefully inside a kitchen drawer. He cleared his throat and nodded toward the breakfast plates. "Have some of those scrambled eggs and toast."

"Smells good," I lied. "I should've set the alarm earlier to fix breakfast."

He offered an empty smile. "Thought I'd give you a break."

I took a few nibbles of a slice of burnt toast before tossing it unceremoniously into the trash.

We drove all the way to the United Methodist Church in silence.

An usher greeted us at the church steps and escorted us to the front pew. The organist was playing "A Mighty Fortress Is Our God" as people filled the church. Soon it was packed with people cooling themselves with cardboard fans advertising Russman's Funeral Home, and a hush fell over the crowd. Pastor Dugin began to speak about life and death and God's glory. And Mama. It hurt to hear him talk in the past tense.

The rest of the service passed in a haze of hallelujahs and amens, all shrouded in the cloying stink of funeral flowers.

At long last, the organist began to pump out "Shall We Gather at the River?" which was mine and Daddy's cue to stand and lead the procession from the church. The pallbearers followed, Sheriff Jingles among them. I couldn't bear to look back at Mama's casket, but the telltale jangling of his keys told me it was on its way.

At the church door, the usher waited to lead us over to the procession car, Bud Lincoln's black Mercury, the one he kept spit-shined to rent to Russman's for funerals. Bud eased out of the lot and followed the hearse past the Unity Baptist Church, the bowling alley, and out toward the Peckinpaw fairgrounds. Patches of bluegrass shimmered in August morning dew.

In the opposite lane, Roy McGee's car slowed just shy of stopping, then quickly passed. Daddy twisted around and stared hotly at McGee until he was well out of sight.

Our car followed close behind the hearse, winding its way lazily toward Cemetery Road, past the good people of Ella Mudas Tilley's hometown. I studied the faces of townsfolk along the way. On the sidewalks, people stopped and nodded, nudging their children to do the same. Farm women backed away from their clotheslines and edged closer to the road in solidarity—women who wouldn't even look Mama in the eye after she married Tommy. Today, the gentlemen and farmers took off their hats and caps. Oncoming cars pulled over to the side of the road and even into ditches as we passed in quiet procession.

We pulled up to Summers Cemetery. Daddy came around to my side and opened the door, leading my body where it didn't want to go. I paused at the tall bur oak and shuffled toward the cemetery's big iron gate, afraid to complete our procession.

It wasn't a fear of the cemetery itself, because I knew the history of most of the 111 graves here in Summers Cemetery, including the four I'd added. The freshest was Patty, buried the year I turned ten, a wolf spider who'd spun a beautiful new web night after night, weaving her orb precisely from the porch railing post to our screen door. It was beautiful. I had become so attached that I wouldn't let anyone use our front door for a whole month. Then, one morning, I found Patty curled up on the ground beside the door. Heartbroken, I'd covered her in cotton, placed her in a match box, and carried her over to the family plot to bury alongside the others: Ricky, a cranky old barn cat who'd belonged to my grandparents and died of old age;

Pauline, the field mouse that Ricky'd caught and delivered to our doorstep; and Speck, the passing monarch butterfly whose short life span had ended on my windowsill. They were all lined up alongside Grammy Essie's and Papaw's graves. Now, Mama would join their somber ranks.

Daddy took my hand and nudged me forward, through the iron gate, and toward the fresh grave and that final step to finality.

ThommaLyn stood beside the casket, waiting for me to join her. I searched the faces of the mourners, hoping to see Bobby Marshall. My heart sank when I saw he hadn't come. Then my eyes lit upon baby Genevieve, snug in Mrs. Whitlock's arms.

I stepped toward them. "Genevieve," I whispered over and over, stroking her chubby little cheeks. "I'm here, baby girl. Sister will never leave you, I promise." I kissed the baby's head, dampening her soft hair with tears. Mrs. Whitlock smiled at me and I saw that she had kind eyes. Genevieve was safe, in steady arms. A lot steadier than mine. I took my place between ThommaLyn and Daddy.

Pastor Dugin took a handkerchief out of his black robe and wiped the August sweat off his brow before giving the eulogy, pausing first to address me and Daddy, then the crowd. He read again from the Bible, the thrum of his voice matching the heightening buzz of the cicadas. Sorrow crept in, sinking deep inside and settling like a handprint in cement. I'd never dreamed my heart could hurt this much.

Time crawled by. I brushed the tip of my shoe over a patch of dandelions and my thoughts drifted to Grammy Essie's famous recipes—and how she'd be having a hissy right now, seeing all these flowers going to waste. We'd called her the *Lion Keeper* because there wasn't a single part of the dandelion she wouldn't put to good use. I'd spent many a Saturday afternoon helping her and Papaw make dandelion wine, dandelion jelly, and even roasted dandelion coffee. They'd shown me how to pluck all the petals and strip the hulls and leaves, releasing their earthy smells to filter through the house. The wine took about five months to cure, but when it was ready, the family would gather 'round the table and everyone, even me, would receive a mug of the sweet wine. I could almost taste the sugary sweetness, the two table-spoons that Grammy Essie allowed, measured out carefully and passed to me with a wink. "To summer's sugar," she'd say.

I gazed across the road to the old Summers Homestead, its 300 acres stretching low and rising like a water snake. Daddy's ancestors settled the land in 1792. My grandparents' two-story farmhouse, its hardwood poplar milled right from the Summerses' treed acres, was now ours. And what was once full of life was now full of nothing but dusty memories and ghosts of yesterday. Gone, all gone.

I looked over to Mrs. Whitlock. From her hip, Genevieve jig-gled a new rattle, smiling, lost in its novelty. I tried to draw strength from her sunshine.

At long last, Pastor closed the burial with a blessing for Mama, pausing a moment for spiritual meditation. Then he rang the brass bell four times to signal Mama's passing.

I bowed my head and pulled from memory one of Grammy Essie's favorite quotes, by Richard Crashaw, the one she'd taught me long ago, and the one I'd said for her when she crossed. I mouthed the farewell blessing to Mama:

> *And when life's sweet fable ends.*
> *Soul and Body part like friends.*
> *No quarrels, murmurs, no delay;*
> *A kiss, a sigh, and so away.*

ThommaLyn hugged me before stepping aside. Mrs. Whit-lock let me kiss a fussy Genevieve good-bye. I clung to her chubby little hands that had once clung to Mama until Mrs. Whitlock promised to bring her by soon. A line of pinched faces, wearing matching pinched shoes and their Sunday finest, came forward to offer their condolences to me and Daddy, some commenting on the beautiful service.

I waited by the graveside, watching while the last of the mourners made their way out of the cemetery and across the road, walking the gravel path up to the Summers Homestead.

I could see ThommaLyn helping the elders set up folding tables, others spreading quilts and blankets under the shade of elms in the meadow for the supper after the burial.

Daddy stood outside the cemetery gate, chewing on his unlit cigar to allow me a moment alone. I ran my hand over the steel casket and pulled a sunflower out of the funeral spray. Mama's favorite.

I plucked off a petal and glided the silk across my face, remembering Daddy's story about the first time he'd come calling on Mama, with roses. Mama had promptly informed him: "It is sunflowers I love, not roses, Adam."

"And why's that, Ella?" he'd asked.

She'd raised her head to the sky, and announced, "Because the sunflower is always planted in the north corner of a garden as the protector over its three corner sisters: bean, corn, and squash. They call it the 'fourth sister,' just like me."

Daddy'd cocked his head in confusion. Everybody knew that Mama was the only Tilley child.

She'd answered his silent question. "I had three big sisters, Adam, but they all died soon after childbirth. I'm the fourth. I never knew my sisters, but I will always guard the memories of what could have been."

Every spring after that, my daddy would load up his old pickup with a bag of seeds and a hand hoe, and head out to the Summers Homestead. He'd spread a quilt down for Mama and she'd read while he worked, stopping to glance up as he labored under sunny skies, knees set on earth's naked field, carving out row after row. He'd tell Mama he envisioned a hundred rows of sunflowers, and promised, "Soon, they'll lift up their brown pancake heads to the sky to pay homage to you, my love." He'd spread out his strong arms in exaggeration and Mama would always laugh, chiding him, "All you'll do is fatten the deer and coons, Adam." But he wouldn't listen, even when the critters came and feasted under the cloak of darkness. Instead, he would curse the beasts and faithfully nurse the few plants that remained.

The field had been barren for years, ever since Mama left with Tommy.

Clutching the sunflower, I lowered myself down onto shaky knees. "Mama," I whispered, "how could you leave me? Why . . . why do you keep leaving me?"

I curled my fingers around the petals of the sunflower, crushing them together and letting the smashed head fall into the deep belly of earth that hungered beside her casket. Looking out across the graves of my kin, I cried for them, and for Daddy and me, left behind with not one of them to cling to. And for baby Genevieve, whose memories of Mama had no chance to take root and would wither just as surely as these graveside flowers.

Daddy called softly to me.

I looked up and spotted a lone colored woman making her way down dusty Summers road. She walked alongside the cemetery fence, dragging a stick across the iron bars, rattling a broken rhythm that sounded a lot like the mournful song of a rain crow that had filled my heart.

Spent, I scooped up a handful of rich Kentucky soil—soil that had already taken too many, and too much. I stood and let the black dirt sieve through my fingers and fall across Mama's grave.

7

The Better Cheater

At sunrise, I awoke to the quarrelsome cries of grackles that punched through the silence of the countryside.

I rolled out from beneath the quilt, rubbing my swollen eyes. I cocked my ear. Oddly quiet. It sounded like Daddy was still in bed, an abnormal beginning for a Wednesday morning in the Summers house. 'Course there was no going back to normal anymore. Not after losing Mama. I never thought I'd wake up with her gone—gone forever and never coming back. I couldn't believe it had been five days since she passed.

Peeling off yesterday's crumpled funeral dress, I picked out a pair of old blue gym shorts and a T-shirt. *What's the use,* I thought. Coach Grider was never going to let females do track. Take a stand, Mama had said. "It's your right!" I picked up my running sneakers and thought about my first pair, the ones Mama bought me when I first visited her in Chicago for the summer. I was ten. Mama and Tommy's arguments had followed them from Nashville to Chicago, growing louder—uglier. That's when I first took up running. After one of their bigger arguments, Mama took me to the city park in Chicago. I'd been surprised to see people running on narrow asphalt paths around the park's boundaries. I'd asked her why they were doing this. I thought this was a fine thing, especially when I saw a woman doing it. Mama'd said she didn't really know why but reckoned it might be they'd gotten a case of the "Lonely Lucys" or "Freddie Fidgets" (what Mama always called my unsettling times). I'd wished I could run around the park and give it my Lonely Lucys. Mama'd laughed a little nervously. The way she sometimes did when the Freddie Fidgets latched on to her.

A week later, Mama'd said she wanted to look at ballet shoes for herself. We'd gone shopping and instead of ballet shoes, we came home carrying a box of funny-looking shoes with waffle-iron bottoms for me. I was hooked, and so was Mama. She'd gotten a kick out of predicting who'd be the next runner I'd catch up with and then pass.

I looked out to my practice track that carved across the back-fields of Summers Homestead, and studied the paths cut into thick scattered tickseed, morning glory, and joe-pye weed. Normally, my homemade running trail was stubbled, but I could see it had been a while since Daddy last bushhogged.

It would have to do. My body was craving a hard run, an escape from the Lucys and Freddies. I hit the path and scared up a doe and her twins about one minute in. I shook off the surprise and ran the first quarter mile, easing into a natural rhythm. Soon, my gait grew strong, and my breathing was lost to the wilds and I let go of yesterday. My legs escaped the earth as I ran the slopes and wore the paths for six miles around. When done, I lifted my hands to the sky and bargained for a better day. For a good hour I cooled down and walked the meadows, almost enjoying its beginning.

With renewed energy, I went back into the house and took a bath; then I picked out a pair of my widest bell-bottoms and a spaghetti-strapped shirt from the clothing already strewn across my bedroom floor. I was surprised to find that the pockets of my jeans were already full—loose change, a few scraps of paper, a lipstick. And Mama's recipe card. I pulled it out and pressed it close to me, inhaling the faint scent of lemon. *Bittersweet.*

I tucked the recipe back into my jeans and turned to the chore of having myself a "normal" morning. I rummaged through my nightstand to find the birth-control package that Mama had bought for me earlier this spring after a visit to her city OB/GYN. She'd had me start on them immediately, and made sure I was kept supplied with them ever since.

I'd shrugged and listened quietly when she'd explained the directions, too embarrassed to ask questions or protest. "It's your senior year," she'd said. "You're going to be smart, get out of here one day, and have a chance at a good life. I don't want you to even think about tying an apron knot or pinning a diaper until you've finished college. That'd be like leaving the birthday party before the cake is served. Here, take them. Just in case. Carry them always."

I never did get around to building up the courage to tell her there hadn't ever been a "just in case" moment, or that there probably wouldn't be one anytime soon. Maybe never, at the rate I was going.

Still, it kept my cycle regular and helped with the cramps some. I popped the tiny yellow pill into my parched mouth and dry-swallowed, all part of my morning ritual.

I cracked open my bedroom door and listened for Daddy.

Silence.

Padding downstairs to the kitchen, I lit the pilot inside the oven so I could get a start on breakfast for us. While I was waiting for it to heat, I picked up the kitchen phone. The party line was busy. I tried three more times and finally asked Widow Sims if I could use it. I knew it was taboo to call a boy for a date, but this was different. I really needed to call Bobby. Not for a date, but for a talk. I paced back and forth a few times before I finally got the courage to pick up the receiver. My windpipe clogged as I fought to find the perfect words. I let his number ring for a long while before hanging up, sorely disappointed. Where could he be?

When the grandfather clock struck nine, I plugged in the percolator.

My stomach grumbled as I lightly kneaded the biscuit dough. After I popped the bread into the oven, I grabbed a peach off the windowsill, soft and warm from days of sitting. When I was through, I spotted the water glass sitting next to the sink. I lifted it quickly to my nose and sniffed for any signs of whiskey—a boot soakin'. *Water.* A great relief, but I couldn't help feeling a snip of anger, because I couldn't trust my daddy.

Standing at the kitchen window, I stared out at the fields, mechanically gnawing on the peach and mentally chewing on yesterday, and what had been brewing inside me for days. Though my run had helped some, my heart helplessly panned for healing. Answers. Now two hours later, my good energy had slowly been replaced, bit by bit, by anger, a churning ball of rage. *I was looking to point the finger.*

If Daddy hadn't boozed, lied, and cheated, I kept thinking. If Mama hadn't left us and hooked up with that good-for-nothing pillhead, none of this would have happened. She would still be here today, living and breathing. If Daddy had never lied to her . . .

At the dinner after the funeral, I'd overheard Ocilla Brown click her false teeth to her nosey group that "if only Adam had never slept around, poor Ella would be here today. Bless her heart," she added, collecting her Jesus points like S&H stamps to trade with the devil.

I tried to shake off these thoughts, especially since Daddy'd been taking such good care of me this past week, letting me sleep in and fixing meals for us. But maybe Ocilla Brown was right and he was responsible from the start, and worse, he was still hiding something from me. And how could I forget what Pastor Dugin's wife had said long ago . . . ?

Yawning, Daddy shuffled through the kitchen door. "Nearly ten o'clock. I can't believe I slept in so late. Good thing I cleared my court calendar for a few days."

I slouched over the sink and watched a flock of crows fuss in the yard. *Why, even the birds are mad at him.*

Daddy peeked out the window beside me. "If those rain clouds would pass, we might have a nice day."

The crows took flight.

If. If. If . . . "Yeah, *if*," I said, looking at him, my anger coiled tight, ready to pounce at the slightest thing or anything that would allow me to unleash. "Been a whole lotta 'ifs' in this house lately." I squeezed past him to hurry upstairs.

I tried to ignore the soft taps on my bedroom door by cramming the pillow tightly over my head, but Daddy was insistent.

"Not feeling well. Go away. Please. Just go away." I pressed my fingers against my temples—squeezing, pushing—and wishing I could just rub him away.

"C'mon, Muddy, let's talk."

My temper sparked, quick and reflexive, like flint on steel. "Mudas, not Muddy."

"Muddy, I—"

"MUD. US. Please stop calling me Muddy, ADAM. My name's Mudas!"

"Watch that sassy mouth, gal."

"Why should I? You can't get anything right! It's your fault! All of it!" I cannoned off my accusations to the door. "If you hadn't cheated on Mama, there'd never have been a divorce or a funeral, and she'd still be here today. Everyone knows it. . . ."

"Muddy, you open this door right now!"

I paced across hardwoods, single-minded with my anger. "You cheated with that secretary, skirt-chased all those women."

"We've been through this before. Just one," he honey-coated. He'd always insisted there'd only been one: just one moment of infidelity with his new secretary, Caroline—the one I'd spilled the beans about when I was five years old. But I knew better, I'd heard about Jackie and Laura, and seems Mama was right, once a snake, always . . .

"Whatever," I mumbled, his past wedged between us, soldiering walls, always blocking. I'd understood little as a child. But Daddy and Mama's heated whispers grew, and my knowledge grew as I did. And I began to understand more of the words I heard and the glimpses of Daddy's cheatin' ways that I saw. The long office hours. The way the town women hovered around him, leaning in close. And him always sidling closer, flirting, being extra nice and talking especially slow when they were around.

He'd always tell Mama, "It's my job to be nice to them, so they'll do me a favor when I need their help with a case or a witness, or even as a juror." I didn't understand back then that a small-town lawyer had to be "everyone's" good friend. I wasn't sure I understood it now.

He jiggled the knob, hard enough to rattle the whole door in its frame.

"You know what people say about you, Daddy? Do you?" I pounded into wood. "I overheard Myrtle Dugin calling you a horndog.... Yeah, that's right, the pastor's wife. She said you're nothin' but a horndog who chased any skirt you could tomcat it up with."

"Muddy Elizabeth Summers!" He battered the door. "You ain't too old for me to take a hickory switch and cut your tail, gal!"

"Myrtle Dugin was only saying what everybody already knows! That you're a cheater. *Lord!* It's your lies that killed Mama!" I picked up my funeral dress off the floor, wadded it into a ball, and threw it at my bedroom door. "Just leave me alone! It's all your fault Mama's dead!" I flung the blame into the charged air, ignoring the voice inside that said the fault was mine for being too weak to stay in the city with her. Leaving her in the yard last week. Or for tattling on Daddy long ago.

I pushed back the guilt, letting anger take the lead. "You had a knot in her noose last Friday! *You* sat on Liar's Bench and swore you didn't cheat on her! You brought women into our house and even had Mama cook for them, letting her think y'all were just business friends, her never suspecting you was doing your business in their beds. And all your drinking ... Lord ... You drove her away!"

"Your mama had her own problems—"

"No, she didn't. . . . Don't say that. *You* were the problem." I chewed on my fist. I'd hardly known much about the danger of refreshments at age nine. But when I turned twelve, I'd over- heard Grammy Essie's whispers to Papaw. "Ella's taken to hard liquor like most folks to sweet tea, and she's got one foot in the trash with Tommy. Respectable lady sips a few tablespoons every now and then ... doesn't nurse a bottle every day. . . . Gonna end up like white-trash Oleanna Hogard if she's not careful," she'd worried to Papaw. I'd fretted for a good week, cried for another, and sulked around for one more after that. I was so ashamed. Ashamed for Mama, and for me. Then Grammy explained to me about the hurts of alcohol, and we'd both prayed for Mama to stop. I'd been praying ever since.

"Open this door right now, young lady." A hint of desperation had snuck into Daddy's voice, beneath the anger, the denials. For a brief moment I felt ill about the words I'd flung. His voice grew soft, like maybe he'd used up all the fight he had left. Maybe I had, too.

"Muddy, please. Jesus. Jesus Christ, please . . ." He slumped against the door, and I heard a gutted breath slip from his mouth.

Soupy, thick air made it difficult to breathe, and I could feel hot tears starting to gather behind my eyes. "Just go, Daddy. *Please.*"

He hesitated outside the door, like he didn't know what I might do if he waited me out. Finally, after a few silent moments, the heavy fall of his steps retreated down the hallway.

Spent, I sat down on the window seat and curled myself up tight against the frame. Reaching for my stuffed tiger, the one I'd received from Grammy Essie on my third Christmas, I stroked Tuffy's ringed tail and cuddled his thinning, fur body. "I'm Mudas. Mudas," I whispered into my tiger's tufted ears. I remembered the lilt Mama always lent to my name when she'd call for me. It was a special name, she'd told me, given as legacy in her family. The meaning: *a seed rising from the mud to blossom as a beautiful flower.* Leaning my head out the window, I drank the fresh air and silently cursed my ancestral name, which I'd once loved as a child, because it was carried by my mama and her mama before that.

But now, Mama was gone. I pressed Tuffy's tail to my eyes, hating that I couldn't stop the hurt, hating my weaknesses then and now. Worst of all, it was not, nor would it ever be, a remembered fact that I was named after my great-great-great grandmother. No. What people did remember was the fact that my daddy, Adam Persis Summers, had gone and ruined the name by marking it with the town's annual summer social: the Cow Plop Bingo.

I looked out the window at the persimmon tree and dredged up the yarn that had damned my name. Oh, how Daddy loved to regale anyone who hadn't already heard or, as a matter of fact, anyone who was too polite to deny Adam Summers one more telling of his braggart's tale: the story of how he'd met and courted Ella Mudas Tilley, my mama. The same ol' story that went like this:

In 1953, Daddy and his friend George were walking across the grounds of the courthouse when he spied a petite woman with gorgeous chestnut hair and green eyes sitting across the road on Liar's Bench. She was "sitting there all propered-up, daisy-like, with legs gracefully long and leading to Heaven," Daddy said.

He immediately stopped and was about to cross over to introduce himself when George held up his hand, and warned, "She's that Casanova Tommy Whitlock's gal. Name's Ella. She was raised in Nashville and Kentucky, same as him, and just moved back here after her parents passed. Easy pickings for Whitlock. So you best mosey on, Adam, before it costs you a whole lotta money and misery. And misery being 'bout the only thing you'd get on ol' Frannie Crow's bench."

Daddy just grinned wide, gave George a friendly whack on the back, and said, "You can't catch a rabbit if you don't muddy up your boots, boy."

And that he did, the following week at the Peckinpaw County Fair, by buying up all the chances for the Cow Plop Bingo, our town's favorite game of chance and an annual tradition. Every year, a particularly unfortunate field was made to look like a bingo card, divided into three-foot squares, each numbered with lime, and the good people of Peckinpaw would place their bets on whether or not a cow would plop on their number. The prize: a dance with the Fair Queen at the Midsummer Dance, the highlight of the Peckinpaw Fair. That year's queen: Ella Mudas Tilley.

Wasn't a year later that Daddy proposed to Mama on Liar's

Bench. I came along in '55, the very next year. In keeping with the Tilley family tradition, they named me Mudas. But Daddy gave me his own special nickname, "Muddy," in homage to his ingenious way of courting Mama and the philosophy that made it special. "Can't catch a rabbit if you don't muddy up your boots, gal," was the refrain of my childhood. My nickname was Daddy's way of reminding me that I needed to strive to be the best and always work extra hard to catch this rabbit of life. To his way of thinking, this was the only path to success.

An all right story. Except for the fact that my daddy didn't know when to end it. He'd puffed up his chest and told the famous Cow Plop Bingo story so many times that, in Peckinpaw, my name would be forever linked to those stupid cows. What a joke and an even bigger joke with the kids at school. Even my best friend, ThommaLyn, couldn't shake off using the name, though I didn't mind much, since she was made fun of for her own tomboy name, same as me. Sharing the misery sort of made it bearable. Still, being named after a boy is one thing, but living down a cow-patty legacy is entirely another. I'd come home from school crying no telling how many times, begging Daddy to let me change my name and to *please* stop telling that stupid story.

Then, one day, he did. It was years ago; three months shy of my ninth birthday. The year he let his rabbit get away. The year Mama decided that Daddy had used up all his chances. She'd had enough of his cheating ways. That's when she resolved to lace up her own shoes to do some stomping. It was in 1964, but it seemed like just yesterday, when Mama had dressed me in my finest cotton dress and driven us down to Liar's Bench to meet Daddy.

Daddy had hurried across the street from his office with a big smile stretched across his face that slowly slid downward with each step closer, until he finally sank down onto the bench next to us, with me in the middle. They wouldn't look at each other. I tapped my thumbs against my fingertips.

Mama crossed her arms and raised her chin. "Adam Summers," she said, "I'm leaving you. Say good-bye to Mudas."

Looking back and forth in confusion, I cried, "I don't wanna go, Mama. I don't want to leave Daddy." Mama wasted no time in marking my cheek with a smart whap. Sighing, Daddy dropped his unlit cigar in the geranium pot and got to work on a stack of lies meant to convince Mama to stay. But I guess that wasn't his day to be the better liar. Mama looked straight ahead as Daddy waded into the thick of his own murky waters and sank lower, and lower still. When he'd just about worn himself out, Mama calmly announced that she'd sold our spacious Bedford ranch and all of its belongings, and was moving us up to the big city of Nashville.

"Ella," he said, "if you'd just stop drinking, too, we could work—"

"Adam!" She looked hard at him.

I tugged on her arm. "Mama?"

"Ella," Daddy whispered, "please, we can both get counseling with the pastor and we can—"

Mama lifted a shaky hand.

Daddy unleashed a fresh pack of lies, promises, protests, and heated declarations that Mama was going to city-me-up and I'd lose all my respectable rural, but Mama wouldn't budge.

"School's out soon. It wouldn't hurt this apron-leashed child to get some citification and learn new cultures. Living her entire life in Peckinpaw will only make her weak and dependent. I need to polish off the edges of this rural." She pinched my arm and I felt shame rising in my cheeks. Confusion riddled my young brain; Mama had pinched me after I told her about Daddy's secretary, too. I wasn't sure what was happening, but I knew I'd done something terribly wrong.

Mama rented us a room over Nettie's Nest until school let out for the summer. Then she loaded us into the car. I cried all the way to Nashville.

Our new home was a tall building full of tiny homes called apartments. We lived on the ninth floor. Mama found a job at a nearby bank and hired Mrs. Barnes, a nice neighbor lady in our building, to babysit me. Sometimes after work, Mama would go out on the avenues with her bank friends and have what she'd always liked to call "refreshments." She'd started smoking, and bought herself a fancy filter like her new friend, Collette. During these times I missed ThommaLyn the most. I even missed school a little.

I began counting the days left in June and those to September. To help me through the "Lonely Lucys," Mrs. Barnes let me open the window and drop breadcrumbs on the ledge. Within two days, I had three feathered friends. I named the pigeons after ThommaLyn, Grammy Essie, and Daddy. But one day Mama came home from work early and saw me talking to all of my new friends. She acted real nervous and led Mrs. Barnes to the door, whispering about "normal." Next thing I knew, Mama had nailed the window shut and put up an ugly green drape. I bawled like a two-year-old and hollered that she was locking my family out, same as she did Daddy. But she'd mixed herself a re-freshment, swatted my tail, and sent me into the bedroom we shared.

It was June 8 when Mama crossed paths again with Tommy Whitlock at the West End juke joint where he worked.

A few days later, we'd all gone out for a Saturday supper to "get to know each other." Tommy flashed a pearly grin to the waitress, and the waitress smiled back, blushing. Tommy and Mama had "refreshments." He'd ordered for us from the menu, making sure to add a big slice of pie for me.

Tommy downed his brown drink like a thirsty man. I soon figured out it was bourbon and water. "More water over that bourbon," the waitress had teased. Mama kept up with him with her refreshment called vodka and tonic. He finished his second one after the first bite of his steak. His voice grew high, loud. Once, he pinched the waitress's rear and Mama'd play-fully chastised him, bent over to me, and said, "He's just fun-nin', ain't he so funny, Mudas?" Like a clown, I'd reckoned, but glued my mouth shut and turned my red face away. Mama gulped down her second refreshment.

I thought about Daddy a lot. At least he drank in private. I

looked over at Tommy. Him, with his mouth full, waving a biscuit, grease on his chin, smacking his lips. Daddy made sure my
elbows were always off the table. . . .

Tommy talked and kept waving his bread. Then I saw it, his
hands. "Like the eyes connect to the soul, the hands talk, too,"
Grammy Essie had once told me. My daddy's hands were
warm, strong, and smooth, but not too soft, like the hands of
men too prissy to turn the dirt of a garden, brick a well, or cradle a fussy baby. Tommy's were different. His pinkie fingernail
was long, like it was made for scooping sand. His nails looked
shiny, like maybe they'd been polished, and his hands hung
limp, like they'd never shook with another. I didn't trust those
hands.

But still, it wasn't long after that supper when Mama settled
into the hands of her former lover. Tommy, acting all sweet and
clownish, courting her with flowers he'd lifted from the park
across the street. And always making sure to give me one of
those daisies, too. His day clothes were always spiffy, like he
was stepping out for a night on the avenues.

He took care of her, too. She'd caught a cold and got a smoking cough. Tommy went out and bought her the codeine cough
syrup, and when she finished that, he bought more bottles. "A
new refreshment," she'd winked.

He made Mama laugh, and they went out dancing a lot. I
reckon that's why she married him right away. But I never did
like clowns. And, after a while, it seemed like this one made both
me and Mama cry more than he made us laugh. Still, he'd always
apologize with a pretty gift and blaze those sharp pearlies. After
he'd gotten over his hangover, that is. Then they'd go dancing
again. I guess that's why she loved him better than my daddy.

Maybe even better than me. Because it was less than two
months later when Mama delivered me back to Liar's Bench.

Daddy was waiting, with arms spread wide. "You didn't let
all that 'fancy' corrupt you, did you, baby?"

I looked up at Mama questioningly and she nodded her approval from behind her sunglasses. I fell happily into Daddy's
hug, sneaking a peek at Mama over his shoulder. And that was

when I saw her heartbreak for the first time—her face seeming to slowly craze like a porcelain bowl picking up the hairline cracks after it hits the floor. I'd never realized just how big her losses were. Her sisters. Her parents. A husband. Now, me, her only child. But in that one glimpse, I saw everything. I was almost nine years old, and I didn't know how to help her. But I knew that she couldn't help me. I buried my face in Daddy's chest, grabbing hold of my immediate little happiness before it could be snatched away.

Wearily, Mama sat down on Liar's Bench and looked across the street toward the old courthouse, lost in thought. When she cleared her throat, the words sounded strange—sad. "Mudas is too puny for the city," she told Daddy. "She mewls like a sick kitten at every loud noise. Tommy and I feel it'd be best if she lived here with you. We're moving north soon, to Chicago. Tommy's been offered a better job. And I don't think she's strong enough for a bigger city."

Confused, I shot her a look. Instead of answering, she adjusted her sunglasses to hide the recent eye whap that Tommy had given her. Instinctively, I felt for the small of my back. It still hurt. Four days ago, I had gotten separated from her and Tommy in the city department store and started crying. Tommy'd called me a big baby—a chicken for making a fuss—and smacked my tail all the way back to the car. When we got back to the apartment, he'd taken off his thick belt and beaten me. But this beating was different.

There'd been a big argument about it afterward. The biggest ruckus ever. Even when I'd clamped my hands over my ears, I could still hear the slaps on skin, the shouts, and the slamming doors. Tommy had finally stormed out of the house, yelling about how he needed some air. His "air" always smelled "a whole lot like whiskey," Mama had screamed back, reaching for a refreshment.

I was so afraid, I ran to hide, pressing my small body way back inside the closet, hiding under a pile of coats until Mama came for me and coaxed me out with a sugar cookie.

Then she'd gone and emptied a bread bag and filled it with

ice to help with the swelling on my back. When Mama had finished, she'd hurried to the medicine chest to get salve to spread
across the welts. I heard her gulping down the bottle of codeine
cough syrup that she kept in there, as she tended to her own
swelling. After she was through nursing our wounds, she'd lit
herself a cigarette and studied me for the longest time. The
smoke settled into our silence, and for a minute I saw wounds
bigger than mine. I'd reached up, hugged her neck, and patted
her back. "It'll be okay, Mama, it'll be okay." I kept petting.

Then, for the first time ever, Mama cried on me. Scared, I patted harder. She finally stood and went into the bathroom. I
heard her open up the cabinet again. Another sip of refreshment, and a few seconds later, she came out. Her breath smelled
a lot stronger, orangier, like fruit and Tommy's bourbon. She'd
knelt down. "Keep your back covered at all times or else it won't
heal," she'd said. "You can't show anyone. Do you understand?"
I'd nodded and sealed the promise with a kiss and two fingers,
just like she'd taught me.

But sitting on that old bench with her now, I couldn't understand anything other than she was leaving me. I hooked my arm
under hers and tightened, scooting closer to her. "No, don't
leave! Please stay, Mama." I grabbed her hand, pulled it on top
of Daddy's and mine, and buried my wet face in the clasp.

Mama stroked my hair. "Hush, sugar," she quieted. "I'll be
back to take you shopping in the big city once we settle in. Now
I've got to get back to Nashville and pack." She untangled our
hands, stood, then smoothed down the creases on her linen skirt
and gave me a tight smile.

Daddy jumped up, clasped her arms, his eyes sorrowful—
pleading. "Don't leave, Ella. Muddy is too young to have her
mama so far away. She's only nine, for God's sake. Whitlock
will just drag you through the gutters with him, and you know
it. We can work this out if you'll just give me another chance."

"Daddy will protect you from Tommy. Don't leave us,
Mama . . . don't leave me." I scrambled up from the bench,
grabbing wildly for both of their hands. When I latched on, I
held them together. "Please, Mama, I'll be strong." I pressed

their hands firmly to show my strength. "Please stay with me, I promise—"

But she turned her head, stiffening.

I tried to run after her, but Daddy caught me. I watched Mama's car head out toward Highway 24. Me and Daddy sat on Liar's Bench for who knows how long—swapping stories, waiting, praying, and me, wearing off the tips of my fingers—all the while clinging to the ragged thread of hope that she'd turn her car back around at the Tennessee line.

Seems I spent most of August sitting on Liar's Bench, waiting for Mama to cross the Kentucky line. It would be almost three months before I'd see her again.

Mama and Tommy ended up staying in Chicago for close to seven years, until Tommy ran out of bartending jobs and his daddy took ill. They moved backed to Peckinpaw at the beginning of '72, just in time for his daddy's burial and Genevieve Louisa's birth.

I looked down to find my thumb gliding over my fingers, nervously tap-tapping away, doing its old dance. I couldn't bear sitting in my bedroom another minute, thinking about the past. I had to get out of this house.

I peeked out my door and heard Daddy rumbling around downstairs in the kitchen. Now if I could just find my car key, I might be able to make it out of here without having to face him. I meant all I'd said, but it had been easier with that door between us. Just the thought of looking him in the eye made me blush with shame.

I needed to get out of here. "Where's my key?" I grumbled. Scanning the room, I realized that Daddy must have hidden it after my little display of emotion at Mama's house, afraid that I'd drive off and do something stupid in my grief.

"Damnit, I'm getting out of here," I said to myself." The key wasn't on the nightstand, where I thought I'd left it. I went over to my window seat bench and lifted the lid, thinking I might have tossed it in there with some clothes. I rummaged through the quilts in the big bench, finding an old picture album, a box of stationery, useless papers, and a few clothes. No key. "Where could it be?"

Then, I caught the shine of my shotgun peeking out from beneath a quilt. It was the old .410 that Papaw had used as a kid. When I turned ten, he had passed it on to me for rabbit hunting, along with his favorite saying: "You can't catch a rabbit lessen you muddy up those boots."

My fingertips touched the cool metal and in one whipcrack of thought, I reflected about Mama—my grandparents—and the final escape of madness—and never-ending sorrow. I licked my lips and pressed a hand over the barrel. Oh, but to drive away this madness . . . to lie down beside them in green pastures and restore my soul!

"Driving is a privilege, and one that I can take away." Daddy's voice was low and stern.

Startled, I piled the quilts over the .410 and dropped the lid. I whipped around to find him standing in the doorway, with his arms crossed and his mouth set in a hard line.

"You're not the Department of Motor Vehicles," I said, shaken.

"I am today." He lifted his coffee mug, before he turned and went back downstairs.

When I heard his footsteps hit the bottom landing, I crossed the hall to his bedroom, intent on finding that key.

I worked my way over to his armoire in the corner and opened its doors, doing a double take in the inlaid mirror. Shocked, I peered closer. My long brown hair was a tangled twist of knots instead of its usual soft curls. My nose, splattered with freckles, what Grammy Essie used to call "a redhead's angel spit," glowed like Peckinpaw's only red light. I groaned. My eyes were road-map red, like the day I'd gotten caught in Grammy Essie's cellar polishing off a jar of sweet dandelion wine. I was nearly thirteen. She'd yanked me out of the cellar and shamed me with a lecture on the evils of alcohol, carefully bringing Mama briefly into it, but I'd only caught two words: *White trash*.

I shut the armoire door. "I've worked three years for that car," I said to the empty room, my resolve growing.

I reached on top of the bureau, fumbling for his leather jewelry box. Finally, I pulled it down and lifted the lid. My nerves lit into my hands, leaving me to fumble. The box slipped from my hands and the contents scattered across the floor.

Dropping to my knees, I scrambled to pick up my car key poking out from beneath the corner of the bed and triumphantly stuffed it into my jean pocket. I stretched my arm across the hardwood to sweep the rest of the mess back into Daddy's box, but I was distracted by a piece of twisted fabric looped around a ring. A small plastic bag labeled "Quality Hair Ribbons, $1.99" lay a foot away, bearing the stamped logo of Nettie's Nest General Store. I scooped it up.

"You leave here without permission, gal, and I will take off your bedroom door and store it in the cellar again," Daddy said from the doorway. "And you will lose your right to privacy for the rest of the summer!" He set down his coffee cup.

"Go—go ahead," I stammered, rubbing my closed hand. "Just need to get out of here . . . I'll be back by four."

"Don't push it, Muddy. You know the rules. Leave the house without consent, you lose my trust—the trust that comes with the protection of privacy—beginning with your door."

"You've taken it off so many times, the lock only works half the time anyways." I stood.

"Muddy—"

"I'm an adult now, seventeen," I said evenly.

"Only ten years older than seven," he shot back, "and damn well showing it."

I raised a shaky fist and opened my palm.

Daddy leaned against the doorframe, arms blocked, eyes tightly scrunched as if he didn't see it, it wouldn't be real.

"Who's—who's the lucky woman this time? Which one of them gets this—the new secretary?" I clutched the piece of jewelry. Slowly, I disentangled a cameo ring from the ribbon and placed the piece down on the nightstand. The ribbon was all too familiar.

"What's this, Daddy? This is the same ribbon Mama was wearing." I raised my fist and let the ribbon slowly unravel. "Everyone knows that Nettie sells in threes." She always put an extra ribbon in the bag in case you lost one out of the set. Nettie was real thoughtful like that. My breath came fast and hot. "Daddy?"

He pressed his fingers to his temples.

"Daddy, you know Mama never wore ribbons and Tommy forbid her from wearing them. Why do you have the same pink ribbon that Mama had on her ankles when . . . ? Oh, oh." I felt a tight squeeze in my throat. "Daddy, what is it that you're not telling me? Please, *please* tell me."

He shook his head dismissively. "Oh, for God's sake, Muddy, you're not making any sense. Settle down! You know it was that horse's ass Whitlock who pushed your mama to the brink. And now, look at you, you're—"

"Stop!" I flailed my arms. "She didn't kill herself. Mama had the other two matching ribbons around her ankles when they . . . when they brought her out of that house. Wait! Did you give those ribbons to Mama? Hurt her? Daddy . . ." I doubled over. "How . . . What Tommy said in the police car . . . you know something about this, about what happened to her, don't you? What did you do? WHAT—"

His face paled. "Enough. I have a lot of grown-up business on my mind." His eyes locked on the ribbon. "Now, Jingles says—"

"I don't care what Jingles says. You know Mama would *never* take her life." Daddy moved over to the bed, lowered himself on its edge, and placed his head in his hands.

I brought my own hands to my forehead in shock and winced as I touched the forgotten bruise I'd caught from Roy McGee last week. McGee. I had to tell someone about what I'd seen, none of it making sense anymore. I worried about breaking my last promise to Mama, disrespecting her last wish. But the story begged to be shared: the argument with McGee . . . I charged forward, teetering between anger and regret. I waved the ribbon in his face. "McGee was over at Mama's when I was visiting last week."

Daddy looked up in surprise. Then recognition.

"Yes. Yes, he was there. And he slapped her. Talk to me. You know something about this. I can see that you do."

He cast his eyes downward.

"Maybe you and McGee both know something and you're *both* hiding it!" I grasped into the heated air. "What is it?" I dangled the ribbon high, waiting. "Are you in deep with McGee? Maybe McGee's pushing out Tommy, huh?"

"Muddy! That's enough! We can talk about all of this later, when you've had some time to calm down. When you can act—"

"I bet you just couldn't stand the thought that she was never coming back to you . . . back to a lying cheatin' horndog!"

Daddy dropped his elbows to his knees. "Jesus," he moaned, looking up at me.

I couldn't look at him. Before all this, I'd never spoken to Daddy or anyone like this. And now, seeing him broken, shattered my own angry heart.

I stared down at the floor, twisting the ribbon. I couldn't bear seeing his hurt—his bewilderment—his disappointment in me. I balled my fists and fought the urge to go over and hug him—to beg his forgiveness.

I studied the ribbon, flowered on one side and pale pink on the other. I looked up and saw his pained expression, a mist settling, red-rimming his eyes. A wave of fury buoyed me. How dare he? How dare he steal my God-given grief for his own!

I rubbed the ribbon between my fingers. Mama's ribbon. My head snapped up and my mind flickered with suspicion. "You have to tell Jingles everything," I said woodenly. "Everything, Daddy. You're the prosecuting attorney. How could you not?" I whispered. "Whatever it takes, I'm going to find out what happened to my mama."

I grabbed the telephone receiver off its black rotary dial base sitting on his nightstand and listened for the dial tone on our party line. I turned the finger wheel, mentally counting out four long rings. "Sheriff Jingles? Sheriff, it's Mudas Summers . . . Yessir, it was a nice service yesterday. . . . Uh-huh. Thank you. I need to tell you, Sheriff; I'm calling because my daddy has some

new information about Mama's death that you really need to—"
The sheriff cut me off with awful news of his own. My mouth
fell open in disbelief. "Oh, oh. That's just, well, I don't know
what to say. . . . All right, yessir."

I set the phone down in its cradle and slowly tied and knotted
the ribbon around my wrist. Daddy's eyes were still glued to the
floor, but he was working his thoughts into his old knee injury,
massaging absently with his hand.

"Jingles says he found Tommy hanged in his cell. They just
sent him off in the coroner's wagon. Daddy, did you hear me?
Tommy's dead . . . dead," I said with a thimble of mixed guilt
and relief. My fingers curled tight around the phone cord. "Justice . . . What he did to Mama after he hung her . . . Daddy?" I
pleaded, waiting—wanting—and desperate for him to make
everything right.

His shoulders dipped lower.

"I'm leaving." I paused at the doorway, deep down hoping he
would stop me if I gave him the opportunity.

He didn't.

"And you called Tommy a horse's ass?" I called coolly over
my shoulder. "You're the pecking chicken. Peck. Peck. Peck. Jus'
pecking away until you've shattered everything and everyone
around you."

I blinked back the tears, making my way blindly down the
stairs and out the porch door. I gave a hard kick to the gravel
drive, scattering up chalk-gray clouds of pebbles and dirt. Another. Then another. "I hate you! Hate you!" I called out,
stomping stupidly and fruitlessly.

I paced back and forth in front of my car. "Daddy," I shouted
to the house, "I'm leaving now! Need your permission, please!"
I paused to catch my breath, and looked up at the house and
then over to Peggy, battling between defiance and duty. And
gripped by the certainty that I would never be able to see home,
or my father, the same way again. When Daddy didn't show his
face in the upstairs window, I cried out, "I'm seventeen, Daddy.
Seventeen!" I raised my hands in the air, clenched my fists once,
then held up seven fingers and swiveled them from my wrists. "Al-

most eighteen—eighteen and free, Daddy . . . an adult! Legal!" I punched through the grieving air. "Free and legal, Daddy!"

I booted more rock, gravel slapped at my leg.

"Hmph. Prosecute that, Mr. Prosecuting Attorney!"

I swiped at the tears scorching over my cheeks as I jumped into the car.

8

Ghost Puppies and Scars

I braked in front of Liar's Bench long enough to glimpse inside the Top Hat Café, searching the busy lunch crowd for Thomma-Lyn, and hoping I'd find Bobby Marshall, too. The last time I'd spoken to him was a week ago, right before I got my car from Daddy. I hadn't seen him at the funeral yesterday, but then again everything was such a blur. Still, I was sure I hadn't seen him in the condolence line. I did a mental tick of time. I couldn't help but to worry why he hadn't called back, or maybe Daddy had said something to chase him off. Surely he'd heard about Mama—everyone had by now. Didn't he care about me? About how I was taking it? He wasn't officially my boyfriend or anything, not my "steady," that is, but we'd grown close, spending easy hours on the phone, hanging out and mixing in some flirtation now and then. I really needed him around right now.

Under the midday sun, a colored woman with a thick scar wired around her neck hobbled her crippled time in front of my car, then lowered herself heavily onto Liar's Bench. I tried to get a closer look, but a bandana swaddled her face. I stole another peek at her scar. A chill shot up my back. Frannie Crow's "cautious reminder" came to me. I was beginning to worry what the elders meant by calling it that. No one's death should be tied to a stupid object that shines everyone's backsides.

I lifted my wrist and inspected the ribbon I'd taken from Daddy's jewelry box. It dangled like a hangman's noose.

I gunned the motor and headed to the outskirts of town trying to shake off my anger—and everyone and everything that had caused it. I drove the hills aimlessly, letting off steam, letting my mind wander, scrolling through the events of the past week. My head was full to bursting with questions: Why had McGee been at Mama's the day she died, talking about his Rooster Run ledger? What was so important about a ledger? Why did Daddy have those ribbons; what had he done and what was he hiding? How could Tommy do what Jingles wrote down . . . and do that to poor Genevieve, too? I needed to talk it all out, sort it all out, or I'd be stuck in it.

The kind of stuck that usually only my Mama or Grammy could unstuck. I used to save those for Sunday. I was going to miss them. Last Sunday, for the first time since the divorce, I'd taken the phone off the hook. I couldn't bear the thought of hearing it ring, knowing it wouldn't be Mama on the other end. When Daddy'd put the receiver back on the hook, I took off running toward the backfields to numb the memories.

Every other Sunday and without fail, and for as long as I could remember, Mama would phone me at exactly 7:00 p.m. Even Daddy helped make it happen. He'd laid down strong words to our party-liners who'd hogged the phone after he found out Mama waited for over an hour in a Chicago snowstorm to talk to me. A lot like her Band-Aids, the calls became tradition, and another small way to keep me in her motherly arms, without the interference of Tommy strong-arming. I'd overheard Tommy arguing with her about our Sunday calls, insisting she use their house phone, but Mama put her foot down, and there it stayed even up until her death. A couple of times he tried to follow her, because I would hear him honking and shouting at her. After that, she took to going out of her way to find different phone booths.

But it didn't matter whether we were separated by one mile or a thousand, we'd talk, and talk, and talk about nothing and everything and anything. A lot of times I could hear the background noises of a big, busy city. Sometimes I'd hear the rain and thunder as a summer storm bounced over her corner phone booth.

I'd spend twice a month on Sundays waiting for the clock to strike seven. When the phone rang, I could barely keep the words from spilling and tangling up with Mama's, worrying about the cost. But the money wasn't important, she would just stuff that phone jaw with more coins and keep going until I'd eventually ticked off my worries and doubts and the week's events to her.

Over the years our conversations turned from lace to lipstick. Last year for my sixteenth birthday, Mama'd bought me *Love Story*, and we'd spent a whole hour and a half discussing Segal's novel. I'd talked a little about boys and the awkwardness I'd felt around them. She'd reminisced about a high-school romance, saying once she'd walked right into a classroom wall and skinned up her nose while trying to catch a boy's eye. The next day she'd accidentally smashed her finger in the library door when the guy passed by her. The week after, she'd been getting a closer look when she missed the bottom step, twisted her ankle, and fell on him. Frustrated, the school nurse sent her home with a note to her parents requesting an eye exam. "I ended up getting that blue pair of cat-eyes I'd been hankering for and the guy's best friend," she'd laughed.

Once in a while, she talked of her dreams and hopes in soft words and quiet pauses. I'd pry and in a bit, she'd tell me about the ballet lessons she'd taken, and her love for art, and soon her words would leap into a world of dances and colors, and laughter would spill.

Her humor couldn't be beat. No one could squeeze a chuckle out of me faster than Mama. She'd told me about the fish Tommy won for her at a church picnic in Chicago and how it almost killed her.

Mama'd said, "I carried the skinny little fella home in a baggie and borrowed a goldfish bowl from my neighbor. I named him Mr. Church. After about a week the goldfish turned sickly. A few days later I found it belly-up in its fishbowl. So, I thought it would be a good idea and the right thing to do to bury Mr. Church in the neighborhood garden before Tommy came home from work.

"Barefoot, I carried the bowl down the apartment stairs, through the corridors, and out the back door, careful not to splash out water, or poor Mr. Church. When I'd finally reached the small garden in the backyard, I straddled its four-foot fence.

"Well, I guess all that sloshing around did something to Mr. Church. Suddenly, the fish jumped up into the air and out of its bowl. It startled me so bad, I lost my footing and the fish bowl went flying, and the next thing I knew I was flat on my back with Mr. Church slapped across my nose. My first thought was the next day's newspaper headline: 'Ballet Dancer Killed by a Flying Fish.' The second: How was I going to explain this to the neighbor lady who was now staring down at me with a peculiar look on her face?"

We'd laughed for at least three nickels' worth over that. And after that, we'd always shout "beware of flying fishes" when one of us had to do a tricky chore.

Mama never hung up the phone until she was sure we'd pounded out my problems, and afterward she'd say, "Not hanging up until I hear a smile in your voice."

Then we'd tease over who'd hang up first, knowing it wouldn't be her, insisting on being last and signing off with "sweet dreams." Sometimes, I'd get real lonely for her after I'd hang up, so I would pick back up the receiver and listen to the nothingness for a minute, in case she'd changed her mind.

"Sweet dreams, Mama." I pulled back into Town Square. Nothing made sense anymore, and thinking on it didn't seem to help. What did Daddy do?

Needing fresh air, I stepped out of the car and walked over to Liar's Bench. I sat a moment and stared into the face of the Town Square clock nestled in the courthouse commons—the matriarch circle of downtown—then looked across the way to my left at Dick's Barber Shop and Peck's Pool Hall, doors wide open, the haze of cigar and cigarette smoke ghosting out into the summer sun.

Nettie's Nest and Shucks Market set to my right, a few crooked abandoned bascarts strewn between them. Shop doorbells from the Parton & Porter and the Top Hat Café and Milton's Hardware jingled behind me. People flitted in and out, and I saw most were just hanging around to swap stories rather than minding any real business. I watched mamas carrying bags full of supper fixings out of Shucks Market. I thought about Mama fixing my cabbage casserole dish. I wrung out the panic that seemed to grab hold of my hands. I needed to do something. I needed to talk to someone and fix this mess in my head.

I got back into my car and headed to the Dixie Bowl, intent on finding ThommaLyn or Bobby. The Dixie Bowl was the "Let's Beat the Drag" area for Peckinpaw's cool kids (at least those who fancied themselves cool) on the outskirts of town. The Dixie Bowl Bowling Alley, where the only things sure to roll were the wheels on cars full of bored teens cruising the lot, the E-Z Wider papers used by a handful of potheads, and the boozehound kids with their empty liquor bottles.

I parked next to a row of other cars and checked out the Dixie Bowl crowd. Jingles pulled his police cruiser onto the edge of the gravel lot, surprising me. I thought he would've been busy at the jail, instead of making his usual circuits. I guess he just flat ran out of busy. How could that be, with Mama fresh in the ground and Tommy dead? How was I going to find the truth about her death with no one on my side? I set my jaw and grabbed the door handle, aiming to give Jingles a piece of my mind.

Nearby, a carload of boys tossed a bottle out their window. Jingles hit his lights. I dropped the handle and studied the broken booze bottle. I couldn't do this here. I'd set this right, but this littered parking lot and cars full of boozehounds didn't feel like the place. I'd seen enough broken bottles in many a broken hand to last a lifetime. I made myself a promise long ago: I'd never pick the splinters of broken glass out of my hand, or the hands of any babies I might have. I thought about going home, the comfort and nothingness of my bed, but I wasn't ready to face Daddy yet. Didn't think I would be for a long while.

I leaned back in my seat, watching as Jingles eased out of his official car and unsnapped the huge key ring from his utility belt. "Get along now, you kids!" Jingles lifted his keys high and rattled hard. Joey Sims balked and raised his own keys, belting out "Jingle Bells." A few of his friends joined in the chorus. The sheriff moved toward Joey. He stopped about two feet in front of the boy, slid the key ring back over his meaty wrist, and squirted out a stream of tobacco juice at Joey's feet.

Digging into his pockets, Jingles pulled out a braid of tobacco and his Boker. He stuffed his mouth with another chaw and then wagged the knife in the boy's face. "Joey Sims, this makes twice lately I've done tol' ya to move along." Jingles scratched his chin with his knife blade. "Didn't you play invisible puppy with me just two months ago?"

Joey took a step back and a few boys woofed and howled in response. I knew from talk, and from the telltale bruises, seat burns, and shiners on some of the boys at school, that "playing invisible puppy" with Sheriff Jingles meant a ride in the back of his cruiser, hands cuffed behind your back, while Jingles locked up his brakes at every other fence post down the road, his metal cage meat-tenderizing your face and body with each forceful slam on the brakes. Him, swerving, laying rubber, and hollering out after each slam, "Well, there goes my invisible puppy, off his leash and in the road again!" Then Jingles would drop the offender off at home, leaving him to explain his sorry state to his parents.

The girls had it worse: They were sent over to Myrtle Dugin's house for six whole weeks of all-day Saturday prayer and evening Bible study.

"You missing the pup? That it?" Jingles asked.

Joey shook his head.

"Then you best move it along real quick, or I'll thump you so hard, boy, you'll be down on your knees searching for your balls with a pair of tweezers."

Joey moved fast. Real fast.

Before Jingles could spy me and make me his next target, I pushed in my clutch and let the car roll back real slow, then turned on the ignition. The radio crackled and let loose a series of loud squawks. A country roads' DJ scratched out another empty song: Elvis's "Queenie Wahine's Papaya." Frustrated, I pounded the dash with my fist, but the King crooned on. I fumbled underneath for speaker wires, hoping to jerk them out.

I didn't know what to do, where to go. A bevy of why-me and what-ifs thumped across my brain. I thought about going back and resting a spell on Liar's Bench. Puddling its worn wood with drops of my brokenness. It reminded me of Grammy Essie, and I was feeling in need of some mothering right now. But if Daddy came looking for me, that'd be the first place he'd look and, well, I just couldn't. I laid my head on the steering wheel, thinking.

After a moment, I sat up and looked around the lot, relieved to see that Jingles was gone. I glided my thumb worriedly over each fingertip again, back and forth, back and forth, picking up speed. I knew it was a maddening habit, one that some folks might call a sign of the crazies to come. Grammy Essie said her own mama'd had the same peculiarity, and she was right in her head all her ninety-eight years long. Still, what if Grammy Essie had been wrong?

Worried, I inspected my fingers, looking for a sign. I peered up at the rearview, bug-eyed. What if the crazy had already sneaked up on me? Here I was, sitting in a parking lot alone, with all these loud thoughts. *That* was a bad sign. I had to find my friends. With a renewed sense of purpose, I hit the gas and peeled out toward Ruby's Dog 'n' Suds.

9

Peckinpaw's
Walking White Liars

I revved the engine before idling alongside the curb of Ruby's Dog 'n' Suds, letting the car radio switch itself back and forth between static and music.

The lot was filled with rows of parked cars packed with teens, bored and hungry. Two carhops roller-skated by with trays of cold dogs, soggy fries, and flat root beer.

Georgianna Deats dropped a tray onto the ground. I knew from working a few shifts with her that it would be one of at least three dumped during her shift. Feigning exasperation, she'd bend over, showing off her black lace panties underneath a too-short pink uniform so she could slut it up with any guy who hadn't had her.

Georgianna was also the reason my ring finger was empty. Up 'til six months ago, I'd been wearing Tripp Seacat's friendship ring. He'd given it to me on Liar's Bench over a year ago and asked me to go steady with him. Promises were made and white lies were told. We'd shared our dreams and secrets, and talked about going to college together. We'd even talked about marriage. But then it changed and got ugly when he started hanging with the boozehounds.

Six months ago, I'd tossed the pearl ring in his face after I caught him sitting on Liar's Bench, trying to wriggle his way into Georgianna's pants. Both of them had stood up and declared their innocence. But it was too late: I'd seen their heads bent, the shared secret, the kiss, and their white-hot lies painted across alcohol-flushed faces. Seeing him like that, I knew Tripp wasn't the guy I wanted to share my secrets or my future with. Always pissed an' pie-eyed, and resembling too much of a passed-out Tommy, he didn't deserve my secrets. I'd wasted enough on him already. He still called me every week or so, talking all silly, begging for one last chance, one last secret to share. When he'd finally come up for air, I'd give him a firm "no" and slam down the phone. It's not like he'd ever earned my secrets anyway, though in his drunken states, he may have thought he had. 'Sides, I couldn't tie up the party line and take a chance on missing Bobby's call. That was my secret.

Now, I just needed to find my friends so I could talk through this mess. I rolled down my window and poked my head out. "Georgianna," I hollered, trying to get her attention. She stopped cold and stared at me.

"Oh, hey, Mud-plop," she cooed, her voice all sugar sweet, dripping with contempt. "Looking for your cows?"

No matter how many times I'd heard it, it was always like the first time, fresh and wounding. I flinched. I tried not to care, but I did. I really did. I wanted my final school year to go smoothly, to wedge myself into that narrow passage of social acceptance.

I shook off her words. "Right, so have you seen ThommaLyn down here today? Or Bobby Marshall? I really need to find them."

"Can't say I have," she smirked, raising a slender hand to her temple. And that's when I saw my pearl ring on her pretty little finger.

"Slut!" I hissed.

I laid rubber across the asphalt and parked in the gravel lot next to Ruby's. I got out and used the pay phone to ring Bobby Marshall. No answer, again. Where *was* he? Next, I dialed ThommaLyn. Her brother answered, saying I'd just missed her—that she'd tried to call my house to let me know she'd be at her granny's for the day, and that I should call her back later in the afternoon. I thought about checking on baby Genevieve, and asked the operator for Mrs. Whitlock's number, but it buzzed the busy signal two times.

I heard a whistle behind me and turned around to see Bobby Marshall waving me over, all lit up with a warm smile, his amber-honey eyes fringed with flecks of gold. A wave of relief came over me; it felt so good to see a friendly face. I made my way between the rows of cars to Bobby, who stood holding a brown package done up with twine wrap.

"Hey, Mudas, there you are!" he said, wrapping me in a big bear hug. "I've been looking all over for you. I got back from Boston 'bout an hour ago. My folks took me to visit the university last week, all at the last minute. I tried calling you before I left. From Boston, too, about a dozen times, but your party line was nonstop busy. I got through once, but your dad said you were resting. It's been busy ever since! What's going on? Is that crazy widow lady hogging the lines again?"

"Yeah, I guess so." I looked into his eyes, searching for the telltale signs of pity, finding nothing. Hadn't he heard about Mama?

"So, what'd you do for your seventeenth birthday? I mailed you a postcard! I was freaking out when I couldn't get you on the pho—"

"Bobby, I've been looking for you. You haven't heard?"

"Heard what? I just got here, Mudas. My truck battery's dead, so I thumbed a ride to come look for you."

Behind him, a group of kids were staring at me. Some looked at me with curiosity, others with pity, and a few with indifference, before shifting their eyes from mine. I pulled him away from the group, and squeaked out, "It's my mama."

"Y'all have a fight?"

"No, no. It's worse than that. Can we go somewhere and talk? My car's over there."

Bobby put his arm around my shoulder as we hurried to my car.

"Wow! Righteous ride. Yours?"

"Yeah, I got her last Thursday. For my birthday."

"Cool! Have you named her yet?"

"Peggy's her name."

"Nice. She's real pretty." Bobby sang the chorus of "Peggy Sue," running his hands across the hood.

I opened the driver's door. "Let's go." I wanted to get out of here before Jingles or my daddy came looking for me. I hit the dash several times with my palm to get a radio station. Sammy Davis, Jr.'s "The Candy Man" dropped into a whir before the radio cut itself off.

"Hey, Mudas, looky-here, I bought you a birthday present." Bobby shoved the brown package into my hand.

The distraction was welcome; with Bobby in the dark about Mama, I could almost pretend that everything was okay. "Oh. Me? Hey, you didn't have to do that." I tore open the wrapping, ever so briefly forgetting my troubles when I saw the two books.

"I got them at the Brattle Book Shop in Boston," he said, sitting straight up. "I remembered you talking about him." He tapped William Faulkner's *Light in August*. "And this one looked pretty cool. My mom picked it out." He reddened. "Uh, well, I hope you like them," he added.

I picked up Mary Rodgers's *Freaky Friday*. For a minute, I was tongue-tied at the thought of him even mentioning me to his mama. Finally, I found my voice. "Yes, thanks. They're awesome, Bobby. Really, super!" I said. 'Course, what I really wanted to tell him was that *he* was super.

"I've missed you, Mudas." Bobby lifted a loose curl off my shoulder and held it between his fingers.

I turned away to hide the sudden candy-cane blush I felt heating into a smile I couldn't help. I loved that he called me by my real name instead of the dirt name. Ages ago, he'd asked me which one I preferred, and never forgot my answer. He always said it all pretty-like, too. It felt good to hear it now. I turned back and gave him an appreciative smile.

Bobby leaned in closer. He placed his hand on my thigh way above the knee, tingling skin, dizzying my mind. Suddenly hungry for life, I leaned into the moment and reached for him, parting my mouth to fill it with something more than the bitterness of the last week. Something like Bobby.

My dangling wristlet cut through the hunger like a sword. I looked at Mama's ribbon and was overcome by emotions. I shook my head. "I'm sorry, Bobby. I can't. Let's go somewhere we can talk, okay?" I said, moving away.

For a minute he looked wounded. But just as quickly, he recovered and the hurt in his eyes turned to confusion and concern. He released his hold and nodded. "So, where are we off to and what's going on?" he asked, pulling up a weak smile and settling into the passenger seat.

10

The Scent of a Lie

We cruised past Liar's Bench. Two elders were sitting there jawing. I circled Town Square twice, then squeezed into a parking spot in front of Peck's Pool Hall.

"I'll grab us a Coke. Be right back," Bobby said. He walked into the pool hall while I waited outside, like all females did—respectable ones, that is.

Crossing over to the bench with my hand in his, we nodded to the two old men, who looked to be deep in reminiscence. Dutifully, we shuffled past and waited. We hung out in silence, sharing the drink, and studying Parton & Porter's window display of leather goods. Bobby looked full to bursting with questions, but he could tell that I wasn't ready to talk. He pointed out the newest leather belts in the window, the ones with turquoise stone buckles.

After about five minutes, the elders stood and adjusted their identical suspenders, then tipped their straw fedoras and bid each other fond farewells. Bobby and I sat down on Liar's Bench, his hand clutching mine, my pink gills slowly speckling green.

"All right, what is it, Mudas? What's wrong? You don't look so good."

I closed my eyes and tried to find the words.

"Please, Mudas, just talk to me. Tell me what's going on."

I took a deep breath. "It's my mama."

He nodded. "Okay. What happened?"

"She's gone, Bobby."

"Back to Nashville?"

I shook my head. "No, gone," I said meaningfully, my voice cracking.

Bobby's eyes widened. "You mean . . . ?"

I nodded. "Yeah, gone forever," I burst out, no longer able to contain the hurricane churning inside me. My mouth seemed to grow a set of runner's legs and soon I was running with the unspeakable words that had been pent up for too long.

"I can't stop seeing it. It was so horrible, Bobby. Tommy was on one of his drug highs that night, as usual—staggered home just as the morning paper hit the stoop and passed out on the bedroom floor. Probably paid no mind to baby Genevieve lying under her music mobile. When he woke up they say he stumbled into the living room and gawped beetle-eyed upward to see my mama . . . her eyes black and her body bruised . . . dangling from one of the exposed rafters."

Bobby knotted up his forehead.

I pinched back the tears and took a breath so I could get the words out. This was hard, but it was a relief to let it out, here, now, with Bobby's hand in mine.

"His neighbor, Higgy Flynn, says he saw it all, watched him come home and everything he did after. When he woke up, Tommy started bellowing, and that's when Higgy made a bee-line to plaster his nose to the windows. I got hold of the report that Sheriff put together after taking down Higgy's story."

Bobby shook his head. "What else did it say?"

"Well, Higgy said Tommy kept cussing and hollering about 'the mess Mommy's done gone and left us.' Higgy could see him cranking Genevieve's mobile and gibbering to her. Then Tommy stumbled into the kitchen, yelling for some sort of 'salvation.' As usual, the bastard found his grace in a bottle of Pabst Blue Ribbon and some other stuff."

"I bet he was lit like the Fourth," Bobby whistled low.

"He was loaded, and headin' into New Year's Eve." I thought about what Higgy said. How he watched Tommy place the rim of the bottle on the edge of the stove and smack the cap off with the palm of his hand, like all the ol' boys do. And I thought how some kids were terrified of noises like police sirens, hornet buzz, or the crack of lightning. But for me, it was the cap popping off the beer bottle sound. The one that would explode in my ears and drop deep into the pit of my stomach. Its alarm meant Tommy-trouble. More than once I'd wet my pants before his fist could meet mine or Mama's flesh, or his belt buckle could cut into our skin. Which only made it worse when Tommy yanked my pants down and made fun of me because I'd wet them.

"Mudas?" Bobby shook my arm. "You okay? You're shivering. Mudas . . ."

Instinctively, I jerked away, feeling light-headed. "I . . . I'm fine." I worried my knuckles over my wrist that Tommy had broken long ago, kneading the same as Daddy did with his ol' knee injury. "Higgy said he saw Tommy pull out an aspirin tin and a baggie full of a rainbow of pills. Said Tommy dropped paper onto his tongue and chased it down with beer and whiskey."

"Acid?" Bobby asked quietly.

"Yeah," I said, "Sheriff said so. Said they found all kinds of other bad stuff. Higgy said that, after Tommy took it, he seemed to sink deeper into a haze, because he lifted the lid on Mama's casserole dish, took one sniff, and shoved it off the counter, roaring something about her cleaning up her own 'slop.' Maybe . . . probably 'cause he knew she'd made me the dish for my birthday."

"Damn, Mudas, that son of—"

"But"—I shook my head, determined to let out the monster—"if that wasn't bad enough, Tommy reached for the whiskey bottle again. Him, always reaching—pounding back the burn that stoked the devil coals inside him. *Bastard.*"

Teary-eyed, I looked up at Bobby to make sure he didn't think I was the high one, the one pounding down the whiskey. His eyes were full in disbelief. He squeezed my hand and whispered, "Pantywaist coward. I bet he was fully jacked by then."

"Higgy told 'em that the phone rang twelve times before Tommy found it. It was Hettie, the fill-in desk clerk. Said she was calling to ask about Mama's missed dispatcher's shift. Hettie said Tommy told her 'she wouldn't be in, though she might be able to pull the graveyard shift.' "

"Shit-fire," Bobby burst.

Bobby had my hand in a near death grip.

I looked down at our hands, mine holding back just as tight, and finished with a scratchy whisper, "Genevieve . . . this . . ." I shook my head. "When Sheriff kicked in the door fifteen minutes later, he said he found Tommy with his foot in the air, winding up her body, right in front of baby Genevieve."

Bobby inhaled a sharp breath.

"Jingles wrote out in his report how Tommy had taken two of Mama's pink hair ribbons from her braids, tied one around each ankle, and fashioned a human mommy-mobile above the playpen. He kept cracking to Genevieve how, 'Mommy always wanted to go to the big city and be a ballerina and look how she's dancing now.' "

I wiped away the tears. Bobby buried his head in his hands and rubbed hard like he was trying to erase dirt.

"Sheriff said Tommy leaned into the ladder-back chair, took his big toe, and prodded Mama's body. Then the very worst. He told baby Genevieve to watch. "Told her, 'Look-a-here, baby . . . Watch Mommy spin!' Sheriff said he saw Genevieve reach her arms up and heard her gurgle out sputters of laughter while Tommy said over and over, Sp-sp . . ." Bobby grasped my hand tighter. " 'Spin,' he said! 'Spin, Mommy, spin a pretty ballerina turn for baby. Spin!' he kept saying! 'Sp—' " I strangled on a sob.

"Bastard," Bobby wheezed.

"Sheriff said he ain't never seen nothing like it and he just stood, shocked, in the doorway for a minute before he snatched Tommy up and busted his jaw."

"Oh my God, Mudas," Bobby hissed out in one wild burst, his face draining. "Crazy bastard! I'm so sorry! Jesus Christ!" He stood, clenched his fists and circled around the bench, and then paced in front of me, before sitting back down.

"Come here, Mudas," he soothed, pulling me closer to him. I felt myself unwind as he rubbed my back and cradled my head in the crook of his shoulder. "I can't believe this. How can this be?" Bobby said. "When—"

"I can't either. It all happened nearly a week ago," I said, my words thickening. "Friday, on my birthday."

"Damn, Mudas. Damn, I'm sorry, I—I really don't know what to say. What's everyone saying?"

"Suicide . . . That's what they're trying to call it, Bobby." I pointed over to the newsstand. "But, my mama would never!"

"I know she wouldn't. No way, no how." Bobby scowled.

My body grew limp. It felt good to have someone squarely on my side. Not having to explain myself, not needing to defend what I knew to be the Gospel truth. Bobby held me with a gentle silence.

"Tommy's dead, too. They found him hanging in the jail cell this morning," I said numbly.

"Jesus." Bobby digested the information. "Wait a minute. Did he finally own up to it? And they're still gonna call it suicide?"

"I don't know. I . . . I think Tommy did it. My daddy does, too. I mean, Tommy always used to beat on Mama. So . . ." I wiped my face with the hem of my shirt. Bobby seized my hand, an unspoken pledge of his support. Still, he was staring over at the Osage tree and stroking his jaw with what Grammy Essie used to call the "disappearing look," the one that appears in a man's eyes when he can't fix it—or fix you.

I blew out a breath. "I need to go into Top Hat and get a napkin."

"Let me go get it for you," Bobby said, patting my knee. "I'll be right back."

I couldn't help worrying if he would.

I saw the Cooper twins slip out of Milton's Hardware, both wearing predictable smiles and carrying a bag of hardware to fix whatever was broke—build whatever it was that needed raising. It seemed most men carried a grin coming out of Milton's, no matter how complex the chore. I couldn't help but think of Papaw's words: "T'aint nothing that's man-made that I can't fix," he'd always declared, his eyes smiling in anticipation.

But if something was just a tad off kilter with a woman, Grammy Essie had said, something intangible, sort of like a Monday morning—a washday-blues sadness that couldn't be explained or fixed by a man's righty-tighty, lefty-loosey wrench— most men would just wring their hands, then amble off. That kind of "brokenness" in a woman had even been known to drive a man or two to drink, Grammy'd said.

Bobby returned with what looked like a whole dispenser of napkins and shoved the clump into my hand. I was so relieved to see that he hadn't scuttled away, I quickly wiped my face and tossed the napkins into the nearby trash can, resolving to get control of my brokenness before I scared him off for good.

"You all right, Mudas?"

"Yeah, thanks. I'll be okay." I attempted a smile. "Still wound up about everything."

"Mudas, I'm real sorry about your mama. I've had my share of hard times, nothing quite like this, but some pretty bad ugly in my life, so if there's anything I can do, well, I'm here for you, okay?"

"Thanks, Bobby."

"You're gonna be just fine, you know that? Just fine. We'll get you through this."

I found calm in his words, but knew they were just that: words. We both knew there wasn't any fixing this—me.

"You hungry? I can grab us a burger," Bobby offered.

I shook my head.

"Sun's starting to heat. Maybe a milkshake?"

"No, really, I'm good." I smiled at his insistence. My gramps was the same way. He thought the best way to cure a woman's tears was by feeding the belly—starting with his own.

"You sure, Mudas? My gramps always says having a milkshake is like having a liquid smile."

Mr. Gooch walked slowly up to the bench with Mrs. Gooch in tow. He stuck out his chin and peered over his spectacles at us. Then he tapped his cane, waiting.

I slowly stood up to let the elders sit a spell. "Your gramps and mine would've gotten along fine." I managed to squeeze out a short, tight laugh, but it felt all wrong. "You know what, Bobby, I could use a little something." I needed to settle my stomach. Maybe a bite would help the nausea. I couldn't risk a repeat of emptying it like I had in Mama's yard.

We walked into the diner. Bobby ordered a grilled cheese and milkshake. I nibbled on a pack of saltine crackers that were stuffed into the basket on our table. After a few of those, my head cleared and my stomach felt somewhat settled. The waitress kept glancing over at me, so I ordered a coke and picked up half of Bobby's grilled cheese. Halfway through our food, I caught the waitress looking again as she whispered something to the cook. The cook gave her a to-go bag. She brought it over to our table and placed it near Bobby's plate.

I started to protest. They didn't want the two of us in here together. But Bobby stood, shook his head, and reached for a tip. "C'mon Mudas, let's warm up, it's getting frosty in here."

I tossed my napkin onto the to-go bag, unsure of what to say.

We settled back onto an empty Liar's Bench. After a few minutes, Bobby asked, "Feeling better?"

"Yeah, thanks. Sorry about that in the diner . . . She's—"

He waved my apology away. "I'm glad you're safe, Mudas. I never knew your stepdad. But the thought of him being alive and out here around you, would've . . . At least that's one less thing to worry about."

"I know. Still, nothing seems to fit. Losing her is bad enough, but on top of that, none of it makes a lick of sense. I don't know what to think anymore. Don't even think I can trust my daddy. He's been lying to me, keeping secrets. I don't know what, but I've got a bad feeling."

Bobby looked at me quizzically.

I sighed. "You know when they found Mama, she had those ribbons. Pink hair ribbons. They weren't even in her hair."

"Jesus Christ," Bobby heated up again. "I just . . . That crazy son of a bitch!"

"I know. The thing is, Mama doesn't—didn't—wear hair ribbons. Tommy made her use plain rubber bands to tie back her hair. Didn't like her to have pretty things."

"I don't understand, Mudas. What's this got to do with your dad?"

"Everything. This morning, I found the same exact kind of ribbon in his room." I lifted my wrist and shook the ribbon. "This."

Bobby took my hand. "Mudas, I'm sure it's just a coincidence."

"No, everyone knows Nettie sells most things in threes, especially all her hair stuff. The ribbons are from her store—I even found the package in his room. I confronted him about it, but he's not talking. We had this huge fight, Bobby, it was awful. I think he's never really accepted that Mama picked Tommy over him." I grew quiet for a moment. "His excuses are full of holes. Yeah, he's hiding something from me. Something big."

Bobby squeezed my hand. "It doesn't make sense, Mudas. Your dad's one of the good guys. There's got to be an explanation for all this."

I nodded, wanting more than anything to believe him. Toying with the threads of the ribbon wrapped around my wrist, I smelled a faint hint of lemon—Mama's scent—now a sad and heart-rending reminder.

"You know, I saw her the day before she died. Last Thursday. I dropped by her house to show her my new ride and, well, I know you've only been in Peckinpaw a short spell, but do you know who Roy McGee is?"

"I've heard the talk. All bad. Why?"

"He was there, right in her house, trying to get information about some book. Called it the 'Rooster Run ledger.' He was really mad, Bobby. I could hear them in the next room: He was smacking her around and accusing her of lying and stealing Rooster Run's money—'his money,' he said. Told her to get to work on his books and get his Rooster Run ledger back to him. When I asked her about it, she said she was helping Tommy keep McGee's books. His accounts and all. But it didn't set right, and I think this ledger has something to do with all this. If I could just find it, maybe I could get a clue. Find out who did this to her. Find the truth."

Bobby let out a long, low whistle, shaking his head. "This is crazy, Mudas. Did you tell Sheriff about all this: your dad's ribbon, McGee's ledger?" He looked at me curiously.

I shook my head. "Haven't told anyone but you. I need to sort everything out. Come up for air a bit. 'Sides, Jingles is busy dealing with the town and everything else. And I don't know . . . I'm not sure I trust him with this. He's pretty much set on calling it a suicide; I think he'd just pooh-pooh anything I have to say, blame it on my grief." I wrapped my fingers over my itching thumb. "But I'm not gonna let him tarnish my mama's name. I owe her that much."

"You know McGee owns the old Anderson mansion now— the Hark Hill Plantation? I've been out there once or twice with the guys," Bobby said. "Nothing special, just snooping around same as most everybody else."

"He's meant to be raising thoroughbreds on that plantation, but I heard it's all a front. Really, he does whatever he likes, thumbing his nose at anyone who tries to stop him." I lowered my voice, making sure nobody was in earshot. "ThommaLyn told me that her brother's friend knows for a fact that McGee holds these exclusive monthlies out there, with private cock-fights, gambling—all kinds of bad stuff."

Bobby wiggled his eyebrows at me. "What kind of 'stuff'?"

"Oh, you know." I blushed.

Bobby shrugged, feigning innocence.

"Whores," I whispered.

"Mudas Elizabeth Summers!" He gave an exaggerated gasp. "How am I ever gonna get that mind of yours out of the gutter?"

"Bobby Wayne Marshall!" I slapped his shoulder playfully. I'd forgotten how easy that boy could make me laugh. Bobby caught my hands and locked them in the air, laughing.

Henrietta Boggs, Peckinpaw's Miss Biggity, waddled past sipping on a Coke float. She stopped, tossed her crumpled napkin onto the sidewalk, and turned to stare at us with her bossy eyes. Raising a prissy penciled brow, she puckered her lips with criticism. I slipped my hands from Bobby's grip and placed them onto my lap. Satisfied, Miss Biggity nodded and continued on, her litter cartwheeling after her in a sudden gust of wind.

Bobby growled at her and rested his hand on my knee. "I really missed you, ya know?" he said, his voice soft, a lazy roll like tufts of cotton clouds drifting in summer winds. A curl tumbled down across his brow.

I waited a minute for Miss Biggity to move a little farther down the sidewalk. "I'm glad you're home," I whispered, looking straight ahead to the Osage tree standing in front of the courthouse. My heart did a few skips, and I felt a slow crawl of warmth creep across my cheeks, numbing my currents. I turned to him. For the first time, I looked closely, studying, seeing things I'd missed in him since we began hanging out. *Feeling things I am not supposed to.*

"I wish I could've been there for you at the funeral," Bobby said, absently shooing away a fly that had landed on Liar's Bench.

"It's okay. You're here now." His fingertips paused on my wrist, then curled over the length of dangling thread. For a second, he peered down the sidewalk toward Miss Biggity, then twisted around to the diner and finally leaned back. He circled the grain of Liar's Bench. "Ya know, Mudas, my great-great-great grandmother was hanged." He pointed across to the Town Square courthouse. "There."

11

Crow Blood

"Right over there near the Osage," Bobby said again.

My gaze veered to follow his over to the courthouse. Streaks of sunshine slipped through the thick canopy of Osage leaves, announcing the afternoon. I watched a catbird forage in grasses beneath the tree. It flew up to a dead branch, mewing out a string of loud notes, then ended its raspy song in a fading whistle. I wiped the sweat off my brow and rubbed my neck, sticky with August heat. "What, Bobby? One of your grammies was hanged over there? Why?"

"Never mind, it's not important," Bobby said, shifting his weight on Liar's Bench. "We need to fix on you, on finding answers about your mama."

"No, tell me. I want to hear about your family and take a break from mine. I hardly know more than your middle name."

He took a deep breath. "My great-great-great grandmother, Frannie Crow, was hanged. This is the bench made from her gallows. And marked from it. Marked *Liar*." He massaged the wooden spot between us.

"But you come from Chetburg...And I thought all the Crows had left Kentucky." I couldn't believe what he was saying: Frannie Crow was one of his grammies? I'd been hearing about Frannie all my life and here was her flesh and blood, sitting right next to me, holding my hand. "But how can you be a Crow? Frannie was darker—colored, and you're almost like me,

Bobby Marshall," I fibbed, my sweaty fingers lingering over a tiny knot in the wood.

"Might not look it, but that's the Lord's truth."

I gave Bobby a quick once-over, searching. His features were exotic, his eyes a rich umber, and his skin darker than mine, but not by much. It didn't matter to me. We'd never really talked about it. Though I knew others had, and I had to tell Daddy that he had a different look than most Kentucky boys. Just didn't know it'd be Crow looks.

I planned on getting Daddy's permission to date him, and once I got it, I'd tell all those elders to kiss my tail. Once you fell into those eyes, nothing much else mattered. I knew he had a different heritage of sorts, though none of us kids seemed to care about that.

And Bobby's skin color had never stopped any of the girls at school from falling all over him, batting their eyes, flirting. The jocks puppy-dogged him, too. Thought he was cool, being from the big city and all.

Most all of us kids were still riding on the coattails of the peace and love movement, trying to find ourselves, to let loose the flower child hidden in our barn-wide bell-bottoms. We were confused about the Vietnam War. It scared us, so lots of kids sought to make sense by protesting it with free love, drugs, and loud rock and roll. This long war seemed so close compared to the other wars our parents and grandparents talked about. The old-timers gave us the notion of romanticism in their wars where the band played festively, while the brave men marched off and came back to a hero's welcome. Not this war. Nuh-huh. Seems like everyone knew someone who came back broken, or in a pine box. There were no bands. We cursed our soldiers, and called them cowards and killers. There seemed to be an insane honor in trying to fight Communism oceans away.

And it splashed out into Any-Small-Town, Kentucky, mud puddles. Peckinpaw's jail overflowed most weekends with pot smokers, noise ordinance criminals, and a few litterbugs who'd covered the historic buildings with their flowery peace signs. We wanted to make real changes, wanted to "teach the world to sing in perfect harmony," just like the cola jingle said. But deep down we all knew that, hell-bound and determined, the God-fearing people of Peckinpaw, Kentucky, would never let that happen. Which, of course, only made us even more determined to make it happen.

I thought about the Klan's never-ending war. "I don't know what to say, Bobby," I said. "I, uh . . . didn't know you had Crow blood. It's gotta be hard knowing one of your grammies was hanged for poisoning and thievery, and you having Negro blood and all. Does anybody know?"

"Now, hold on—Frannie Crow wasn't a murderer or a thief! And I'm proud of my family's heritage. Frannie's mama was kidnapped from the Indian nation and sold into slavery to the Andersons of Hark Hill Plantation. So it's not just my Negro blood. I've got some Chickasaw in me, too. I'm a Melungeon. Damnit, Mudas, do you think I care what this hick-ass town's inbreds think of me? Hell's bells, girl! You think it's fair that Peckinpaw built a community of shanty houses over there"—he jerked his thumb behind him—"and confined the coloreds up on a crumbling hillside and marked it Nigger Hill?"

"No, I—"

"I have people up there, for chrissakes! That's where my kin lives, up on that hill."

"Oh."

"That's right. Kin." Bobby stood up and paced. "This is 1972, Mudas, not 1862. What? Are you gonna call a town meeting, cry Negro, and have me sent up there on Nigger Hill?" he barked, his voice hugging an edge that cut across my heart.

A scalding-hot blush crept up and spread across my face, flaming my words. "Stop! Just stop!" I shouted, jumping up from my seat. "That's not fair and you know it, Bobby Marshall. It's not what I mean!" I wiped the heat from my brow. "Bobby, I'm sorry for what your family's been through, real sorry." I jabbed my fists into my hips and set my chin. "But this ain't the North. It's Peckinpaw—just another pick-any-name small town, USA. Things don't end well in Peckinpaw, Bobby! You have to understand that. Maybe you just haven't been here long enough to feel the slap of the South." I felt my nostrils flare. And I found myself biting back words best left unspoken.

"You're wrong about that," Bobby whispered.

Fear took hold. I sat back down and braced my back against the bench, waiting for the worst.

"My first week back in Kentucky," he began, "my parents took me over to the spring festival in Mallardsburg. My parents met up with some old friends. I got bored with all the chitchat and so I set off to grab a burger and Coke. There were three Klansmen handing out pamphlets and, well, I guess they didn't like my winter tan. They jumped me and dragged me to the back of the concession stand. Two of them pinned me to the wall, while the other tried to put my eye out with a cigarette. He said, 'The last thing our county needs is another nigger-mutt. But, just in case you decide to stay, here's a reminder that we'll be watching.' The guy took a long drag off his cigarette and put it real close to my eye. But I got blind lucky. A concession stand worker came around to dump out his grease pan just in time, and they startled and ran off." Bobby paused and pulled his lips back tight. "But not before Kentucky's Welcome Wagon committee could leave their hospitality card." He twisted sideways and lifted his shirt.

I gasped at the ugly scar that bubbled on his back. "Oh, Bobby." I gently rubbed my hand across it. "Those sick cone-headed cowards! I'm so sorry this happened to you. I had no idea."

"The guy used me as an ashtray. Said I was lucky this time, and here was my carny prize to prove it." Bobby dropped the shirt back down. "When we left New York, I didn't realize I was leaving freedom behind. I do love these hills, Mudas, but I love freedom more."

My ears torched with a deep shame and sorrow at what this place—my home—had done to Bobby. Though I didn't often have cause to confront it, I knew some of these hills' ugly secrets, and knew there was plenty more in the past.

12

Bitter Fruit

"Bobby, I whispered, and stared out to Town Square, "I was twelve years old in the spring of 1968. I remember when I sat on the red stepstool in my kitchen and watched as Grammy Essie helped Daddy knot his tie. Daddy was so wound up, I'd feared Grammy was going to strangle him with it. She kept fussing at him to quit fidgeting, and once she even snapped at me to take off my wrinkly Sunday dress and press it again—and then she added: 'Church is not the day to show God lazy.' I was getting ready to protest when I caught the look that said it'd be best if I didn't."

"I don't know what's got into Pastor Dugin," Daddy huffed. "Him, going over to Grove Hill Baptist Church for Colored and inviting the choir . . . There's enough trouble 'round here than folks having to go looking for it . . . Good God, Mama, stop. . . ." He leaned away from Grammy Essie. "Stop. You're choking me!" Daddy raised his brow. "Now, Mama, it's a fine thing, but rooting for trouble on the broken heel of another is—"

Grammy Essie gave another sharp tug to Daddy's tie and horned him "the look."

I quickly turned away, lest those eyes dagger into mine.

"The troublemakers 'round here will burn the church," Daddy warned. "Muddy"—he snapped his finger for my attention—"maybe it's best you stay home, baby. Yeah, that would be best and—"

I stopped my thumb from cuckooing over my fingers and carefully folded my hands over my fresh-pressed church dress. I held my breath. Coloreds had never been allowed in our church.

"She'll do no such thing, Adam," Grammy Essie insisted. "She is going to hear the gospel choir that Pastor has invited to our church."

"When that black choir strolls in, they'll likely be singing to empty pews," Daddy worried. "Don't you see . . . Mama, now is not the right time to be doing this. They called out the National Guard to Louisville last week. They've deployed over two thousand guardsmen to the streets. And you're trying to have a social . . . Mama, two kids died last week in the Louisville race riots and—"

"Can you think of a better time?" Grammy Essie shot back as she grabbed her Bible off the kitchen table.

When we arrived at the church parking lot, we found it full.

I followed Grammy Essie up to the Summers' pew and squeezed in alongside Daddy. The packed church sounded like a swarm of bees, angry ones, that is. When Grammy wasn't looking, I peeked over my shoulder. I spied Mrs. Elliot wearing her prettiest hat, a stiff worry fastened to her poppy-red cheeks.

Mr. Edward rested his fingers against his knotted forehead, narrow eyes spitting grease. His wife looked pale-faced and agity.

Rita Bosly was stuck on painting her lips, twisting them cattywampus-like at anyone looking. And Patrick McCall and his pew mates had their heads bowed in feverish prayer. Nearby, Mrs. Moss flashed me a look that meant to do a'hurting.

I whipped my head back around and fired up my worrying hands.

After a few minutes, Pastor Dugin crossed to the pulpit. Everyone quieted.

Daddy stretched his arm around me, and Grammy picked up my nervous hand and squeezed. Then behind us, the church doors creaked opened, and people turned and stretched their necks, me included.

Ten black women in long crimson robes formed two lines to the choir box. They stood in the box and waited, shifting their feet, sneaking glances at us.

Pastor Dugin cleared his throat, and announced, "Let's bow our head in prayer." After a short lapse, Pastor said, "Thank you, oh Lord, for this glorious day. . . ." When he was through, he said, "We are pleased to have the visiting choir from Grove Hill Baptist Church for Colored here this morning. They'll lead our service with a hymn."

I looked over at the women and their shiny dark faces wearing jittery smiles. I smiled back. A commotion broke out behind me. I heard Daddy hiss through his teeth, and I turned to see what the rustling was about.

Mrs. Moss stood up with her pocketbook hooked over her arm. Behind her, a red-faced Mr. Cooper stood between his twins. Farther back, I saw three others slowly rise.

Then they spilled out of their pews and hurried out of our church.

After a long hush, a round woman with dark, kind eyes stepped forward from the choir and began to sing "Oh Happy Day." Soon, the church was filled with a glory that I thought could only be found in Heaven, or at the very least, in the seasons of Christmas and the Fourth of July, all rolled into a beautiful celebration. Never had I'd heard such true harmony. I even enjoyed Pastor Dugin's sermon, especially the lively declarations that the black choir shouted with their spontaneous "Hallelujahs" and multiple "Praise be to God."

At the end of the service, the choir sang "The Church in the Wildwood." Daddy teared up and hummed along. Everyone kept repeating "pretty" like it was the new amen.

And although blacks were still turned away from our church doors, most agreed they'd enjoyed the pretty left behind.

* * *

"Grammy Essie said it seemed like it would take root, but in the end it wasn't strong enough to strangle the ugly, pushy kudzu." I sighed to Bobby. "Still . . ."

Bobby picked up my hand and pressed it to his mouth.

"Some people aren't born, they just fall out of the ugly tree and crash into stupidity branches," I said. I traced a finger lightly over his back, worrying it over the scar.

"And grow bird-shit brains," Bobby muttered.

I knew that bigotry ran deep here. Confederate flags flew proud, snapping in the Kentucky winds like leather straps against skin. And, on occasion, the KKK kicked up dirt at dusk.

But I'd been taught from a young age that those people—those champions of hatred—were cowards. Daddy had taken on more than a few cases involving racial discord, business that would send him up to Nigger Hill from time to time, looking for witnesses or victims. I loved that about Daddy. The fearless way he took on criminals and sought to bring justice to the under-dog. The respect and kindness he gave to all victims. And Mama too. She'd always rush to put together a lil feed sack full of cookies, candies, and some flower seeds, and insist that Daddy give it to the family he was visiting. Then she would give me the nod and I'd run to my bedroom to rummage through my toys, looking to find one to stick inside her package.

Sometimes Daddy'd even let me ride along with him, but I was never allowed to step out of the car, which I didn't under-stand. And whenever I'd asked, "Why not?" he wouldn't ex-plain, just said those were the rules. So I'd sat dutifully in the car, fascinated by the tiny hill community—the one-room shacks and little shotgun houses tentacling across the hillside like ivy leaves to the vine. The inviting smell of outdoor cookers, the pools of summer shade, and the musical laughter that punc-tuated front-porch storytelling. I hadn't been up to Nigger Hill in years.

"Bobby, I didn't know you had Crow color in you. I, well," I shrugged, "I just thought you might have a mix of something from further back and far away. I'm real sorry they hurt you—

sorry your home state steals what another gives so freely," I said, conjuring up those redneck cowards hurting him.

Bobby looked away, trying to unwind his anger. "Yeah, well, one more year of school and then I'm out of here."

I bent down for an Osage ball and massaged the tough fruit against my forehead to hide the shame of my ancestors. I thought about Grammy Essie, how she'd finally set Frannie's story to pen for history's sake, since nobody else would. And telling me how after *it* happened (the *it* always squeezed out in a tight whisper), nothing would grow in front of the courthouse: every shrub, flower, and tree they'd planted would just shrivel up and die. That is, until the Osage tree took root. It was planted next to the courthouse nearly seventy-five years after Frannie's kin built the bench here, with the seat positioned to face the courthouse commons, as if they knew the tree would be coming and wanted to get a good view. Now those funny little fruits always seemed to make their way across the street from the courthouse, to rest beneath the shade of Liar's Bench.

Bobby took my hands and lowered me down on Liar's Bench, looking at me all serious-like. "Most of my relatives had color, Mudas. They were passed around in wills and deeds, same as the silverware and the mules. Just a piece of property, something to be owned."

I grimaced. "Bobby, you're the same as me. Look." I pulled up a lock of my mix of brown hair and put it next to my gray eyes. Pointed to the splay of light and dark freckles across my nose. I smiled, clicked my white teeth, and stuck out my pink tongue. "See. I'm just full of rainbows."

"So, you don't care that I have color in me? That Frannie Crow was my relative, my blood-kin?"

"No," I said quietly.

"Then say it."

"Say what?"

"That you don't care that I'm colored—a nigger Injun."

"I told you, I don't care. And I don't care what ignorant rednecks think."

"Say it, Mudas. Say you don't care that I'm a nig—"

"Stop, Bobby."

"Just say it."

"I said stop it! I'm not gonna insult you with those words."

"C'mon, Mudas—"

I looked at him carefully, not sure why he wanted me to blaspheme him like this. His eyes were determined. "Okay, Bobby, okay, you're colored! A half-breed. A nigger! And I don't give a spit! Happy now?" He looked anything but. I sighed. "Bobby, it doesn't matter to me. But, we've got to worry about the Klan and their kin scattered about these parts, always lurking—as you know—waiting to target anyone a split-hair different than their scumbag selves."

"I'm not afraid of cowardly jerkwads," Bobby sneered.

"I'm not either," I whispered, waving the lie off Liar's Bench.

Bobby softened and pulled back. "I'm sorry for upsetting you," he said, shaking his head. "I know you've got bigger worries than a century-old hanging and my family." Stretching his long legs outward, he slouched down on Liar's Bench, linked his hands behind his head. "It's just this bench . . . it punches up all these feelings in my bones I can't control. It's like whenever I sit here, I can picture my gramma sitting right next to me. Hell, sometimes it feels like she's trying to tell me something. Hah, how's that for crazy?"

I gave an involuntary shudder. "I can feel something, too. It makes me feel closer to my grammy. And, you know what? I think it's kind of cool that one of your grammies was Frannie Crow."

"We're cool, then?" He flicked my dangling ribbon.

"Cool," I replied, slipping into a smile. It felt good to share worries.

"Hmm, that's strange." Bobby lifted my wrist in the air, twisted, then sniffed the ribbon. He aimed the fabric toward the sun and squinted.

"What is it?"

"I'll be damned." He whistled. "Looks to me like this ribbon has writing on it. Real faint. Maybe you've got yourself some sort of message here, darlin'."

"Pfft, you're joshing?"

"Nope." He grinned. "See right here, on the back of the ribbon? The pink side?" He turned it over. "Not the flowered side. The pink here has turned a bit blue-brown. It's got a scrawl of chicken scratch."

"Huh." I inspected the ribbon.

"Maybe it's a secret message," he said, growing excited. "My gramps Jessum served in the war and he told me all about how army intelligence used invisible ink to send their secrets back and forth. Way cool. He even showed me how to make my own invisible ink out of vinegar or lemon. Even milk. Here, take it off and let me see."

"Ah, lemon. That's it! Mama told me, too, that her daddy was a soldier and he taught her how to make the ink. We were just talking about it, Bobby. She dug up my old chemistry set last week." I picked out the knots and handed the ribbon to Bobby. "That was the last time I saw her."

He held the ribbon up to the sun and examined it closely, twisting his head to get a better look. "I'm guessing an *R* and an *O*, or *P*, it looks like an *S* . . . maybe, hmm, maybe two *O*s and a *T*? That mean anything to you?"

"Really?" I leaned into him. "Roo? Rop? Root, Roos. Aha!" I jumped up from Liar's Bench. "Rooster! ROOSTER RUN! Wow, Bobby! It's got to be Rooster Run, right? Maybe the ribbon is connected to McGee's Rooster Run ledger that Mama was working on. It's got to be."

I peered at the ribbon, and sure enough saw the faded words. Excitement, fear, and dread ran through me.

Bobby stood up and clasped my hand. "Let's go out to McGee's and look around. Maybe we'll find the answers you need."

"What?" I pulled away. "No way, Bobby. I want to, but what if we get caught? McGee is dangerous. Everybody knows it. He hangs with a bunch of politicians—has them all in his pocket so he can do whatever he likes. He's untouchable." I felt my still-sore forehead, picturing the evil that had spilled out of McGee's eyes and hung thick to his body, before taking a chokehold on me.

"It's important we get you some answers, Mudas. Find out who killed your mama." Bobby drew me close and nuzzled my hair. "Don't worry; I'll be right there with you."

I took the ribbon from him, wrapped it back around my wrist, and tied it tight. "I want to find out the truth, Bobby, I do. But if Daddy ever found out, there'd be hell to pay. I just, I can't. . . ." My words jumped, then parachuted into a whispered cowardice.

He frowned. "Nothing's stopping you. I'll help. And," he reasoned, "I know it's scary, but it's not half as scary as knowing there's somebody out there who did that to your mama."

"I'm too afraid," I said, embarrassed—embarrassed because I admitted it and embarrassed because I didn't want to admit it to another. "Mewls like a sick kitten," Mama'd said when she dropped me back off in Peckinpaw all those years ago. I knew it was just another way of her saying "coward." The words had settled like gravel in my belly. "Too afraid," I repeated.

Bobby shook his head slowly and extended his hand. "I'd be afraid not to."

If only I'd stayed with her at Tommy's, she would be here today. *Mewls like a sick kitten.* Could it be all along I was the one who'd been doing the actual leaving. I stood, rubbed the ribbon across my lips. Back and forth, back and forth, the memories scratched: *Jingles saying Mama was tired of living. Daddy saying it was Tommy who drove her to the brink.* The words slipped in between twirling ribbons.

I looked over my shoulder to the half stack of Wednesday's papers left over in the newsstand, the *Smitt County Herald,* with Mama's name inserted under the word *Suicide* in big bold print. If I didn't stop them, they were going to let the truth stay buried with her. Smear her name worse than it already was.

In one thunderclap of thought, I cast off the whole scene—what the officials said, what my daddy thought, and what that stinking birdcage liner of a newspaper wrote. "She didn't kill herself, Bobby." I glared at the metal box. "She wouldn't do that."

Bobby gripped my shoulder.

"You're right," I said, "I have to find Mama's killer, find the truth. This ribbon is a compass pointing us straight to McGee and that Rooster Run ledger. We've got to go to Hark Hill," I said, full of purpose and promise. "C'mon, Bobby, I'm ready, let's go."

13

Rooster Run

Bobby placed his hand in mine, his fingers wrapping securely, like armor against fear, and for a moment I felt empowered—strong and protected. We crossed over to my car and headed out to the old Hark Hill Plantation, Roy McGee's horse farm. Five miles outside of Town Square, we passed over two wooden bridges and then drove several more miles down tree-canopied lanes. The farther away from town we got, the fewer cars we passed. The country roads were empty, except for John Webb's creaky water delivery truck making its normal Wednesday rounds.

Bobby said to take the second fork to Kat Walk Road, a dragon tail of a path, and then follow another mile alongside the Persimmon Branch Creek, where we could park and slip in unnoticed through the back of McGee's property. "No one will ever see it tucked there," Bobby promised.

I could only hope. Any kid who'd accepted a dare had, at one time or another, snooped around the 500-acre plantation that McGee called Rooster Run. Others, more foolish, would drive out to nestle their cars in the dense woods, thinking them a perfect lovers' hideaway. But really, the risk of getting caught was half the fun. We'd all heard the horror stories about McGee sneaking up on unsuspecting teens necking in their cars. Catching the kids heated an' hitting third base, he'd angrily thump the hood and force the startled, buck-naked lovers outside with a double-barrel twelve gauge. Then he'd gather up their carelessly strewn clothes from inside the car, forcing the sobbing, begging lovers to drive home in their birthday suits.

I wondered how many times Bobby had been to McGee's and, more so, what or who had brought him out there.

I'd never tried anything so bold as all that. But I had been up to Rooster Run once before, when I was maybe ten or eleven, and Daddy'd had legal business with McGee. He'd let me ride along up to the plantation, but left me sitting in McGee's garden for what seemed like forever. Surrounded by life-size statues, with ivy and roses trailing, and twisting macabre around their marble bodies, I'd been scared half to death. I'll never forget how relieved I was when Daddy and McGee finally walked out from behind the barn—him bragging about how much money he'd spent restoring the 150-year-old fieldstone Spring House behind it, turning it into his office. I ran up, interrupting, begging a tummy ache and pleading with Daddy to take me home.

Now, I pulled my Mustang behind some bushes, snugged it up to a mulberry alongside the creek, and parked, not fussing that the birds would release purple bombs onto its shiny new wax job. Didn't matter, so long as we weren't found. Bobby and I edged out and quietly shut the doors. I shoved my car key into the back pocket of my jeans.

A steady breeze accompanied the day, making the August heat just a little more tolerable.

Bobby held out a hand and I took it.

He stooped over to pick up a branch. Using it to help clear a path before us, we made our way slowly through the wood's whistling pines and moss-sheltered oaks. We stopped more than once when our rustling of the leaves and broken twigs had caused a rabbit to flee across our path, or brought out a squirrel to chatter and scold.

I kept my eyes peeled for copperheads, carefully sniffing the air for cucumber—their signature musk—and pausing every now and then to cock my ear and listen for the warning whir of a rattlesnake's tail. Balsam pines, wild berry plants, honeysuckle, and damp leaves perfumed the air, in equal measure.

As Bobby pushed away branches, the long twigs sprung back to shape after we'd passed, throwing shivers of half shadows across the earth. The summery breeze lifted, and cooled, abandoning leaves to quiver in its wake. I stopped to pause before I passed a Kentucky warbler perched on top of a rotting stump, calling loudly to its mate. The ugliness of death and sorrow seemed to slip, and a hopeful glow of life and renewal rushed over me.

Shortly before we reached the clearing, Bobby dug inside his jean pocket and pulled out a Buck knife, then crouched down on an apron of leaves. He peeled off his T-shirt. His muscular body was suddenly awash in gold sunspots that snuck through the trees, accentuating each curved cut of flesh. I felt my face warm.

"What are you doing, Bobby?"

"Making us some trail markers, so we don't get lost." Gripping the shirt in one hand and the knife in another, he secured the T-shirt under his knee, then jerked upward and sliced the bottom hem off quick, leaving the edge jagged.

For a brief second, maybe longer, I thought hard about grabbing the cotton rag and burying my face in it, soaking up Bobby's scent, just like Grammy Essie'd taught me.

My obsession with eau de boy had started the year I turned twelve, when Clyde Cole stole a kiss from me on Liar's Bench, my very first. The next day, he'd snuck another behind the school bleachers: a genuine spit-swapper, that is, not a passing peck. And, truth be told, they weren't really stolen, because I had surrendered to those kisses easily. But still, it was unexpected and confusing. I'd marched right on over to Grammy Essie's (after I'd sat on Liar's Bench and bragged to a few, just a few girls from school), where I'd hem-hawed and turned beet-faced before I finally got my nerve up to ask: "Grammy, how do you know when it's true love?" I'd climbed up onto the old metal-red stepstool next to her stove and perched, waiting for her answer.

Grammy Essie'd been frying up jowl bacon and peppered

chops for dinner. She wiped her palm on her apron, and said, "Since you're a big twelve now, I reckon' you're old enough to know a few things."

I'd sat up straight, pulling up all the bigginess that my twelve-year-old body could muster.

Then she'd picked up her spatula, tapped the iron skillet, and said, "It's the scent, chil'. The scent."

Perplexed, I'd looked up at her and waited. Grammy Essie peeled back the aluminum foil from the plate of cooked meats and handed me a small piece of bacon. "It's a scent like that piece of jowl that's making your mouth water. Go ahead," she'd nudged. "Smell it and take a bite."

I'd taken a whiff, then a bite, before a grin spread across my face.

Grammy Essie had grabbed a piece for herself. "Mm-mm." She smacked her lips after each bite. "It leaves you drooling for more, eh? A slow feed that fuels the belly and heart." Grammy Essie handed me a whole slice of bacon. "But"—she'd raised her spatula—"sometimes the nose will mislead you and you get the bellyache. The bellyaching scent is the one you'll want to be cautious of. Fickle, that one is."

"Bellyache?"

"S'okay, chil', you'll know the difference between the two when it's time. But before you go getting the mind-set to take up with just any Kentucky boy"—she'd playfully tweaked my nose—"be mindful of your scents." She'd lightly rapped my head with her knuckles. "An' the common sense God gave you," she'd added softly.

I had blushed and quickly taken another bite of bacon to hide behind.

"Muddy, smell that pot of turnips cooking on the back burner?" Leaning over the stove, she'd lifted the lid and dipped her utensil inside the pan, giving a whirl to the boiling water.

I'd wrinkled my nose and fanned away the pungent steam.

Grammy Essie had picked up a dishtowel and opened the oven. "Sometimes you'll have to wade through the scent of bitter to get to the sweet," she'd winked, pulling out a bubbling brown peach pie. The smell of buttery pastry and cinnamon wafted, drawing me close. "Mmm. True love." She'd sat the pie on the windowsill to cool and, satisfied, stepped back to gather me in a hug. "The nose'll show you, and your heart will follow, chil'. Now, why don't you scoot down to the cellar and fetch me two small potatoes so you can help me make up a few loaves of Potato Candy for the church social."

I had paid extra special attention after that, carefully sniffing—sneaking around to lean in close, give a friendly hug or whisper when I found myself around a boy. I became fascinated by the scent of boy. Consumed with curiosity and a strange bellyache of want—the hunger had driven me to pay an unexpected overnight visit to ThommaLyn's house.

ThommaLyn had four older brothers, each one different and cuter than the next. And, if there was any sure way to understand and explore Grammy Essie's mystery scent, the how-you'll-know-it's-love scent, I'd figured, surely I'd find my answers there. The next morning, I'd awoke before ThommaLyn, snuck into her brothers' bedrooms, found their worn T-shirts, and stuffed one from each into my overnight bag.

Mortified about getting caught and labeled a freak (and a shirt thief to boot), I'd excused myself from the breakfast table early and made a hasty retreat across the meadows toward home. When I reached one of our fields, I'd plopped down under a blossoming apple tree, the one closest to the running brook, and pulled out the brothers' T-shirts from my bag. I buried my face in each one, inhaling deeply. Boys. All similar, musky and a little sweaty, but the most curious and alluring shirt, by far, was that of the second-oldest brother, Bernie. I couldn't put a finger on why I liked it the best. I just did.

I'd stretched out under the tree, picked up Bernie's thread-worn shirt, and inhaled as I trailed the scent of boy across my face. It wasn't enough. Stripping off my blouse, I'd pulled on his T-shirt, buried my nose in the collar, and took several deep breaths. Drowsy, tingly, and feeling blissfully happy, I'd drifted off to sleep. I don't recall coming to terms with any one understanding of scent, but I did find a sweetness somewhere amidst the salty musk of male, the apple-blossom breezes, the late-morning birdcalls, and the whir of honeybees that left me surrendering to a heated blush that crept ever so slowly over my entire being.

I'd slept with Bernie's T-shirt for a good month, and puppy-dogged him around for another, until ThommaLyn threatened to end our friendship if I didn't stop acting all fool-zappy.

But I didn't truly understand the first thing about the scent until I met Tripp Seacat, my first serious "steady." His was a wild and confusing chemical-like mix that had eventually turned to turnips, trailing like wet dog on a rainy day. But Bobby, he was nothing like that. Bobby was the scent of warm berry cobbler, the calming allure of fresh-turned earth and coming home—a soul-feed that sated and, not uncomfortably, left me yearning for more.

Nonchalantly, I tilted toward Bobby and inhaled a generous dose of him. I couldn't help wondering if *I* was a good scent for him, too.

"Looks like we have the woods to ourselves right now," Bobby remarked.

I backed up to the trunk of a tree, looking up, my face heated—red. Still a virgin, cherry, that is, unless I was sitting on Liar's Bench chatting it up with the girls from school. Then I might've white-lied my way around the truth and bragged a little, just *a little,* that I was broken.

I sighed. Still a virgin, though I had planned to change all that before I'd caught Tripp with Georgianna Deats. Reeling from the blow, I convinced myself that a new boy would be the balm for revenge. But not just any boy. Nuh-huh. I had set my sights on Tripp's best friend, Kevin. But when I finally got the chance to make my move, I was distracted by Kevin's scent, or rather the lack thereof. With him, all I could smell was myself, a pathetic mixture of stupid steeped in revenge. I'd left Kevin in a hurry, alone and no doubt bewildered by my very mixed signals. I'd been so embarrassed—angry with myself for letting a boy like Tripp get the best of me—and had decided to take some time away from boys. To give my heart a chance to heal and my nose a chance to hone its love-finding abilities.

But now, with Bobby, the scent of *boy* was getting harder and harder to ignore. And my vow was getting harder to keep. His was the one scent that screamed so loud, so true, and felt like a safe harbor in the midst of all this sadness and calamity.

Bobby tossed me a lopsided grin and raised several ragged hems from his shirt like a trophy, surfacing the memory of Mama's ankle ribbons, and reminding me why we were here. *Mama.* I stepped back, my rush for Bobby fading. I fanned my face and the silly childhood memory away.

"August heat," I mumbled.

Satisfied with his work, Bobby wedged the knife back into his pocket. "We'll leave these as markers to wrap around a trunk or branch. To find our way back to this path once we're through at McGee's." He stood up and planted a kiss on my mouth.

Surprised, I backed up another step. "Bobby, we're here for my mama. To find the ledger and see if it's—"

"Sorry, Mudas." He tucked his chin under. "I thought . . . well, I guess I wasn't thinking. I didn't mean to disrespect, I just, uh . . ." Awkwardly, he raised the marker. "I'll just find a tree for this one."

"Bobby, I really like you. But, well, I have Mama to think about and . . ." I trailed off, unsure of how to justify myself.

"I understand, Mudas. Let's go find out what happened." He pulled the T-shirt easily over his head. As he turned, I saw the angry scar on his back and, instinctively, protectively, moved to touch it. Just as quickly, I withdrew my hand, sorrow and anger burning my face. Bobby's body grew stiff when he saw my eyes focus on his mark. He swiftly stretched the shirt across his dark, broad chest. "Let's go get that ledger and find out what happened to your mama, Mudas." He took my hand and gave me a determined nod.

We walked several minutes in silence, the dappled sunshine spreading larger through the trees with each careful step taken.

Stopping at the wood's edge, we stared ahead. McGee's sprawling white plantation house rose up from the thick, lush bluegrass, looking like some sort of royal country club. I inhaled deeply, scanning the fields painted with Queen Anne's lace, patches of hound's-tongue, and stalks of goldenrod. Clumps of wild rose bushes provided nesting for songbirds.

We both jumped at a sudden rat-a-tap tapping. I spotted a woodpecker plowing its beak into a nearby trunk, and my shoulders relaxed. Bobby saw the pecker, too, and let out a low whistle of relief. Then, trying to fuse some light into the dark that brought us here, he dropped to his knees, scooped up a handful of soil, and struck his fist to the sky, mocking a Scarlett O'Hara, "As God is my witness . . ." victory for leading us to the plantation house.

I laughed uneasily and redirected my gaze back to Hark Hill Plantation, slowly edging my way to the white plank fence that separated us from McGee's land. Resting my elbows on the horse fence, I leaned over and spied a small bush of jimson weed. The devil's weed trumpeted pale purple blooms, hugging the fence alongside the trailing honeysuckle. The picture was deceptive: bucolic, but gunpowdered with poison. The Greek revival mansion stood proud. Such breathtaking pastoral beauty, but elements of sad and ugly seemed to blanket it. Gooseflesh prickled my skin.

The summer wind raked up grasses, leaving blades shivering. A smatter of wild strawberries mottled the landscape. Scattered clumps of field mint tickled my nose, and fresh-cut hay sweetened the air. But it wasn't enough to smother the sour of the place. *I shouldn't have come,* I thought, a sudden sneezing fit echoing my regrets.

Bobby responded with a "God bless," and pointed to the distant barns. "His horses live better than people."

"I bet he holds his cockfights in one of them." I counted five large horse barns, all well-kept, dotting the land like oversized red poppies. Horses and colts grazed lazily on generous turf, while others stood resting, shaded under elms and chestnuts.

Bobby tied another torn-off piece of shirt around the fence, then came to stand beside me. "You okay?"

"Uh-huh. What about you? It must be hard to see where your grammy lived."

"Slaved. Where she *slaved*. Look at those long rows of stone fencing—the slave walls."

"Yeah, most folks think Kentucky slave fences are pretty, but they always make me sad."

Bobby spit into the wind. "Remember where McGee's office is?"

"Uh-huh. Unless he's moved it, the Spring House should be right over there." I picked up a stick and pointed. A horse nickered softly, then quieted into a rooster's startled crow. "Yeah, I'm pretty sure McGee's office will be somewhere behind that horse barn from what I remember when Daddy brought me out. See over to the far left of the garden? The big barn sitting close to the house? It's behind that."

Bobby stepped forward and lifted himself easily over the fence. Following, I scampered up the boards and dropped down beside him.

A dog barked, then another joined in. I shaded my eyes with my hands, searching for the source. A gruff male voice hollered out, shushing the dogs. They answered back, each yap lifting, carrying across the meadows.

"Beagles," Bobby said, releasing a burst of air.

"Yeah, beagles," I repeated numbly, still worried about where they kept the guard dogs, the Dobermans.

We stared in the direction of a small barn, waiting for an opening. At last, an engine came to life, and slowly the hum of a tractor rose, making its way somewhere behind a building. The distant thrum of its motor faded.

I swallowed my fear, shoving down the urge to turn around and hightail it back to my car.

"Okay, it's gonna be a helluva stretch to get from here to there without anyone seeing us," Bobby warned. "We're gonna have to run between brush, horse, and tree. Ready?"

The pounding in my chest climbed up to my ears, leaving a rush in my head. I nodded. Bobby sprinted away from me, but I caught up and we rested under a tree. "I hope McGee will be gone. Daddy says he really doesn't live here all the time. Lives mostly in Nashville . . . uses this place as a tax write-off and for his fancy parties."

"Hope so, too."

"Maybe he'll only have a few farmhands around." I smiled. "You got one more lap in you? We need it."

Bobby grinned. "I'll give you a five-second head start."

"On." We moved on and made it to the first barn, poking our heads in to see the backside of a lone worker shoveling manure into the far stall. Speeding past, we reached the main garden. Once inside the tall maze of hedges, we slowed our pace.

Bobby stopped to stare at the huge marbled statues. I shifted uneasily, remembering my last visit to Rooster Run.

"Let's go," I said in a tiny voice. "The Spring House is up there, past those hedges." I stepped away from the bush and started trailing behind my shadow. I glanced up to the western sky to check on the time. It was possibly four, maybe five o'clock. . . .

When we made it to the far end of the maze, Bobby separated pieces of the hedge so we could get a good look at where we were headed. The Spring House sat about thirty yards away from the main house.

"It's like a ghost town," he whispered. "And on hump day at that. You'd think a place like this would be buzzing midweek . . . creepy."

"Uh-huh. This place gives me the heebie-jeebies." I thought about McGee, his cold eyes. I wondered if he had slipped into Mama's funeral after he sped by the procession line. I didn't recall seeing him. Would he go to Tommy's funeral?

We squeezed through the hedgerow and shuffled toward the Spring House, looking over our shoulders as we went. Making our way around to the side of the old fieldstone building, we stopped under the window and looked up, trying to figure out how we could hoist ourselves up to peek inside.

The window, old leaden glass in a wooden lattice, stared out seven or eight feet above the ground.

I glanced over my shoulder to the towering mansion. It looked like there were sneaky eyes tracking us from its many tall panes of glass.

Bobby turned to face the Spring House and scrunched down into a crouch. Tapping his shoulder, he motioned for me to climb on, then placed his palms flat against the stone wall. Straddling his shoulders, I eased into a sitting position and placed my hands on the wall. He interlocked his arms securely above my ankles and lifted me slowly up to the window.

I cupped the sides of my face and smashed my nose to the window, searching. "No one's here," I whispered. "There's just some file cabinets . . . two chairs, a desk and a lamp, a sofa and TV. A closet. Hmm. And looks like a cage over in the corner—an animal cage of sorts. But I can't really tell."

"Let's go around. Try the front door first," Bobby grunted, lowering me to the ground.

The old arched door of McGee's office pushed open easily. A blast of damp clay and musty stone hit us. Hurrying inside, we shut the door tight.

We stood in silence, waiting as our eyes adjusted to the darkness. The only light, slivers of sunshine slipping through the one latticed window, spilled onto a dark wooden floor.

"Let's find a lamp," Bobby whispered.

I moved toward the desk, but stopped dead cold when I heard a low squawk, and a series of clucks followed by a *whoosh whoosh*. Panicked, I looked over to the cage in the corner, then to Bobby who was already moving across the room. I made it to the cage just as a rooster puffed up and let out a startling high-pitched crow, then another.

Bobby crouched down and made patterned clucking sounds, strumming his fingers along the cage's wire. Soothed, the rooster settled his feathers, cocked his head, and stared at us beady-eyed.

"A cockfighter," he said. "Look at his tail and saddle feathers. Man, these colors are righteous!"

I scanned the room, looking for the ledger, or anything that might be useful to us. I spotted a piece of paper atop a file cabinet that butted up to the wall. I hurried over and snatched it off, lifting it up to a stream of light.

"Find something?" Bobby asked, eyeing the rooster.

"A note of sorts." I moved back to Bobby.

"What does it say?"

"It's an invoice. Says here"—I flicked the paper—*"August 5th, Cock #114—Fire-Rooster.* It's some sort of transportation document to McGee from Senator John Yinsey's estate. And it's got a handwritten note at the bottom: *Sen. Yinsey will be attending the August 19th Rooster Run cockfight and will be fighting his prized cock, Fire-Rooster. Sen. Yinsey requests two female companions for the weekend."*

Bobby sucked in a breath. "Man! THE Senator John Yinsey of Tennessee?"

"Yeah," I breathed, shaking my head in disbelief. "It's even got his signature—*Senator John Yinsey, Esq.*—right next to McGee's. Whoa. Can you believe it?"

Bobby shook his head, eyes wide.

"Sure looks like the good senator enjoys a few Kentucky sins," I said as a shiver circled my neck and crawled up, tightening my scalp. "Hmm. Wonder what the citizens of Tennessee would think if they found out their tax money goes to illegal cockfights and whores?"

The rooster ruffled its feathers and *clucked, clucked, clucked.*

"Wonder what the Mrs. Yinsey would say?" Bobby *tut, tut, tutted,* mocking the rooster, who responded with silence. "Good boy, Fire-Rooster." He raised a brow and gave a devilish smile. "Ya know, maybe I should release him. . . ."

"Daddy says cockfighting and dogfighting are cruel—that men who do this to animals will do it to people, too." I thought about what Tommy had done to the pregnant cat that had made a home under Mama's front porch, after he caught her sneaking scraps to it. A cold fury streaked across my heart. "Bobby, don't release him while we're in here, or he might flog us. Wait 'til we're ready to leave and then free him." I winked. "Outside."

Bobby grinned as he poked his fingers inside the cage wire and rubbed the rooster's wattle. Fire-Rooster stretched a shank as if he agreed.

I folded the invoice and slid it into the pocket of my jeans. "We better hurry up and try to find that ledger, Bobby. The door was unlocked—probably means someone just stepped out for a bit. If McGee catches us, we'll be walking home buck naked or worse."

"Okay. Pass me that chair," he said, pointing to a wooden one beside the desk. I dragged it across old planks to Bobby, who set it under the window and climbed up onto the seat. He motioned to the desk. "See what else you can find. I'll keep watch."

I opened the tiny closet. "Oh, wow, Bobby, have a look." I held up the satin white Klan robe. "Whoa, who would've thought ol' man McGee was into this?"

"Coward," Bobby hissed, and jumped to the floor.

"See these plum stripes on the arm, Bobby?"

"What are they?"

"There's a lady who lives out near Tubertown Road. Name's Edgarita Bower. She's a fifth-generation Klan who sews the robes and hoods. She buys most of her fabric from Nettie's Nest. I pulled out the wrong color bolt one day and she got mad, and gave me a lecture about their colors. The purplish color is for leaders."

"Should be *yeller* for coward," Bobby spit.

"Look here, Bobby, there's a flyer in the side pocket." I studied the drawing of a robed Klansman and read the words:

KKK RALLY. JOIN THE LOYAL WHITE KNIGHTS.
KEEP AMERICA WHITE AND STRONG.
8:00 TONIGHT AT FOX TRAIL ROAD.

"That's McGee's address here," Bobby spit. "How can Sheriff let them do it?"

"I heard last year that a bunch of Klan went up to Louisville and rallied on the courthouse steps. A colored girl stepped into their protest area and they threw *rocks* at her. The police escorted the girl back over to her side, calling it 'freedom of speech.'" I dropped the robe. Bobby ground his sneaker into it, before climbing back onto the chair.

I made my way over to the couch, raised the sofa cushions,

and looked on top of the expensive cherry desk. Empty, except for a crystal-cut lamp, some coins, and a calendar. I turned on the light, then tried to pull out each of the desk's six drawers. All of them were locked except for the top left. I rummaged through it. Nothing but pens, a wooden box of old knifelike gaffes used for rooster fighting, and the usual junk.

"Nothing here but razored gaffes. There might be something in the rest of these drawers, but he's got them locked up tight . . . No keys." Puzzled, I tapped my foot. "There's got to be some other hiding place in here, big enough to hold real secrets."

"Check the cabinets over there where you found the invoice," Bobby whispered over his shoulder.

I tapped my foot again. "Yeah, I'm gonna check the floorboards, too." I walked back and forth and up and down over the oak planks, bending over to inspect any creaky boards, trying to see if I could pry one free, hoping I'd find the ledger hidden beneath. I peered at the walls, running my palms over the cracks, searching for loose stones. "Hmm." I looked carefully at the stones.

"Anything?" Bobby asked.

"No, but I remember Grammy Essie had a big ol' loose creek stone inside the house, by the mantel. She said it was a safe place for her jewelry. And when ol' man Higgins passed, his niece said they found two bags of silver dollars hidden behind a field stone in his Spring House."

"Keep looking!"

I hurried over to the file cabinets. "Locked," I said, kneeling down to tug on the bottom drawer. Out of the corner of my eye, I glimpsed paper peeking out from behind the cabinet. The wind must've blown it off the top when we came in. I reached around and pulled out two tiny scraps of paper. One had a string of numbers inked across, the other, a receipt with names:

RESERVED Escorts for Sen. J. Yinsey, Aug. 19, 1972
Lana Thompson—$75.00
Ella Whitlock—$75.00
PAID—Aug. 9, 1972

I choked on muggy air. The page blurred. I blinked and stared again at the paper. I stood up, remembering my last visit with Mama. How she'd handed me a ten-dollar bill, and I'd fretted about taking her diaper and milk money. Seventy-five dollars was a lot of money, more than what she made in a whole week working at the sheriff's office. It hadn't occurred to me that she might've got that ten-dollar bill somewhere else. Doing something else. Whoring for McGee. "A whore?" I breathed.

"Find anything, Mudas?" Bobby called over his shoulder.

"Whor . . . Hur . . . Let's hurry up here," my voice cracked. I curled my shaky fingers around the paper.

Then Bobby hissed out a "Shit-fire!" and landed with a thud, kicking the chair out of his way.

I quickly stuffed the note inside my pocket. Anxiety thumped in my chest. Sorrow and disbelief coursed through my veins. I latched on to the metal pull on the file cabinet, my body a magnet, my brain a launched missile of alarms.

"Mudas, we gotta book! Now! Someone just came out of the mansion. They're heading this way. C'mon!"

His voice seemed soft and distant, like he was trapped at the bottom of a jelly jar. He latched on to my hand and jerked hard, pulling me out of my stupor.

I stumbled behind him.

Bobby flung open the door.

"Oh no, oh no . . ." I caterwauled. Roy McGee was headed straight for us, making his way across the lawn toward the Spring House in a tight line. His hands clenched to his sides, cold eyes locked to mine, he took long, purposeful strides.

I sagged against the doorjamb.

"Muddy Summers, you and your friend are trespassing." McGee lifted the bottom of his linen shirt and I caught the wink of a nickel-plated Colt revolver tucked halfway down his trousers. "You got a lot of 'splaining to do," McGee bellowed. Sweat bubbled on his red forehead, his jaw cutting steel.

I felt a blaze of fire lick my body, then suddenly snuff, weakening.

McGee pulled out the gun and pointed.

Bobby squeezed my hand. "Stay put, Mudas."

I couldn't move if I tried. My eyes were glued to the gun, my feet to the ground.

Bobby let go of me. Surprised, I peered over my shoulder for a quick look. Flipping open the animal cage, Bobby snatched up Fire-Rooster by the legs and tucked the cock close to his body, snug underneath his armpit. He pushed past me, standing as a shield between me and McGee.

"Put that gamecock back, boy!" McGee boomed. Not five long strides from us, he stopped. His hand shook as he set the gun sight on Bobby. "I shoot thieves and trespassers!"

I looked at a rock lying a foot away to my right and tried to do the math. The distance, the speed. Summing up how good of a shot he was, him holding the gun wobbly-like, setting the sight off center. Me, how comet-fast I could snag that rock and throw.

Fire-Rooster let out a low, mangled squawk. Bobby had his hand wrapped around its neck. He lifted the cock, leaving its claws to windmill frantically, his tiny eyes bugged.

"Bobby, stop!" I cried. "No!"

"You stay right there and put that gun away, or I'm gonna ring his neck!" Bobby exploded.

McGee cursed. "Boy, I will have *your* neck on a platter! You hear me?"

"Not before I can snap his!" Bobby grabbed hold of Fire-Rooster's shanks and took a step toward McGee. Then two more until he was a very short stone's throw away.

"Son of a bitch!" McGee roared. "Put down my bird! I will load up your black ass with lead!"

Bobby hoisted the bird high, tightening his grip. "Mmm! Fried chicken!" He gave a shake, jiggling the bird's comb. "White or dark?"

McGee straightened out his arm, the short gun barrel looming closer to Bobby's head.

"Bobby, no! Bobby—"

"I said put down that bird!" McGee screamed.

"Mmm, chicken!" Bobby taunted.

I snatched up the rock and threw it with all my might. McGee raised his upper arm and it bounced off his shoulder. I saw the muzzle's flash an instant before I heard the explosion. I screamed out and pitched my body onto the ground.

Bobby thrust the rooster at McGee. The feisty cock flew up, squawking, hit the ground once, then bounced up and charged McGee, its four-inch spurs spread, seeking revenge.

I scrambled to my feet.

"Book!" Bobby said, shooting McGee a middle-finger salute before bolting. McGee flailed his arms trying to get the rooster off him.

I ran. Our bell-bottom jeans rippling, swooshing in disharmony, scattering up grasshoppers.

"The maze, the maze. Get into the maze!" Bobby urged.

We slipped into the garden maze.

Another piercing explosion rang out, followed by one more. I fought the urge to scream and, instead, lock-jawed my mouth and pumped my arms harder, catching up with Bobby, my lungs full and burning.

We took a sharp right at the roses, another before the circle of statues, and then slowed near the middle of one of the maze's paths. Bobby called out, "Can you believe that crazy coot, shooting at us? Let's hurry! Here! Here!" He stopped and held out his hand, then moved in front of me. "Close your eyes, lower your head, and try to cover yourself. We're gonna have to barrel our way through one of these hedges to get out," he panted. "Ready?"

I patted my pockets and felt the crinkly paper, worrying what other surprises lie in wait.

14

Coward's Notched Trophies

I eyed McGee's hedgerow rising in front of us. Each bush seemed separated from the next by a mere half foot, if that.

I took one look back. Fire-Rooster strutted past a statue, then slipped easily between the bushes, taking a string of gargled clucks with him.

Bobby plunged forward, catching the brunt of the branches. By the time we'd both rambled through, my hair was in twig-snagged clumps full of leaves, my arms and hands were scratched and bloodied, and my shirt was barely holding itself together. I looked up at Bobby, his hair tined like a pitchfork and his arms and face chock-full of scratches and trickles of trailing blood.

I glanced over my shoulder, then back to the land ahead of us. I poked Bobby. "See that clump of trees ahead? If we can get to it, we should be able to cross over to the big woods and work our way back down to our trail. Find your rag marker."

Angry shouts echoed not far behind us. McGee wasn't alone. Someone yelled, "Find that goddamn rooster first! And, Toby, you go and head those kids off at Town Square." Another man called, "Check her daddy's house." And another shouted, "Fan the woods." A chill took hold of my legs, rattling.

"Let's go," Bobby nudged. "Now!"

I bent over slightly, rocked a trembling knee, and sprang off the ground. Speeding to the grove of trees, Bobby's sneakers thumped close to mine. Swatting at the vines, thorns, and branches, I fought my way through clumps of overgrowth, only to trip over a log, landing facedown in rotting leaves and damp earth.

Bobby skidded to my side. He quickly lifted me into a sitting position. "Okay?"

I nodded, wiping away the leaves that had stuck to my sweaty face.

Bobby cocked his head toward the clearing we had just passed through and listened for activity. It was quiet—no one had seen us.

I looked at my wrist, thankful to see I hadn't lost Mama's ribbon, but my eyes filled as I remembered the scrap of paper in my pocket. The thought of her going out to McGee's parties, sleeping with men for money—it was too much to bear. If anyone ever found out, they'd say Mama deserved her ending. Right then, I made a vow to take this to my grave. I could never tell a soul, not even Bobby.

"Are you okay?" Bobby worried. "Your cheek's puffed up. I shouldn't have brought you here."

I felt my sore cheek. "I'm okay." I attempted a smile, but my brain reached down and corkscrewed it stiff with doubt. "Wish we'd found that ledger."

Bobby frowned. "Mudas, I know you didn't want to take this to Jingles, but I think we have to. I mean, I thought it wouldn't be that bad, us coming up here, but now we've got McGee shooting at us, running for our lives! And dirt on a senator? Pretty serious, if you ask me."

I had to admit it, he was right. This little expedition had turned out to be way more than either of us had bargained for. "Okay," I agreed. "And it'd probably be best if we hand over this rooster invoice to Jingles. I'd like to see Yinsey go down for illegal cockfighting." I patted my pockets. I still didn't trust Jingles, but now that we had some hard evidence, I thought he might be willing to see things my way. Daddy would make copies and see to it.

"Good, I'm taking you right back to town and then we'll go straight to Jingles. If we drive around the knobs, then circle back, we can easily confuse any tail they might have thought about sending after us."

A revving and roaring of engines kicked up over McGee's fields. Bobby hurried over to the clearing and parted the branches of a pine. "It's a Mercedes. Silver," he reported back.

"McGee's. I saw it parked over at Mama's house last week."

"He's pulling out now. And there's a white farm truck following him. They're heading in the opposite direction. Come see." He motioned.

I joined him at the edge of the clearing. "Oh, man, there's so many of 'em," I said, unable to stuff down my fear. "How will we get back to the woods and your rag marker without one of 'em spotting us? And what about my car? The only way back is through those woods and past McGee's property to the spot beside the creek."

"They're probably expecting us to go back through the woods," Bobby guessed. "I bet they'll check there first. But they'll never see your car tucked by Persimmon Branch Creek." He paused to calculate. "When they don't spot us or a car in the woods, they'll split up and take Monk Road to Town Square, and the back roads to get to your homestead. So we'll do the opposite: trail behind 'em instead of them trailing us. We'll wait them out. For now, we're safe in this clump of trees."

"Makes sense." I was glad Bobby was thinking so coolly. I looked over his shoulder, scanning the plantation grounds, and spied the tail of McGee's car barreling a fair distance away from us. Bobby was right. My body slacked in relief.

"If only we could've found the Rooster Run ledger," I said, defeated.

"I know, Mudas. We'll come back and look again if Jingles doesn't find it. I promise. And the next time, I'll be ready." He peered out of the clearing once more, to make sure McGee and his cronies had really gone. Taking my hand, Bobby said, "C'mon, let's get out of here."

We made our way through the island of trees and to the edge of the clearing, then paused near an oak and scanned our surroundings. An old cemetery sat to our left, carpeted with weeds. The graveyard was bordered by a knee-high limestone fence—a slave fence—same as the walls that enclosed McGee's property. Headstones and chipped markers, darkened from weather and time, poked up and dotted the small area.

"Probably slave graves," I said. My throat was dry and itchy, my lips cracked and baked. "Looks like no one's been tending the graves for a while. It's odd, actually: Most of the family plots around here have some of the slaves buried in them, or right next to them. It's strange that this is all by itself, instead of with the Andersons."

"Well, it's a big plantation. They could afford to spare a scrap of land," Bobby said matter-of-factly. "For their slaves."

I did a quick mental count of the stones. "There's got to be at least seven here. Look at them, Bobby." I studied the cemetery, feeling sad for the souls it held, untended and unloved. "Do you think McGee's in town by now or—?"

"I dunno, but I don't think he's giving up. Especially when he finds out that rooster invoice is gone. Don't worry." Bobby hugged me. "I'll get you to safety."

In his arms, it was hard to remember I had worries, only the promises they held. Still, I pulled back slightly, looking toward the tiny cemetery and thinking about Mama being put to rest only yesterday. I raised Mama's dangling ribbon and rubbed the dangling threads across my lips. Back and forth. Back and forth. "I want to go in and have a quick look." I nodded toward the iron gate, half-broken away from its hinge and tipping to the ground. "C'mon," I pushed. "It's our only chance! It's not exactly like we're gonna be invited back anytime soon." I didn't tell him that there was an urgency—something about the graveyard that whispered, pulling me in.

"Well . . ." he hesitated, "I guess we can rest a minute. McGee and his men are gone for now. But just a minute, Mudas," he warned. "I want to get you on back to Jingles."

We stopped at the entrance. A tired old catalpa tree shaded half of the graves. Its Indian cigar buds sagged and strained in the light breeze, while a skirt of its spent white blossoms and chocolate bean-pods swelled, scattered around the trunk.

A white-hot memory rocketed to the surface and then tunneled back down just as quickly as it had come. A noose—black and white legs intertwined, one with a dangling white sock, the other, a pink ribbon. What did it mean? I tried to think about something else. Like when Mama had made my favorite dish, red cabbage casserole. It didn't work. Feeling light-headed, I slanted toward the bark of a burly oak for support.

"You okay, Mudas?"

It was difficult to define the hieroglyphics in my mind—the juxtaposition of Mama, Frannie, rope, and ribbons. Easier to swallow the thoughts. "I'm fine," I said, brushing Bobby's concern away.

Above, a cluster of swollen storm clouds covered the blue skies and filled the air with puffs of wind. The cool breeze lifted, leaving the prickly rise of gooseflesh in its wake. Below, an overgrowth of milkweeds, toothy bull thistle, horse nettle, and tall bluegrass had turned feral, blanketing the small area. Vines of beggarweed and wood sorrel crept and all but choked out the fieldstone markers, the sorrowful seven I had counted. A lone titmouse eyed us from atop a cluster of chicory, riding the bright blue rosette as the wind lifted and rocked the stems.

Cautiously, we crunched our way through patches of cheatgrass and dead leaves to the center of the plot, where the cigar tree stood looming over most of the graves. I swatted at a veil of spider webs and made my way under the big old catalpa. Reaching up, I brushed the cobwebs off his shoulders, then snapped off a dying bough near his head.

Bobby shoved his hands deep into his pockets and narrowed his eyes. "Forgotten souls, condemned to an eternity on their tormentors' land. Can't be bigger than twenty feet long by wide." His eyes scoured the area, measuring, calculating. "And leaving them to rot like this? No one looking after? It's not right."

"Ginny Meade usually looks after these sorts of places; I think she's in charge of Peckinpaw's historical cemeteries. Maybe McGee won't give her passage onto his land. Or," I suggested, "maybe no one's ever gotten around to documenting it."

"More like no one ever cared," Bobby grunted.

A light wind gusted over my face like a guarded whisper, followed by a loud crack slicing through the quiet. I looked up and gasped. A large branch, half torn, dangled by threads of bark.

Bobby charged, uprooting me from where I stood. Startled, I cried out. Just as he landed on top of me, a thud vibrated the earth beneath us. Breathing heavily, I turned my head to see the big log resting a foot away from us.

"Jesus, Mudas! What the hell is going on today?" Bobby squeezed out in rapid breaths. "That was crazy!"

I felt his heart against mine, thumping hard, furious. I felt strangely energized by the near miss, somehow confident that luck was on my side.

"That's it, get up. I'm taking you home." He stood up, towering above me. I didn't move. "That was a sign if I ever saw one, Mudas. We've got to get out of here," he demanded as he pulled me up.

I backed myself up to the catalpa and glared at him. "I'm not leaving 'til I have my look-see. We have time, you said so yourself. McGee's probably long gone. Maybe even down at Town Square by now."

"What are we even doing here, Mudas? You're not gonna find that Rooster Run ledger here, that's for damn sure. So, what now? Are you gonna start digging up graves?"

Fumbling in my back pocket, I pulled out my car key and threw it at him. It bounced off his chest and landed in the tall grass beside him. "Just leave if you need to. I'm staying, Bobby Marshall."

His tawny eyes narrowed and met mine, arsenic gray, cold as a wintry storm sky. Defiant of anyone who might try to stop me—searching for anything that would help me find answers. My gut told me I had to stay.

Bobby had his jaw set tight, too. For a minute, I thought he might actually throw me over his shoulder and carry me away.

Then, with a grunt, he began to dig around in the tall weeds, muttering something about mules. At last, Bobby found the key. He stood, arms folded and eyes tired. "Look, Mudas, I know you want answers, but we're not gonna find any here. It's not worth the risk."

"I can't leave, Bobby, I just can't. I know it sounds crazy, but I feel like there's a reason we happened upon this graveyard. Like there's something here we're meant to find, or see. Bear witness to, even." I didn't know how to explain it, but there was something here in this precious abandoned patch of woe-begotten history and forgotten spirits that called to me. It tugged at my soul. I turned away and ran my fingers over the jagged grayish brown bark of the catalpa and peered up at the large sweet-heart-shaped leaves.

"Come here; I want to show you this." I extended my arm, keeping my eyes focused upward on the tree's trunk. "Please, Bobby." Pulling him to the tree, I took his hand and gently placed his fingertips on the trunk, then placed mine on top of his and began guiding our fingers back and forth across the bark.

"Feel that?"

"Nothin' but peeling bark." He shrugged.

"No." I rolled his fingertips back and forth across a burrow. "Look closer. It's notched," I coaxed.

He leaned in.

"See it?" I rubbed the bark.

"What does it mean?"

"It's a hangman's notch." I ran my finger along the crevice. "Here. Feel it, Bobby. There's got to be at least a dozen notches."

I traced the notches in the catalpa, a tier of ruts trailing upward. Some were gouged with definition, others aged and swelling with warty knots, while others were faint scars with tiny specks of budding leaves. But one cut in particular seemed fresh, its bark broom colored and raw. The furrow, deep and long.

"That one seems new," Bobby said.

A chill shot up. I thought about Mama, hanged, and briefly wondered if this notch was hers. No, I reminded myself, this was a Klan-marked tree, for coloreds; it couldn't have anything to do with her. But still, the freshness of the mark seeped in cold. "These notches were put here by bad men—more than likely the Klan. Daddy once showed me a hangman's tree over in Kasey just like this. The pattern was identical. He told me that after the Klan strings up a man, the bastards take a hatchet, knife, whatever, and notch the tree to show how many coloreds they've hanged. The notches are like a ledger of their evils—their sick trophies and twisted warnings."

Bobby looked at them in disgust, then withdrew his hand as if it had been scalded.

We moved on to a cracked, lopsided fieldstone that poked up amidst a cluster of tall fescue. We bent to inspect it. Bobby dusted off the headstone with the tail of his shirt, and we both squinted to make out the rough etchings. What looked like DENNALEE CROW, or maybe PENNALEE, was chiseled in the stone and, underneath it, DIED 1860. There were no other markings.

Bobby's face lit up. "See that, Mudas? Dennalee Crow? Could be my kin." He rubbed his palm harder across the stone, tiny bits of pebble spraying into the thick clump of leaves and weeds.

I plopped down on the grass. "Hold on, I'll try and make you a rag," I said. Sitting cross-legged, I snatched up the wide bottom of my jeans and tugged until I made a tiny rip.

Bobby leaned over me and in a swift and easy movement, grabbed the hem, tearing off a generous strip—a near-perfect rag. He raised it and tossed me a grin. "Thanks."

I stretched out my legs, studying the bottom of my jeans—my favorite jeans, now ruined. "I'm gonna have a lot of explaining to do when Mama sees this. She just bought these last month." The words tumbled out before I could stop them. I looked up at Bobby, stricken that there was no more Mama—no one to answer to, no more explaining anything to anyone. Period.

Bobby stiffened. "I'm sorry, Mudas. I had no idea she bought these jeans for you. Here." He handed me the rag.

I raised it to my face, blocking the sorrow. "I can't paste it back on now. It's okay, you keep it. I'll turn them into cutoffs." I shoved it back into his hand. A burst of wind swooped across my neck, parting, twisting hairs. Then, just as quick, somewhere in the dark cranny of my mind, an image flitted out. Frannie, Mama, and a hangman's noose cinched tight.

Bobby sat beside me, knotting the rag, staring off. His mind, I knew, was working to fix the problem—me.

I shrugged off the grisly mental snapshots and crawled over his legs to examine the stone. " 'Dennalee Crow.' Wonder who she was."

He pondered a moment. "Gramps said Frannie was one of six kids. The youngest, I think. Two brothers and three sisters." He edged closer to get a better look at the words.

"Ah, my mama was a fourth sister, too." A reaching sunflower, I thought. I walked over to a different stone and lightly pressed down the grass, exposing mostly rubble. "This one's too busted to read."

"Bummer. But here's another," Bobby announced, growing excited. "Says here, 'Amos Crow, died 1925.' Come see."

"Amos . . . the name sounds familiar. I think Grammy Essie told me about him once. . . . Oh, that's right: It's Frannie's son! Yeah, I remember now. Amos built Liar's Bench." I ogled the half-chipped stone.

Amazed, Bobby shook his head. "Wow! I never knew that."

"I wonder if Frannie's here. . . ." We both jumped up and began checking the other headstones for her name, as if she were some kind of local celebrity. Which, I guess, she was.

Behind me, I heard a loud thump as Bobby stumbled over a grave marker, falling hard on the ground. A whoosh of what sounded like mud-suck oozed up. About a foot away, a gravestone lay flat. Reaching over, I placed my hand over his and shook hard. I felt my heartbeat in the tips of my fingers. "Bobby? Bobby, are you okay?"

Bobby moaned and lifted his head slightly off the ground. He slowly shoved himself up to a sitting stance, one leg extended, the other crooked upward. He rested an elbow on his knee. "You okay?" he mumbled, rubbing his head.

"Who, me? I'm worried about *you*, Bobby. You hit the ground hard."

"I'm fine, I'm fine," he said.

"Christ, Bobby, you could've killed yourself. . . . You scared me to death!"

The second I said it, our eyes locked and we collapsed in a fit of nervous laughter.

"Death?" Bobby chuckled. "In my own family cemetery! No hearse needed."

"Pretty convenient!" I giggled. We lay back on the cool earth and laughed ourselves silly. Laughed and laughed 'til it wasn't even funny anymore.

When we quieted, Bobby crooked his head toward me and stretched out a hand. I took it and let myself fall into his gaze. For a long minute I was dizzy with a wanting. A hawk soared above and shrilled its warning, anchoring me.

Spooked, we both laughed weakly. "C'mon." I tugged at his hand. "I think we better leave. You were right. We need to get to Jingles, before McGee gets to us. There's nothing here."

"Told 'ya so," he said playfully, and, together, we sat up, taking one last look around the lonely graveyard.

"Wait." He pointed to a headstone lying flat on the ground.

"That's what you tripped over. Jeez, the weeds are so thick an' tall, it's hard to see where you're stepping in parts."

"No, look at it," he said quietly. I turned to Bobby, surprised to see that his eyes were full of turmoil. I leaned toward the stone to get a closer look and saw that it had landed faceup: FRANNIE CROW—DIED 1860, read the moss-darkened etching.

"Oh, wow."

"It's Frannie. My gramma Frannie," he said, surprise and sorrow coating his voice.

I rested my hand lightly on Bobby's arm. "We should try and set it upright before we go, okay?" He nodded. I crawled toward the grave marker but stopped as my flesh scraped against something sharp. Yelping, I grabbed my knee. Tracks of blood dripped down, spreading crimson onto my jeans. A foot away, glints of sunshine bounced off glass.

Bobby came running to my side and examined my knee

through the freshly ripped hole in my jeans. Once he wiped away the mess, we could see that the cut wasn't deep, just bloody. "Not really our lucky day, huh?"

"What is that, anyway?" I asked, nodding toward the half-exposed glass sparkling in the mud. "Looks like a jar or something."

Pulling out his pocketknife, Bobby cut into the earth, trying to pry loose what appeared to be a Mason jar buried just below the surface. His knife plunged deeper into the muck and, with a hard flick to the soil, uprooted the old fruit jar. Tossing aside his knife, he clawed the earth around the object, forming a pocket between the dirt and the glass, finally lifting it out. Bobby grinned wide, sweat dampening his forehead.

"Beware of flying fishes, Bobby!" flew out before I could think.

"Huh?"

I swallowed Mama's old adage and pointed to the Mason jar.

He inspected the jar, which appeared to be whole, lightly tracing his finger across the tip of the clamp. "Sharp. You must have cut yourself on that clamp." He raised the large Mason jar to me.

I hesitated, then grasped the jar, turning it over and back again (carefully avoiding the clasp), marveling at what was sealed inside: a small package wrapped in yellowed-brown leather. Like a message in a bottle. I brushed away the copper dirt coating the surface and ran my fingers across the smooth, clear finish. The jar was thick and heavy, probably about a half gallon in size, if I remembered correctly from my canning lessons with Grammy Essie years before. It was sealed tight by a glass lid with a rusted thumbscrew clamp that was crusted, caked with earth. Avoiding the sharp point, I tried to lift the clamp, but it wouldn't budge. I handed the jar back to Bobby. "Maybe you can do better."

He used his knife to scrape off the corrosion and dirt that had glued the jar shut, working carefully around the mouth of the lid. Then he gently pried the knife into the sliver of space between the lip and glass stopper. At last, the clamp flung back, banging against the glass. The force popped the lid right off, showering us both in tiny specks of confetti glass and pieces of gray wax.

I gasped and quickly shook them off my arms and clothing, lest they burn or, worse, had someone's remains mixed in. Undeterred, Bobby poked his fingers inside the wide mouth of the jar, pulled them back out, sniffed, and then massaged the oily glow between his fingertips. Leaning over his shoulders, I took a whiff and wiggled my fingers into the jar's mouth, pulling out the leather package. Carefully, I unwrapped the layers of soft leather. Beneath those, an aged handkerchief. When I'd finished, I held a thin dark navy book of sorts, hand-tooled in gold letters: *E.A.A.* Could it be the Rooster Run ledger? My hands shook.

"Go on, open it!"

"Yes," I whispered. I swiped my dirty hands over my jeans and, ever so carefully, opened the small journal, gently separating the cotton rag pages. It looked to be a diary of sorts. No numbers, no names, no clues to Mama's death, and nothing to incriminate McGee. "Just an old journal," I said, trying to tamp my disappointment. I leaned my head against Bobby's chest and began to flip through the old pages. What was I thinking? That I'd just walk into a slave graveyard and find my answers here? I'd been foolish, naïve. As I came to the end of the first entry, *Evelyn Amaris Anderson,* in petite faded script, sat at the bottom of the page. "Whoa—look, Bobby! It's the Hark Hill lady, Anderson."

Bobby winced in recognition.

I tilted the journal toward a stream of sunlight to get a better look, and continued to flip through the pages. Chills scuttled up my spine when I saw the date on the book's final entry. "Bobby, look—the date here—it was written on my birthday—Mama's death day . . ." I reached my hand into the rippled shadows for his. Church mouse quiet, we put our heads together and began to read.

11 August 1862

Last night I failed to choose a suitable piece to play on the pianoforte for our Dinner Guests, and received the full brunt of Mr. Anderson's temper for my error.

His disappointment in me grows, and my small failures serve only to exacerbate his great ire at my truly unforgivable crime of having yet to provide an heir.

In the wee hours of this morning's budding sunlight, I began my monthly courses.

This is the third child I have lost since the death of Frannie Crow, and I must now declare here what I fear to say aloud.

Frannie haunts me in my dreams and in the weight of my waking hours. I see her everywhere. I am certain I see her. Down the hall, through the window, in the eye of my mind, and every time I close my eyes to rest. I have come to dread the mere notion of sleep. Frannie demands exoneration, I am certain of this, just as I am certain of my own suffering until she shall have it.

Three lost babes in the time since her death. Surely I have been cursed for the enormity of my lies.

O, but for the courage to confess my wrong-doing. I cannot. I cannot relinquish what little value I have to the world of the living to appease the world of the departed. But perhaps in penning this confession, I might be granted some level of atonement. Perhaps I might be free of Frannie's ghost and be granted the Lord's forgiveness.

For shield against Hell's might, I must release this journal and the tormented spirits that beg to be released. Mine and Frannie's. By doing so and

*by placing this last entry in the earth alongside
Frannie's eternal shadow, I pray it shall give rest
to us both.*

*I do confess that I, Evelyn Amaris Anderson,
mistress of Hark Hill, unjustly accused my good
and loyal slave, Frannie Crow, of poisoning me
and knowingly so plotted her demise. I did so in
fear of my husband's wrath, and now do whole-
heartedly repent my sin.*

*As recompense, I shall ask Mr. Anderson for
the Freedom Papers of Frannie's son, Amos, along
with two hogs and the wood to build a pen. I
shall also deed to Amos and his heirs the two-acre
field to the north of the black oak bordering
Anderson Woods and the small Slave Cemetery,
so that he might begin life anew.*

*My husband will wish to know the reason for
such generosity, but I am certain a lie can be had.
As our good and vengeful Lord knows, I am ever
adept at lying.*

Bobby and I reached the end of the page at the same time, our
eyes meeting, widened by the revelation. The journal felt heavy
in my hands. *"Signed, Evelyn Amaris Anderson,"* I read, releasing a burst of air.

"Evelyn Amaris Anderson," Bobby repeated, mulling over
the name. He pressed his palms to his thighs, jumped to his feet,
and growled. "Bastards," he spat, not hiding his contempt. His
eyes drifted to Frannie's headstone. He squatted down and tried
to place it upright, secure in the plug of muck it had been ripped
up from, but it kept tipping listlessly to the left. Pulling himself
up, he spun around and gave a violent kick to the ground, scattering the leaves and dirt.

"Hey," I said, rising slowly, wincing from my wounds as I
stood. "This here bastard just exonerated your grammy." I pat-

ted the mistress's diary. "To think, Frannie Crow left this world cradled in bigotry and lies. And now, a hundred years later, she can finally have her justice." I studied Bobby's face, rigid from anger and pain. "Let's go," I said gently. "We need to make sure Ginny Meade records this. This book can right your family history."

"Yeah, okay. Let's get out of here." Absorbed in the diary, he began to walk slowly toward the gate, rereading the mistress's words—a century overdue.

Kneeling over Frannie's grave, I righted her stone, pushing it down into the earth so that it stood strong and straight. At least now her name would be displayed for anyone else who happened upon this forgotten graveyard. She deserved that, at least. Lingering, I reached inside my pocket and pulled out the scrap of paper with Mama's name on it. The one that would forever brand her a whore. No one could ever know about it, and I couldn't bear to have the awful thing burning a hole in my pocket for another second longer. Neatly, I folded the receipt into quarters and plugged it deep into the hole the Mason jar had left behind. "Mama," I whispered, "I'm burying your secret." I covered it with grave dirt and tamped down the soil with the heel of my palm. "Dear God," I murmured, "bless Frannie and all her kin. Don't let them be forgotten. And, please, make sure Frannie watches over Mama's secret."

"Mudas?" Bobby stood at the iron gate, waiting.

"Coming. Just straightening Frannie's stone." I stood, feeling peace wash over me, cool and refreshing, for the first time in days. "Bobby," I said, walking up to him, "we'll get a'hold of Ginny Meade as soon as we get back."

"Mud—" Bobby launched. I sealed my mouth over his before he could say another word. I was tired of talking, tired of trying. A well of emotions drained into the balm of a long kiss. Surprised, Bobby stepped back before wrapping me in a perfect hug. "My family would love that. Thank you."

I raised my chin and rested it on top of his shoulder, my mind racing and my heart *thump-thumping*. Like my mama, Frannie Crow was buried in the northern corner—the sunflower sentinel of this cemetery, a true guardian.

The cigar tree swayed ghoulishly, the sunlight filtering through its leaves cast bands of greenish yellow on the tall grasses and weeds. A warbler clung to a gnarled twig, trilling sweetly, soft and slow, while a solitary dove perched on the slave fence and mourned the day's sadness.

I snuggled into Bobby's embrace. The world seemed to shift and suddenly everything was beautiful. Wondrous.

And, for a minute, I could feel Frannie smiling down on us, saying it was true.

15

A Stench

Bobby and I trekked back to his rag marker, through the big woods, and beyond to the side of Persimmon Branch Creek.

We found Peggy sitting under the mulberry right where I'd parked her and, thankfully, exactly as I had left her.

Bobby let out a joyful whoop and leaned against the car in relief.

Exhausted, I cradled the journal and tucked the Mason jar into the crook of my arm. "I just wish we'd had more time in McGee's office. I know that Rooster Run ledger is in there somewhere. Has to be."

"C'mon, Mudas. Let's head on to Town Square and find Jingles. He'll sort this all out."

Sapped, I tossed the key to Bobby and slipped into the passenger seat, placing the jar on the floorboard. With the journal cradled on my lap, I let my head fall back against the seat and crooked my neck sideways to watch Bobby.

In a series of small movements, he slid the key into the ignition, pressed in the clutch, and put the gear in first—lickety-split and smooth. Bobby turned to me, smiling. "Tighter than my pickup." He leaned over and kissed me fully. I pressed into a sun's midday kiss, hot and heating, then backed away.

Again, Bobby and I stared at each other for a second. Hesitant, I turned to the window, before that second could claim the hour.

He gave a slow, low whistle, before easing us out onto the

road. After a few minutes driving down Kat Walk, Bobby turned left onto Harper Road. We traveled about two miles before spotting old man Harper's huge round Texaco sign, its red star faded and rusted, the Kelly green signature *T* blistered and peeling from years in the Kentucky sun.

"I'm dying of thirst. Can we stop to use their water fountain?" I asked, pointing to the station. I was so desperate for a long, cool drink that I was even willing to put up with old man Harper's gross advances for a minute.

Bobby worked his jaw back and forth, studying, then quietly said, "Suppose it wouldn't hurt."

He pulled into the gravel lot and parked by a gas pump sporting a metal sign of a Fire Chief's hat. Before I could reach for the door handle, Bobby had hopped out of the car, and said, "Be right back." He winked at me and headed inside.

I started to protest, wanting to go inside and hog the water fountain—slurp up cool water till my eyes swam, my tongue waterlogged with satisfaction. I slumped back in my seat, waiting.

Gasoline fumes hazed the air, seeping in through the open window. I stared down at the journal clasped in my hands. Rubbing my fingers across the blue leather, I traced the gold scripted initials, *E.A.A.* I marveled at its age and, even more, its condition, the delicate fine cotton paper brown and yellowed, the ink smudged in parts, but still legible. I wished Grammy Essie was still alive to record this; it would've made her so happy. I brought the journal up to my nose, closed my eyes, and inhaled its earthy, aged scent, lost in thoughts about Frannie. Frannie and Mama. It would have been so much easier if Mama had left a journal behind instead of a strange ribbon with an even stranger encrypted message. And what if Mama hadn't left the message after all? Maybe Daddy had put it there, I despaired, or maybe Bobby and I'd been looking for something that wasn't even there—seeing what we wanted to see. Maybe this was all for naught, nothing but a snipe hunt. I thought of the receipt I'd buried alongside Frannie's grave, sick with the knowledge that Mama'd been reduced to whoring.

Bobby jerked open the door, startling me. The journal fell to my lap and sprung off onto the floorboard before I could snatch it up.

"Bobby, you sca—" I stopped, looked at his hands, and squealed, bouncing up and down on the bucket seat and clapping my hands. I felt my eyes balloon into moon pies as I momentarily tossed my worries over my shoulder.

Bobby flashed a grin, ducked his head inside the car, and handed me an ice-cold Coke and a tall, narrow bag of peanuts. He slid in behind the steering wheel and silenced my girlish peals of laughter with a friendly smooch.

I knocked back a huge swallow of Coke and felt its burn slide down, soothing my bone-dry throat. "I was *so* thirsty!" With shaky hands, I ripped open one of the bags of nuts and shoveled a handful into my mouth. "Thank you . . . mmm," I said, mumbling with a mouthful, leaning forward to snatch up a nut that had slipped off my tongue and landed on my chest.

Bobby laughed and took a long swig of his Coke, then opened his peanuts. He popped them into his mouth and crunched away.

I funneled some of my own peanuts into my Coke. "Mmm," I moaned, taking a sip, slurping and crunching, savoring each jaw-full as if it was a fried chicken Sunday dinner. "Mmm, mmm!" I stuffed more peanuts into my mouth, famished. My tongue quivered from the salt. I washed it down with a swill of icy Coke flavored with softened nuts. Savoring the fizz, I tossed Bobby a chipmunk grin.

Then, out of the corner of my eye, I saw old man Harper approaching our car, red-faced, wearing a tight grin with even tighter eyes. He gave a sharp whack to the hood and whisked around to the driver's side. Resting his meaty hand on the roof, he leaned down to Bobby.

"Ain't you ol' man Jessum's kin?"

"Yessir," Bobby said slowly.

"Nigga Jessum's grandson?"

"Sir?" Bobby replied, gripping the steering wheel and tucking his head down low. His eyes were fixed to the wheel.

Mr. Harper turned his head, opened his mouth, and squirted out a trail of spit. "I've seen ya wid him a couple of times when he comes in to git tires to take to the recap center. Ain't that right?"

"Uh—"

He pounded the roof. "Answer me, boy."

I pulled Bobby slightly back and craned forward, peering over his shoulder to give Mr. Harper a puzzled look.

"Why, Miz Muddy, is that you?" Mr. Harper acted surprised, his mouth contorted—twisted all sourball candy-like—his red lips jutted, settling into a sneering pout. He plucked off his dirty ball cap and poked his sweaty face inside the car. "Me an' Missus Harper was jus' talking 'bout yore loss an' the fine service Pastor gave yore Mama yesterday. An' 'bout the good riddance of that no-good white-trash Whitlock today. Tut, tut." He picked at his oily nose, ratlike.

"Yessir," I answered, growing alarmed. The stench of his grease, dirt, and sweat wafted close and settled into the car, causing me to take short, tiny breaths.

"This boy running errands for ya today?" He glanced at Bobby.

"Huh? I—"

Bobby grabbed my knee and gave a soft, loaded squeeze, before returning his hands to the steering wheel.

"Ya know, iffin' you wanting some gasoline, Miz Muddy, I can't serve ya wid him sitting 'hind the wheel. Only you."

"Mr. Harper, Bobby goes to my school. And, he's—"

"Educated nigga or not, I ain't serving him. 'Course he can always git out an' pump for ya." Mr. Harper's face was pinched, his eyes hardened to slits as he stood there studying Bobby.

Stunned, I looked over to Bobby, whose head was slightly down, his jaw clenched, and his knuckles turning stark white on the steering wheel.

"Mr. Harper, sir," I replied, "we were just stopping by for a drink from the fountain. And we, um, bought Cokes and peanuts." I lifted my empty Coke bottle, feeling the syrupy liquid begin to crawl up the back of my throat, like the sticky sap of a hedge ball.

"That so?" he said, his eyes darting over us. He dug into the pocket of his sweat-stained blue union suit and pulled out a palm full of change. Picking over the coins, he lifted up a nickel. "Looks like I owe my customer a bottle refund." Mr. Harper brought his arm up to his mouth, wiping his spittle on his already dirty sleeve, and dangled the nickel toward me, waiting.

Shaking, I extended my arm past Bobby to hand Mr. Harper my Coke bottle for the standard refund. He plunked the coin into my open palm and smirked at Bobby. Mr. Harper just stood there—staring, waiting—his neck all stretched out like a turkey's wattle, with veins threaded and pulsing below warty skin.

I lowered my eyes and murmured a polite thank you.

Satisfied, he nodded twice, jowls flapping with each bob.

Bobby sat quietly, but I could feel his contained anger threatening to spill over, a hotness oozing out.

I tugged at Bobby's Coke bottle, but he wouldn't let go.

Mr. Harper gloated. "That's right. He knows the rules, Miz Muddy. We don't refund to coloreds." He snarled at Bobby. "They take their bottles down to Skeeter's for their refunds. Ain't that right, boy?"

Bobby fixed his eyes on the steering wheel.

"Answer me, boy!" Mr. Harper cursed.

Bobby gradually turned toward him.

Taking a step back, Mr. Harper stuck out his lips and spit. Thick goo landed on Bobby's cheek, a few wayward droplets hitting my face. I gasped and hurriedly swiped my hand over my face, repulsed.

Bobby turned away, shutting his eyes.

Harper whacked the roof and edged farther away from the car to swagger around the front. Giving a fisted thump to the hood, he called over his shoulder and waggled a stubby finger in the air: "Ya tell ol' Jessum we won't be needing him for tire pickups anymore. Maybe he can find work over in Mallardsburg. Ya hear me, boy?"

Bobby fumbled for the door handle.

I squeezed out a sharp "No!" and quickly opened the glove box to find a handful of tissue paper. "Bobby . . . Hey, Bobby, look at me. Please." I gently guided his face away from Harper and toward me.

Slowly, he relented, but his eyes bore into mine, heated, pained. He held the Coke bottle vicelike, the green glass threatening to burst.

"S'okay. It's okay, c'mon," I whispered, carefully wiping the sputter off with a tissue. "Let him go. Let *it* go, Bobby. My grammy always said you gotta choose your battles carefully. 'Cause the enemies, and the offspring of your enemies"—I tapped his temple— "are gonna be setting up shop in there. So you best make sure they're worthy, 'cause I know you've got better things to think about. Need to leave space for all the good stuff, okay?" I wrapped my hand over his and gently stroked. His muscles relaxed and the grip on the bottle loosened.

I let out a tiny sigh of relief.

Bobby rested his forehead against mine.

"C'mon, Bobby, let's get outta here."

He shrugged and tossed the tissue out the window. "Prick," he muttered, his voice rattling back up from the hurt. Setting the pop bottle between his legs, Bobby started the car and eased out onto Harper's Road. "We'd best take Harper's straight down to Town Square, in case McGee and his men are lurking on the back roads," he speculated. "I reckon it'd be safer to stay on the busier road."

It was. No more than five minutes later, we passed Jewel Johnson on Harper's Road, her station wagon bulging with six children squeezed inside. She waved and I smiled, remembering how, just a few weeks ago, I'd babysat for her and Mr. Johnson. I especially remembered how their house had been loud and full of love, peppered with plenty of cussing an' kissing. She'd told me she was plumb worn-out from popping out babies. "Thankfully," she'd said, "as soon as we lugged our first TV set home, Mr. Johnson's attentions turned." I'd blushed at her frankness.

We sped into town, driving past the Cooper twins carrying bales of hay in the back of their pickup truck and past Joel Irving in his mail truck, slowing only to swerve around a deer and brake for a pokey box turtle.

With my belly full, and feeling drowsy and spent, I leaned my head against the passenger window, watching as the car whizzed past the tall weeds and pines. It wasn't long until the scene became a comfortable blur, and the hum of wheels on asphalt lulled me into nothingness. I felt Bobby reach for my hand, a gentle caress, before my eyelids grew heavy.

I awoke to the sun setting behind the Peckinpaw Jail, the late-afternoon shadows casting a freakish blue haze over the pea-green building. Peeling my forehead from the car window, I groaned. "Here already?"

"I cut over Knobmole Hill. You hit a brick wall 'bout fifteen minutes back."

"Feels more like fifteen seconds," I yawned, blinking twice to stretch my eyes.

Bobby leaned over the seat and lifted the Mason jar.

I grabbed the journal and met him on the sidewalk. We stared up at the old brick building. "What do you think Jingles will do?" I asked.

"Dunno. Would you rather go find your dad first? We could head to your house?"

I looked over my shoulder, worrying and wondering about McGee. "No." I shook my head firmly. "I can't go back there," I announced. "I don't trust him. I'll be sleeping in Peggy until I can figure out where home's gonna be."

"I'll be damned if I'll let that happen," Bobby replied, his jaw set firm. "No way."

I shrugged.

"Listen, my gramps has a breezeway off the back of his house and if you don't mind sharing it with Cassie, I'm sure Gramps wouldn't mind a bit."

"Cassie? Your grammy?"

"No, she passed."

"Oh, sorry."

"Years ago. But thanks."

"So . . . Cassie is?"

"Dog breath, and lazy."

"Hmm."

"You don't mind bunking with a hound dog?"

"Hah." I tousled his hair. "I'll study on it," I said gratefully.

"All right, you ready to go see Jingles?" I nodded. We climbed the concrete steps of Peckinpaw Jail. I moaned when I spotted the faded blue WILL RETURN IN AN HOUR sign, knowing that, in Peckinpaw time, that could mean a second, a minute, or a day.

The old jailhouse—one room with a holding cell and what was once my mama's desk—was locked up tight. Beneath the sign was a sticker saying, IN CASE OF AN EMERGENCY CALL: KENTUCKY STATE POLICE POST 126.

"It must be 'round suppertime," Bobby said, glancing up at the sun. "I didn't realize how late it'd gotten. Well, Jingles should be home eating. If he doesn't doze off after, he'll be making his rounds at the Dixie Bowl and Ruby's. Maybe sooner if the kids split up and set off firecrackers at each end of town to keep him hopping, and away from the hangouts."

"I 'spect Jingles hasn't had time to replace Mama. His wife's probably playing receptionist for the time being." I leaned over the iron railing and pressed my face to the old wrought-iron bars covering the tall, narrow pane of glass, fixing my gaze on Mama's desk. I spied a picture of me and Genevieve, the frame sitting angled beside her big sunglasses, all regular, like she'd just stepped away from her desk. I clamped my hand over my mouth.

"What?" Bobby leaned over my shoulder to peer into the window. "Shit-fire," he mumbled.

I ran down the steps to Peggy and buried my face in my hands, straining to quiet myself. I felt Bobby touch my shoulder, but then his hand dropped away, like maybe I was made of porcelain, too fragile to touch. I turned to see him staring at the ground, Grammy Essie's "disappearing look" creeping into his eyes.

"Sorry, I . . . I wasn't expecting to see that." I wiped my eyes, wishing I hadn't, and wishing I'd control what was inside of me that was always wanting out. I gathered up my resolve, and said flatly, "I think you best go, Bobby."

"Go *where?*" His voice was sharp.

I bit down on my quivering lips, fighting to keep my composure. "Just leave. It would probably be for the best. I think I need to be alone so I can try and work this out—"

"What the hell are you saying, Mudas? You expect me to go? Just shuffle on home after everything that's happened today? Leave you here like a sitting duck for McGee and his bastards?" Before I could protest, he'd opened the passenger door, swept me off my feet, and placed me firmly on the seat, muttering "Hell, no," about three times under his breath all the while.

"Bobby! What are you doing?"

He leaned into the car. "I'm not about to let you get rid of me, Mudas Summers. Thought you knew me better than that," he winked. "I intend to make sure you're safe. And I know the perfect place."

Outwardly, I scowled, ever so slightly miffed at Bobby for being so downright contrary. But inside, I was breathing a big ol' sigh of relief, grateful that he hadn't left me sitting in the middle of Town Square, soaking in my own misery, drowning in abandonment. I couldn't stop a teeny smile from tugging at the corners of my mouth. "All right, Bobby Marshall, we'll do it your way. Where we going?"

"You'll see."

"Wait, hold on just a minute. I forgot something. Let me go use the phone—I need to call ThommaLyn." I reached inside and opened the glove box and raked up some change.

"Fine. But you best come back now, ya hear? I've done enough running for one day; last thing I need is to come chasin' after you."

"I'll be right back," I promised.

I crossed over to the diner and slipped inside the phone booth. ThommaLyn answered on the first ring. "Hey," I said, glancing out at Bobby, "I need you to cover for me. . . . No, I'm fine, everything's fine, really. . . . Listen, ThommaLyn, my daddy's probably gonna come looking for me later and I need you to cover for me. . . . Well, we had a big fight and—I actually don't have time to talk right now, I'll explain everything later, I promise. . . . Yeah, okay. Just promise you'll . . . Okay, thanks. . . . See ya soon." Satisfied, I hung up.

Bobby was in the car, waiting for me. I smiled as I slipped back into the passenger seat.

"All right, mister. Where to?"

16

The Hill

Bobby drove us toward the outskirts of town. The car filled with the quiet of two people who'd done plenty enough for one day, and the sorting that comes with it. Strange emotions bubbled up inside me. This was the worst time of my life: Mama gone, her memory tarnished, Daddy a stranger, McGee and his henchmen on my tail. But here with Bobby—my cheeks rosy and my heart aflutter—I felt wholly loved and protected, like never before. It was hard to find a middle ground. I wasn't even sure if one existed.

"I think we both need to get some rest," Bobby interrupted my musings, "so we can think clearly in the morning. We can try to find Sheriff then, okay?" He glanced at my thumb, again flying over each finger.

Basking in his comfort and in ThommaLyn's promise, I slowly tucked my worrying fingers into a fist. "Sleep sounds good."

Bobby turned onto Nigger Hill Road. "So, where is this mysterious place?" I asked, watching the whir of passing trees as Bobby navigated the car easily up the narrow gravel trails, winding higher and higher up the hilltop.

"Well, like I told you, my Gramps Jessum's got a breezeway you can sleep in. His house is just up here. Real quiet, tucked outta the way. You'll be safe there for the night."

"Oh, yeah." He'd told me on Liar's Bench that he had kin living up on Nigger Hill, but I hadn't put two and two together. I wasn't so sure that this was a good idea. I *had* been up here before, but, then again, I'd never actually gotten out of the car.

"This okay with you?" Bobby asked.

"Sure," I said. "Of course." Still, I couldn't help but worry. What would Daddy say if he found out? Worse, what if word spread and the Klan came looking for us? I'd never forgive myself if somebody hurt Bobby or his gramps on my account.

"It'll be cool," he said, as if he'd Polaroid'ed my thoughts. "You'll be safe here, Mudas, I promise."

I leaned my head slightly out the window and inhaled deeply. Honeysuckle and wild onion perfumed the cool air. The song of the katydids swelled and waned, an ongoing cycle. From farther up the hill, I could hear the tickle of a fiddle climb up, up, up, and descend slowly back down. A harmonica leaped in to join the fading strings, colorful and sweet. The barking of dogs and the laughter of children echoed through the small hillside community. Dark pines cooled, cradling tiny homes. This hill comforted me, distilled all my troubled thoughts and fears, and soon, I felt my mind slipping into a cool and placid place, and then trail into a warmer one with thoughts of Bobby.

Bobby turned onto a dirt drive in front of a tiny house with a wooden porch and an old swing that hung from sagging eaves. The home was bordered by a worn but freshly painted white picket fence. He parked under a sugar maple and grabbed the Mason jar and journal from the backseat.

Stepping out cautiously, I took notice of the mimosa trees scattered around the yard, their feathery puffs of pink blossoms crayoned against the white clapboard. Clumps of daisies bordered the porch. Nearby, a snowball bush showed off its sky-blue blossoms, and pink ladies skirted high around a chipped, concrete swan. We crossed through a latticed arched gate with trails of crimson rose blooms and ivy clinging roly-poly snug to the white slats.

An old man in faded trousers opened the screen door, his eyes narrowed, studying on his visitors. Then he flashed a wide, toothy grin in recognition and motioned us up onto the porch, his dark skin glowing from the heat of the evening. Bobby led me up the wooden steps.

"Mudas, meet my gramps, Jessum Crow. Gramps, this is my friend, Mudas Summers."

Bobby's gramps set aside his cane and clasped my hand in a friendly squeeze. "Pleasure, Miz Summers." He tipped his head and a smile rippled across weathered, map-lined lips, stretching wide, and then settling comfortably into the corners of his mouth.

"Hi," I mumbled, feeling my face slowly warm from shyness.

"Have a seat, chil'. Here, Bobby, grab Miz Summers a seat on the porch where it's cool. And fetch her a glass of sweet tea. There's a bucket of fresh ice chips in the cold box."

"Mudas. Please call me Mudas, sir."

Bobby pulled up a wooden rocker for me.

"How was Boston, Bobby?" his gramps asked, settling into the swing.

"Great, Gramps." He bent over and gave the old man a hug. "I'll tell you all about it later. Be right back with that sweet tea." He ducked inside the house, leaving me and Gramps Jessum smiling awkwardly at each other. I fidgeted with my hands, inspecting my ragged, dirty nails.

"Uh-huh," Jessum drawled. "Uh-huh, fine Wednesday evenin' for fine company." His amber eyes beamed bright.

"Yessir." I stared longingly at a wooden washstand perched against the porch wall beside me. A white ceramic bowl and a jug bearing lilac flowers sat on top of it, while an embroidered hand towel and bar of soap cozied nearby. A small mirror hung above the stand. I couldn't wait to get myself cleaned up.

"Yore daddy, Adam Persis Summers," Bobby's gramps stated matter-of-factly.

"Uh, yessir, that's my daddy."

"Be fine to call me Jessum, chil'," he invited. Leaning back, he tucked the toes of his worn leather oxfords under the swing, lifted his feet, settling into a soft rock.

"You know my daddy?"

"Known Adam since he was wearing the cloth." Jessum raised his hands cradle-like, swooping back and forth. "A fine boy, a finer man. Hmm-mmm," he hummed. "An' his mama, Miz Essie, lawsy, wasn't a finer soul on this sweet earth, 'ceptn' my angel, Sara, God rest her soul. Me an' my missus used to go over to the Summers Homestead to look after Adam when the folks went down to Nashville. Lawd, he was wearing the cloth, just a tiny little thing back then, yore daddy was." He lifted his hands again and held them maybe a foot wide. I laughed to think of my Daddy so little, so young. It was hard to imagine. "My Sara passed through the gates shortly after Miz Essie," Jessum said, standing.

"I'm so sorry. . . ." I paused as Bobby came through the door, handing me a jelly jar full of sweet tea. I sipped it slowly, savoring the flavor. "Bobby, you didn't tell me that your grammy babysat my daddy."

"Never knew," he said, looking up at his gramps in surprise.

"Uh-huh," Jessum said. "Used to ride him 'round on the tractor in yore backfield. He always loved to stop and play in that ol' Penitentiary Hole."

"ThommaLyn and I used to play in that cave," I laughed, twisting to Bobby. "That's what they called it. Daddy said his great-grandparents allowed it to be used as a safe haven. Grammy Essie even had this old picture from the 1800s. It's of a small group of slaves standing at the entrance of the cave. Really neat." I blushed. "I mean, a neat piece of history, that is."

"That's cool having your own piece of history in your backyard," Bobby said.

"You knew my Grammy Essie, too?" I looked at Jessum. I couldn't imagine her as a young person either. Somehow I had a feeling she'd always been wise beyond her years. "What was she like when she was younger?" I ventured.

Jessum picked up a glass of water sitting on a stool fashioned from a log and walked over to a hanging basket of leggy, peppermint-swirled petunias. After pinching off a few spent flowers, he slowly watered the plant.

"Miz Essie looked a lot like you, chil'. She was a good mama, too. Toted baby Adam everywhere. Worked hard at the library. When Adam got bigger, he helped her stack the books there. And, on Saturdays, he'd carry books up to the hill here for our youngin's and our sickly elders. Gave us all those books and them books take us to places we couldn't ever go. 'Travelin', Adam said.'" Jessum spread his arms. "Every Saturday morn'. Adam never missed one that I knew of, even when he went to high school. Toting all those heavy books up an' down this big ol' hill. Uh-huh. . . . Miz Essie—a fine, thoughtful lady—raised a fine, thoughtful son. Mmm-hmm." He set the empty glass down and seated himself back onto the swing.

I never knew this about Daddy. A day of wonders. For a moment, I closed my eyes, picturing Daddy toting a big bag of books, just like Santa Claus. Spreading Christmas joy and knowledge to the people of this hill each and every Saturday, in the rain, sunshine, and snow. And my heart was happy and proud—and suddenly a bit lonely for a hug from him, a little mad at myself.

"Gramps, you mind if I take Mudas inside?"

"You chil'un' go on ahead." Jessum hiked his arm up on the swing's chain and rocked.

Bobby held open the door as I stepped into a one-room home. The walls were clean, whitewashed a robin's-egg blue. A huge potbelly stove hugged a corner of the room. Pine floors gleamed. A cot, neatly made with a coverlet, nestled near the wall under an open window. Breezes trailed through lace curtains and an old box fan's whirl cooled the room. On the opposite wall, flashes of sunlight bounced off glass whatnots and canning jars on a shelf hanging above a narrow window. An enamel sink with a ruffled bottom curtain stood beneath. Next to the sink, a small wooden table with four mismatched chairs, all neatly tucked under, held a Mason jar full of crimson roses.

Bobby walked over to the stove and opened its heavy door. The heavenly scent of hoecakes laced with onion bits rode the warm breeze, nearly causing me to sway. Bobby flashed a wicked grin, and then crooked his finger, motioning for me to come closer. He lifted the lid off a simmering cast-iron pot that brimmed with mixed beans, onion, a sprinkling of red-hot peppers, and a huge meaty ham hock.

"Smells divine," I said, turning to Bobby. Sunbeams dropped warm rays across his face. His eyes rested hungrily on my lips, leaving me with a different and greater hunger.

The porch swing creaked and the moment was lost, swiftly magpie'd away.

He shifted his gaze to the door, and said softly, "Guess I'll set the table."

I nodded. "Let me help."

Bobby pulled down dishes and grabbed silverware from the drawer.

"Here," I said, opening my hands. "Why don't I take these and you can go out and visit with your gramps. I'm sure he's missed you. You two can catch up on your trip to Boston."

Bobby nodded appreciatively. "Thanks. With my truck battery busted, I haven't had time."

I stacked the dishes and silver in the drain dry, but not until I took my time washing my face and hands in the sink. I stirred the soup for a few minutes. Then I wiped down the table and set it. I poked my head out the screen door and signaled to Bobby. They joined me inside.

Bobby pulled out a chair for me. I snuck a peek at Jessum, suddenly self-conscious. But if Bobby had told him anything about McGee, Rooster Run, the journal, or Frannie, Jessum didn't let on. He padded around with a contented smile.

More than once, I found myself drawn to the old man. His face was cut strong, his color, more light brown than dark. It was obvious that he'd been a startlingly attractive young man, and time had been gracious with him. I wondered if Jessum got his looks from his grammy, Frannie Crow. Wondered how he'd feel about Mistress Anderson's old journal, her confession. I suspected it would all be taken with ease—the gift that comes with age.

Jessum placed two cups of coffee on the table. Then, humming, he shuffled over to the stove, returning with a huge bowl of bean soup that he set in front of me. Smiling, he moved leisurely back to the stove, filling two more bowls for Bobby and himself, and placing them on the table.

Bobby jumped up to help. I heard the thump of the metal stove door and my stomach growled back in response. The smell of buttery hoecakes wafted heavenly, filling my nostrils.

I spooned up the thick bean soup, eating every last drop. Bobby drained the juice from his second bowl before taking two large hunks of sweet bread from the basket, complimenting Jessum's cooking after each swallow.

The bread was heavy and sweet, hitting the spot. Full, I forced myself back from the table and raised my hands. "Delicious, Jessum. Thank you for having me."

A smile blossomed on Jessum's face. He lifted a mug of steaming coffee to his lips and blew lightly. "Fetch yourself some dessert up on the shelf above the dish dry, chil'. Mighty good bonbons that Widow Brown brought back from her visit with family in Savannah last week. Mmm-hmm! Mighty nice of the widow to think of ol' Jessum, while she was down there laying Mr. Brown to rest." He took a long sip.

"Oh, no," I lamented. "I'm sorry."

"Mmm-hmm." Jessum set his coffee onto the table. "Peoples talkin', sayin' jus' a matter of time 'fore the moonshine an' cigarettes would kill ol' Billy Brown. Uh-huh, yessum. Always had the thirst of a willow root, an' smoked like the ol' Owl Runner freight train, that one did. Uh-huh, his light plumb snuffed, near to the exact day 'fore his ninetieth birthday candles took spark. So, chil'un, best eat all yore bonbons 'fore the candles can spark." He winked. Then Jessum and Bobby exchanged secret smiles.

I looked back and forth at the two of them. Bobby began to hum a teasing rendition of "Happy Birthday." Jessum kicked it up a notch, singing the words in a rich timbre. Their voices slowed and blended together in a thick, gravelly, charmed harmony. My eyes filled at their kindness, the bigness of their hearts.

When they finished, I was struck by an overwhelming spasm

of homesickness for home. And a family that didn't exist any-more. I dabbed the corners of my eyes with my napkin. "Thank you, thanks so much for the wishes." I smiled gratefully, and jumped up and hugged Jessum.

Jessum winked. "Look for the brightest star tonight and toss your wish to the heavens."

I helped Bobby carry the dishes to the sink. Jessum picked up his pipe, poured himself another cup of coffee, and headed out to the porch still humming my birthday wishes, while Bobby and I washed the supperware. Above the clatter of dishes, we talked about the hearty food, his Grammy Sara, Jessum's gar-den, all light conversation after a long day of heaviness. Out-side, the porch swing creaked in methodical rhythm, while crickets called the darkness.

Bobby told me Jessum offered his home for as long as I needed; then we talked a little about seeing Sheriff Jingles in the morning.

I hung the dishtowel across the rack and we shared a few of the chewy coconut candies, with Bobby eating the vanilla ones and saving the strawberry ones for me. When we finished, I poked my head out the screen door and thanked Jessum again. "Gramps, you need another cup of coffee?" Bobby asked over my shoulder.

"Nah," he said. "Might take me a walk over yonder, pay a visit to the widow an' see how her batch of blackberry wine turned out." He winked again.

"Okay, I'm going to show Mudas to her room."

Jessum raised his arm and wagged a good-bye.

Bobby took my hand and led me past the sink to the back door. He pushed it open and stepped aside, letting me walk into a small attached breezeway. The walls were screened at the top half, with a waist-high skirt of wormy chestnut running down to the wooden floor. I laughed when I spotted a hound dog lying atop a narrow iron bed covered with a chenille bedspread.

"Aw, Cassie, c'mon, get off now." Bobby stepped around me and scooted the big dog off the bed and onto the floor. Cassie peered up at us with somber eyes. Bobby scratched her long, silky ears. She gave a short snort and turned in a circle before curling up on a green braided rug.

Bobby leaped over her and dug into a wicker basket. He pulled out a green T-shirt, PJ bottoms, and two ratty towels. "This is my room when I come and visit," he explained, his face beginning to color. "Tonight I'll use Gramps's sleeping bag and sleep on the porch. I do that sometimes anyway." He tossed the wrinkled clothes and the towels onto the bed. "Here. They're clean." He crossed to the wooden stand beside the bed and tossed me a little package wrapped in cheesecloth. "And take this." I removed the gauze and brought a heavy bar of sweet-smelling soap to my nose, caught a whiff of flowers, and sighed happily.

"My gramma was a soap maker," he said, digging into the clothes basket again. "She had two goats on the back of the hill here. Fine goat's milk soap. Shopkeepers in Nashville would even order it. She made it all out there." He stood and jerked his thumb over to the screened wall. A dense thicket of trees trailed up, a nature-made curtain of privacy.

I pressed the bar of soap to my nose and drank in long draws of sweetness. "Thank you." My heart swelled with gratitude at everything Bobby had done for me and I sprang across the room. Bobby lifted me up and I wound my legs and arms around him. His face shone with boyish cheer. Laughing, he spun us around.

Setting me down, he said, "Okay, then. Well, the door's here." He knocked on the obvious. "And out back, there's a water hose and the bathing bucket, and—" He hesitated, embarrassed. "Sorry it's not inside."

"Bobby, it's perfect. Thank you." I looked up at him. Then I bent in and gave him a soft kiss. He tasted like sweet earth. And the curiosity of everything good.

"Okay"—he took a breath—"I'm going to take a towel and head down to the creek. I'll be back in a jiff, so be sure and holler if you need anything." He grabbed a towel and slipped out the door, shutting it quietly behind him.

I brought my fingertips up to my mouth and then pirouetted around the room. All of this felt good. And this room . . . It was like a Grammy Essie hug. Home. I could see her now, padding around her worn but spotless pine floors, rugged over with puddles of sunshine. Standing in her kitchen with the wide, wallpapered border of cherries that popped off of the yellow walls like big ol' sunny lipstick smiles. Her head bent over the heavy iron skillets that sizzled in tune with the morning song of birds perched on the window's ledge. Thick jowl bacon and peppered eggs dancing on the skillet and spitting at the air, filling the kitchen with their familiar aroma.

All that changed after she and Papaw passed. Daddy'd said he "fancied some change" and brought renovators into the homestead to change the furnishings and "freshen up" the paint. I didn't think a new coat of paint was going to change anything. We were still alone. To me, the newness was a reminder of their absence, a symbol of all that we'd lost.

I shook my head, pushing the grief away. No, no, I thought. I wanted to be happy, and I didn't want to let anything take away my happy. For this day, this minute, even a second, I prayed, dear God, please let me have my happy.

I thought about Bobby, what it would feel like to find that happy in his arms.

Cassie lifted her head and sighed a hound-dog amen. I laughed and bent over and stroked her slick fur, then drank in more of my surroundings. Stepping over Cassie, I ran my hands across the soft, plush bedspread, tracing the needle-tufted yellow flowers, remembering how Grammy Essie used to have the same pattern. I pictured her and Sara sitting, sewing together, talking about life, children, and family. In my mind, I clung to her ghosted apron strings and a warm homecoming swept over me.

I untied my sneakers and gladly kicked them off. Picking up the soap and towel, I walked to the back door and stepped outside. About twenty feet to my right, an outhouse butted up to the steep hill rising behind it, and a well with a red-flaked iron pump stood nearby. To my left, a water hose snaked behind a tightly woven grapevine screen. I spied the spigot at the far end of the house and hurried over to turn on the water, then followed the hose trail back to the screen.

I stepped behind the thick grapevine and wiggled my toes in the cool grasses, digging them into the thick fescue. Lifting the water hose to my mouth, I gulped—each swallow a sweet charge surging through me like electric nectar. I carried the soap and towel, along with the hose, over to an old wooden bathing bucket lined with thick cowhide, and scooped up the stringed cork stopper dangling off its side to plug the drain. After I tossed in the soap, I slung the spout over the rim and watched as the bucket began to fill.

Taking one last look over my shoulder, I glanced at the grapevine screen, then back to the tree-thick hill rising in front of me, offering privacy. Satisfied, I stripped off my clothes and draped them over the tall screen. A breeze tousled my hair and a rise of gooseflesh crept over my body.

Ever so slow, I dipped my toe into the tub, shuddered, and then forced myself to step fully into the water bucket, gasping at the shock. The water, witch-tit cold, lapped at the hollows of my flesh. I took a deep breath and stared up to the evening sky. Fireflies ghosted light across the dusk as an evening chill floated down the mountain. The sun disappeared behind the hilltop and the silver moon hid behind her shadow.

I shrugged off the cold and washed briskly, eager to escape the frigid water. I dried off and couldn't help notice the sweet scent that Bobby's goat soap left on me. I sniffed my hand. Dear Lord, I thought, I hope that what I smell is Grammy Essie's true scent, and it doesn't turn sour. I want more than kisses from that man, but I want it to be right, too. Mama'd always said there's only one first at anything in life, and you get only one chance to do anything the first time, so make sure that when you grab that first, it's right.

When I walked around the screen in my towel, I found Bobby pacing, holding a bottle of Calamine lotion and a tattered old army jacket, with an oil lantern hooked over his arm. His wet hair was slicked back, and drops of water glossed across his bare chest. "Thought you might need this." He placed the lotion on top of the screen and rubbed a wet hand on his jeans. "And this," he said, setting down the lantern and holding up the huge jacket. "I just . . . I reckoned you might get cold," he blushed.

"Oh. Thanks," I managed, my throat suddenly dry.

Taking a step forward to hand me the coat, Bobby tucked a lock of wet hair behind my ear. I shivered at his touch. His eyes darted over my mottled skin, goose bumped from the cold. I looked at the coat, then back to him.

"Oh," he said, turning his back so I could slip it on. "Yeah, sorry."

I pressed one side of the enormous jacket across me and folded the other side over it. Underneath, the towel loosened and fell to the ground. I pulled the coat closer to my body, soft against my skin. "Thanks," I murmured.

Turning back around, he pointed to the path up the hill. "I was just heading back down to Soldier Creek. It's over the hill and down a little bit. I can't seem to find my knife—it must've dropped out when, uh . . . while I was putting on my jeans. Can't lose that. Gramps gave it to me when I was ten." He started for the path. "I'll meet you back at the house."

"Wait."

Bobby turned back.

"I'll go with you. I can help you look for it."

He stood studying me a bit, then finally nodded and lit the lantern, a smile tugging at the corners of his mouth. I followed him through the pines, a carpet of soft pine needles cushioning my bare feet.

Slips of moonlight flickered through the trees. The howl of a lone coyote lent song to the orchestral swell and fade of crickets, accompanied by the *quonk* of tree frogs. I ducked under an orb weaver's web, where drops of dew were suspended, shimmering like jeweled beads on gossamer.

After a few minutes, the slope leveled out and we came to a small clearing. A nearby creek came to life. Rushing water splashed over the rocks, misting into the sweet air. Bobby stopped and raised the lantern high. "It should be close."

I scanned the ground and immediately spotted the knife lying next to a dead branch at the edge of the clearing. "Over there, Bobby," I pointed.

"Sharp eyes, Mudas!" He slipped the knife into his back pocket and set the lantern back down on the stump. He smiled. "Thanks. A Kentucky boy's best friend."

"Sharp knife," I grinned back.

I stood under a tall pine and watched the fireflies light along the path and into the trees. "When I was little, Mama used to help me catch lightning bugs. She always said the best part was setting them free." I smiled, remembering the joy that used to light up Mama's eyes. She'd always worn the most beautiful smile. I couldn't help thinking that she'd want me to wear one now, too. I pushed back a curl from my face and caught a whiff of the lovely goat soap again. "Pretty up here," I said.

Bobby was staring at me, his brow knitted, all thoughtful-like.

"What is it, Bobby?"

He shook his head. "It's just . . . well, I just can't believe how pretty *you* are."

A warm, swooping sensation hit my midsection and my breath quickened.

"Even now," he laughed, "barefoot and wearing that big ol' ugly jacket. Especially now."

His scent carried, trailing thick on the night breeze. Feeling giddy, light-headed, I leaned against a tree trunk, my eyes never leaving Bobby's.

After a moment, Bobby shifted and cleared his throat. "Well, I guess that's that. We should get back to the house." He turned and began walking back down to the house, lantern in hand.

I took another breath of the hill.

"You coming, Mudas?" He turned back.

I shifted and dropped my gaze. The coat slipped down over my shoulder.

His broad chest rose, falling into a slow, deep rhythm. "Mudas . . ."

I grappled for my sleeve, fumbling with a shaky hand.

"Here. I . . . don't want to take advantage of you," he said hoarsely, helping me pull it back up with his own shaky talking hand.

I slowly shook my head.

"Mudas?"

We both took a hesitant step toward each other. Cupping the back of my head, he seized a fistful of tangled wet curls and pulled me closer, his bare chest warm again mine. For the first time in a week, I felt my muscles relax—an emotional nod to surrender—and was gripped by an urgency to take this protected break from all the bad and churn it into a sweet physical release.

Pulling back, Bobby tenderly traced a thumb along my cheeks, my lips.

I looked up at him, searching.

Dark with wanting, his eyes met mine, questioning.

I let myself fall into those wide wading pools of sunlit amber and nodded a hungry yes.

Bobby pulled me down to the damp, cool earth and rolled me over onto the soft army coat.

Somewhere amidst the soar of nature's sweet music and the bitterness of life's gritty, we surrendered and laid down our burdens. Letting go of everything and anything that could steal our attention, we fed gloriously on the sweet.

17

The Knowing

I stretched to the sweet, low-pitched hoot of an owl. Running my hand across the earth, I scrunched up a patch of damp leaves and brought them to my face. I inhaled the aromas sweetened with the scent of life—him. Tossing leaves into the air, I let them fall like confetti on my bare skin, celebrating my passage into womanhood, marveling at the rush of immortality.

Bobby rested on his elbow, watching me. His crooked smile warmed. I'd always thought this would be an awkward moment. Instead, it felt right, like Grammy Essie's true-love tale. There were no pangs of regret or guilt—just us, hungry to know more, eager to reveal the pieces of ourselves we'd never been brave enough to share before. I sat up and covered myself with the coat, leaning into him.

"This field jacket sure does look better on you than it does on me. Or my brother." He laughed and gave me a quick kiss.

"Oh, wow"—I touched the collar—"it's Henry's?"

Bobby lifted the sleeve draped across me. "Yeah, he left it for me last time he was home."

"Does he get to come home soon? I heard that President Nixon is pulling out all the troops now."

His eyes lit up, jeweled like tiger-eye stones. "Yeah, I can't wait 'til he gets here! The last ground combat battalion is coming home in two weeks. I've sorely missed him. Can't wait for this crazy war to end."

I nodded. "I read about what that actress, Jane Fonda, did last month. Horrible."

Bobby scratched the whiskers budding on his jaw. "Yeah, traitor. When I was in Boston, I saw the photo of her sitting on the North Vietnamese battery. . . . Henry served this country for two tours in Vietnam, and for others, they served with their lives, and that's how she repays them. Jesus, I'm just relieved it's almost over."

I snuggled the coat, feeling safe and a part of Bobby, and all that he was a part of. "I can't wait to meet him."

He brought his mouth down and kissed me lightly, our mouths still trembly. We laughed off the awkwardness and snuggled closer.

"Do you spend a lot of time here with your gramps?"

"Yeah, in between looking at colleges, I'm here for the summer." He frowned. "I like it here, and it makes it easier . . . my dad's really uptight."

I rested my head against his chest. "Didn't you say your daddy worked in numbers in Nashville? Gone a lot?"

"Yeah, he's a corporate accountant. Hardly ever see him anymore," he sighed. "But when he's around, he expects everybody to bow—struts around with a grin that looks like he's just swallowed a pail of Kentucky coal and crapped out the Hope Diamond." He shook his head. "I dunno, it makes me nervous. Like I told you a few weeks ago, he's just so unpredictable. Easy to rile."

I reached up and massaged his shoulder. "How's your mama doing? You said she was sick. . . ."

"She's . . . she's still not well." He looked away.

"I'm sorry, Bobby."

"It's those damn pills—Black Beauties," he grimaced. "Spends half her time shopping 'round for them, the rest hopped up and driving everyone around her batty."

"Oh, I . . . I'm sorry to hear that," I said, thinking of Daddy's drinking, Mama's hidden refreshments, and suddenly seeing a glimpse of the little boy Bobby had been, his sadness bruising my heart. "I know what that's like."

"You do?" he looked up, surprised.

"Daddy has a weakness for the bottle," I confessed, my face heating at the thought of outing Mama, or having another person thinking her "white trash." And latching it on to me like a Mason jar lid.

His eyebrows shot up. "But he's so . . . together."

"Yeah, he gave it up. It's been years since . . . but still, the worry's always lurking in the shadows."

"That's good that he turned it around, Mudas. Real good."

"Maybe your mama will, too," I said, sending a silent wish and prayer for her like I'd done for Mama so many times.

"Naw." Bobby shook his head. "She hasn't been the same since . . . Well, when I was six, Mom found out my dad cheated on her, and went"—Bobby drew air circles next to his temple—"cuckoo. I came in from school and found her sitting on the floor in our living room, next to a big ol' pile of family photos. She'd taken a red crayon and waxed an *A* for adultery over Dad's face in every single one. Then about a week later, he caught her with—if you can believe it—the deputy sheriff of our town."

"Oh, no, Bobby, really?"

"Yeah, got her revenge, I guess." He hesitated. "My old man drove me and my brother over here to Gramps, then took Mom up to Louisville to one of those asylums where they give electric shock treatments. We moved up north the very next year, a fresh start. But Mom never could get right after all that. Never seemed to care much about me or Henry. Never knew how to take care of us."

"Oh, Bobby." I wanted to take a soft cloth and wipe off the misery puttying his face. Instead, I took his hand and squeezed.

"Well, I'll be gone soon enough." A spasm of pain seeped out and haloed Bobby's voice.

I thought about Mama letting me take up running and those funny shoes she'd bought long ago. How she was forever giving me Band-Aids and our tradition of phone calls. Grammy Essie insisting I sign up for track. . . . Like most my age, I wasn't entirely sure of a lot of things, especially now, but despite everything I'd been going through, I was beginning to realize how much I'd been blessed with the surety of love from two women, and I almost felt the urge to apologize.

Lacing his fingers between mine, Bobby raised our fists to the sky and gave a little shake. "What about you, Mudas Summers? What do you want?"

I felt a catch in my throat. I couldn't remember the last time someone had bothered to ask. What I wanted, more than anything, was to clear up all this mess about Mama. Clear her name, and the guilt I'd been carrying for leaving her on that porch. Or, better still, for it to have never happened. But I didn't want to talk about that now, not when I'd just been gifted with life's perfect release.

"You know I love the track team, but I'm giving it up this year." I paused. "I'm an okay runner, and I thought that maybe I could get a scholarship. The coach from Mallardsburg came over and said I was really good. Said that I had better times in me, and the right amount of coaching and workouts, and should try out for one."

"What? Really? Man, Coach Hall's a top coach!"

"I know. But, hell, nothing's gonna happen unless they give us a good coach—a coach who thinks it's okay for girls to play sports. We can't even use the school track most times."

"I've seen you over on the boys' track. You're faster than some boys I know." Bobby slid his leg down over mine. "I hope it works out that you can go to college, even without a scholarship."

"I don't know . . . ThommaLyn's not going. She's gonna stay to marry Paul Jameson. Her daddy wants her to help out the family."

"PJ seems like a nice fella and a hard worker. They'll make a great couple. It's good she's going to stay and have her babies here."

I wasn't so sure. ThommaLyn was a whiz at biology, pulling straight As and dreaming about being a nurse in the big city. We even talked about how we'd get a cute little apartment together, a place of our own with bright wallpaper and a lazy cat. But her daddy let her start dating at thirteen. "The quicker she gets hitched," he'd said, "the quicker her man can help me grow more crops that'll bring in bigger cash." ThommaLyn fell hard for Paul within a year. Her daddy couldn't have been happier. And I knew we wouldn't be getting that cat after all.

"Maybe," I said, "but I had hoped ThommaLyn would get out of this Podunk town."

"Well, I can't wait. I hope our senior year goes by real fast."

"It can't get here soon enough. My daddy rides me pretty hard, expects me to make all As." I didn't mention how the kids at school made fun of me and my cow-plop name. I'm sure he already knew about it; he was just too cool to bring it up.

"The year will go by quick, Mudas, you'll see," he said, tapping into my thoughts.

"I really can't wait to get out of this town one day, but now I may have to back-burner that for a bit." Life in a small town moved slowly enough—even slower in sadness. "I've been thinking a lot about it this past week. Thinking maybe I should stick around here another year before going. Because of my baby sister, Genevieve, and all that's happened. I dunno. . . . She's going to need me." And if I was being perfectly honest with myself, I knew that I was going to need her. She was the very last reminder of Mama.

Bobby looked at me as if deep in thought about plans. His, mine.

"If I ever do get out of Peckinpaw, I'm cutting a path straight across western Kentucky to Louisville for a degree in business." I picked up a leaf and traced it, thinking about what Daddy expected me to do: stand beside his lawyering boots and do secretarial law, *and* become a female Olympic runner. "I'd really love to run . . . maybe make it to the Olympics one day." I laughed even though I was dead serious. When Bobby didn't snicker back, I dipped farther into the water. "And I'd also like to follow in my grammy's footsteps as the county librarian. Who knows . . . maybe even open the first bookstore in these parts."

"Neato," Bobby said, his eyes holding mine.

"I even know what I'd call it . . ."

"Yeah? C'mon, spill," Bobby teased, lightly tickling my ribs.

"Okay, okay. Dandelion Books. It's for my Grammy Essie; she used to make all kinds of things with them. Jelly, coffee, wine, you name it. Anyway, it's silly, but dandelions make me think of her, and she would've loved to have a bookstore here in town, like they do in Louisville. It's silly," I shrugged.

I held my breath, waiting for him to laugh at me. But he didn't. Instead, Bobby smiled warmly and stretched for a buttercup. He ran the petals over my lips. "Bet you could serve those book lovers a Mason jar of that recipe and they'd empty their wallets, big time."

"Mmm." I grinned lazily, savoring.

"Mmm-hmm," he echoed. The corners of his mouth lifted and, in a swift and easy movement, he sat up and pulled me on top of him, scattering pine needles and leaves. Cupping my face with both hands, Bobby dragged my mouth to his. I watched as his long, thick lashes fluttered open to expose his deep amber eyes. He let out a long sigh and ran his fingers through my twisted curls, and brought the strands to his mouth. "Mudas," he breathed my name, sweetening its syllables. I loved the way he abandoned my nickname—loved the sweet drawl he sowed into my given name when he spoke it.

I felt a deep warmth torch my ears. "We should probably scoot, before your gramps comes looking."

Laughing, Bobby placed one arm behind him, wrapped the other around me, and lifted us both off the ground. He swung me around, then planted me on my feet and brushed his lips over my temple. He tilted my chin and looked up with sincerity and determination. "Mudas Elizabeth Summers, I mean to make you mine one day, to honor, love, and protect, like no other. To love you right an' tight." My eyes widened, but before I could react, he plowed forward. "In the meantime and before anybody else can lay claim: Will you come to senior prom with me?"

Gasping, my hands flew to my cheeks and tears sprang to my eyes. I had resigned myself years ago that I wouldn't be attending senior prom. Sure, for a moment I'd thought I had a chance with Tripp, but not now that I'd kicked him to the curb. And it was practically here, like tomorrow-here. People were already talking about it. Sewing machines had been dusted and tuned, and people were going to White's department store in the city.

Still, I would have been content to see it through Thomma-Lyn's eyes. She hadn't missed a single dance in all the years I'd known her. And it was a given that I'd go over and fix her hair and makeup before every date or dance. Then her mama would pull out the old Polaroid. I always tried to beg an excuse, but Mrs. Green never failed to huddle me, ThommaLyn, and her date into a semicircle and snap our picture, leaving me embarrassed, a third wheel splotched with red paint.

Afterward, I'd go home to my running field. There, I'd wear myself out until I numbed the hurt, the rejection, and the loneliness. The next day, I'd break and beg ThommaLyn for details. Watching her eyes light up as she recounted the dance was the next best thing to being there, I reckoned, and about as close to Heaven as I'd ever get.

"Mudas?" Bobby took my hand and squeezed, pulling me back to the present.

I grinned wide and nodded, before he could change his mind and before the what-ifs could take hold of my thought-ticking hands and send them flying. "Yes, yes!" I blurted out, bursting with that "prism full of colors" Mama had told me about.

"Yes!" he beamed, planting a big ol' kiss on my lips, leaving me lighter than air. Snatching up his jeans, Bobby dressed and turned to grab the lantern. I slipped the army coat back on. Gathering our things, both of us were quiet in the newness of us, our expectations, the possibilities, and the undeniable tugging scent of our physical and emotional oneness.

Bobby came up behind me, plucked an orange leaf from my hair, and handed it to me. I studied the color and what my Grammy said long ago. Oddly, orange meant change, and desire and warmth. All the things I needed. *And all the things Bobby gives me.*

"Mudas"—Bobby rested his jaw on my shoulder—"you're so

beautiful," he whispered hoarsely, nuzzling my neck. Protectively, he looped his arm around my waist and we headed back to the house.

Bobby followed me into the breezeway. "C'mon, Cassie, let's go for a walk." He clicked his tongue for her to follow him outside, winking at me before the screen door slammed shut.

I pulled back the coverlet and eased myself onto the old tick mattress. I took in a breath of rain and sun-washed cotton sheets. Night song whirred outside. Cassie gave off two throaty barks, followed by a shouted greeting from Gramps Jessum. In a moment, Jessum and Bobby's shared laughter dissolved into murmurs of warm conversation, lighting the dark.

I picked up the leaf I'd brought in and studied it. "Change," I whispered. Curling myself into a ball, I closed my eyes and thought about how lucky Bobby was to have his gramps, his family. This.

Oh, how I missed my grandparents! I missed Papaw letting me run the fence row to kick up rabbits for a supper stew, whispering, "You can't catch a rabbit 'less you muddy up them boots, gal." I missed him chasing me around the pond with frogs and then gently tossing me in to learn how to swim like one. I missed helping him plant the pumpkin patch. Missed his four-in-the-morning wakeup calls on opening day of deer season, though I didn't miss them back then. Missed getting bundled up in Papaw's worn tobacco barn coat so I could help him track game. I missed the evenings when we'd curl up in his leather recliner and he'd read *Heidi* aloud. But mostly, I missed trailing after him, my five-year-old arms winding around his legs, both of us laughing as we tumbled into a twisty-tangled hug.

And Grammy Essie, who'd patched the heartbreak and filled the holes when Mama moved to the city. I especially missed her. Who would patch this new break? I missed my grammy dabbing her expensive Evening in Paris perfume behind my ears. I missed her reading me *Ladies' Home Journal* magazines, then asking me what I thought about a particular article. I missed the old *Webster's Dictionary* sitting next to the Family Bible on her library table. Missed her quotes and the hours we'd spent poring over the marbled-edge dictionary pages, Grammy teaching me how to use the harder words and to spell them the right way. Chuckling at the words that tickled our tongues and at the made-up sentences that gave us belly-roaring laughter. More than anything, I longed for her lavender-scented hugs.

And little Genevieve. Oh, to hug her, tell her we were going to be okay, that I'd never leave her like I'd been left so long ago! Genevieve was my last piece of Mama, the very last. I felt a stabbing homesickness for Mama . . . and even Daddy, a little. My family. It was now beginning to hit home that I was alone. Completely, horribly alone. I could feel the power and consequence of that solitude. In my mind's eye, I saw the ribbons candy-caned around Mama's ankles, twirling, jubilant—mocking me.

Fighting a thunderbolt of panic, I slipped my hands prayer-like between the pillow and my cheek and, heaving a long sigh, forced my thoughts to turn to Bobby.

Plumb exhausted, my racing thumb forgot to whisper worries to my now-still fingers.

18

Change

Dawn streamed through the breezeway's screen, gleaming like shards of broken glass. The nattering of tree squirrels and a mockingbird's imitation nudged the morning light, awakening the buzz of insects and my memories of last night.

A smile tugged at my heart. Making love to Bobby had been easy, like I'd somehow reclaimed myself, found something rare and truthful in the midst of all this deceit, sorrow, and confusion. I was not ashamed, or embarrassed or regretful. Instead, I felt empowered by what we'd done, by our discovery. And I vowed to use this newness as shelter to safeguard during whatever stormy weather lay ahead.

I climbed out of bed and called softly to Cassie, who was sprawled out on her side, wheezing out tiny yelps in a doggy dreamland critter pursuit. She stirred at my voice and followed me out the back door. I took in a breath of pine before slipping into the outhouse. Staring into a wood-framed mirror, I peered into the darkened glass.

My face was streaked with scratches. Bruises were beginning to banana-ripen across my cheek. I wrinkled my nose and a dusting of freckles leaped across its bridge. My hair needed a good hundred-stroke brushing, and my cheeks were sunburned, begging for balm butter. After a few minutes of troubled inspection, I smiled. Again, I warmed from last night's memories.

I searched the yard and the breezeway for my clothes, but they were nowhere to be found. Dismayed, I poked my head into the kitchen, hoping my face wouldn't reveal last night's secrets to Jessum's all-knowing eyes.

Steam rose from a kettle atop the potbelly stove, ghosting upward. To my great relief, Bobby sat alone at the table, sipping coffee and reading newsprint. His breakfast plate was half empty.

"Morn'," I said crossing the room, my heart feeling light at the sight of him, a glow pinking my cheeks.

"Good morning," he said softly, carefully trailing me with his eyes.

"Is that today's paper?"

"Yeah, I ran down the hill and picked one up. The latest, see?" Bobby pointed to the date: *Thursday, August 17, 1972.* He bit into a sausage patty and chewed as he studied me when he felt I wasn't looking.

I looked over his shoulder, searching for Tommy's obituary. His name leaped up, the story of his death splattered across the front page, bigger than life. Feigning interest in the weather report, I flicked to the next page. "Paper says another hot day." I plopped down onto the chair beside him. The scent of apple sausage drifted through the aromas of coffee beans and the wood-burning stove.

"Breakfast's over there waiting." Bobby buttered a biscuit and made it disappear in two large bites. He took a big gulp of coffee and flashed a small, shy-like grin.

I grabbed some coffee and joined him at the table. Taking a sip, I peeked over the lip of the cup, trying to see if anything had changed.

"Did you sleep good in there?" he asked genuinely and in his same Bobby style.

I pulled one of Jessum's crimson roses out of the jar and blushed behind it. I hadn't slept that good in a week. "Smells good," I murmured, and set it back. "Uh-huh, your room is really comfortable, Bobby."

He smiled back, coloring a bit. "Hey." He tugged at my sleeve, grinning a little mischievously.

"Hey yourself," I blushed.

"I, er . . . well, I enjoyed . . . uh, talking . . . last night."

I nodded slowly. "Yeah?" I tucked my hair behind my ear. "Me too."

"Yup." He lit up a smile and reached over to lightly tickle me. "Girl, are you gonna kiss me good morning or not?"

"I am." I breathed out a laugh, sweeping my lips across his, grateful for his ease and humor. "Hey, Bobby." I pulled back, noting the clean T-shirt and jeans he wore. "I couldn't find my clothes. Seen them?"

The porch swing creaked.

"Gramps gave your clothes a good stone scrubbing early this morning with Gramma's lye soap, and hooked them over there behind the stove to dry." He pointed. "Your shirt was nothing but a rag, but you can keep my T-shirt." He stretched out his long legs.

"I could've washed them," I said guiltily. I'd been taking care of all the washing and most of the cooking for Daddy for so long I'd forgotten what it felt like to have someone take care of me. "That's really super of your gramps to go through all that trouble."

"No big deal." Bobby smiled. "I put the things that were in your pockets inside the basket in the breezeway."

The screen door squeaked. Jessum walked in, carrying his pipe and coffee mug.

"Ah, a good Thursday morn' to you, Miz Mudas. I hope you slept well." He smiled kindly. "Will you be having a bit of breakfast?"

"Morning, sir." I jumped up. "Thank you, Jessum, for the clean clothes. And I can fetch breakfast, don't you worry," I called over my shoulder. I grabbed a plate from the drain dry and loaded it up with a biscuit and two scrapple patties.

Much hungrier than I realized, I dug in and quickly polished off the meal. When I'd finished, I pushed away, ready to stand, but Bobby reached for the ribbon around my wrist and pulled.

"I hope you don't mind, Mudas, but I told Gramps about the ribbon."

Gramps smiled wide. "Miz Mudas, Bobby did, and, well, I served in the war," he added with pride. "I know about codes."

Bobby said, "Your mom probably used lemon juice to make the message."

"Yeah," I said. "Mama taught me all about that and her daddy taught her. He was in the war, too." I thought back to the chemistry set days, when Mama had shown me how to make invisible ink from lemon juice and vinegar. How the acid had stayed on the paper after the juice dried, like magic.

"When I was a soldier," Jessum explained, "they taught us all 'bout ink an' codes. Lots of ways to make ink, uh-huh. We used words like *heat* an' *red cabbage* to let ya know there's a secret. That's 'cause you can spray red cabbage water on invisible ink or heat the paper to bring out the words." He winked. "I ate my share of cabbage during the war . . . uh-huh. Don't have much of a taste for it anymore."

"I love it," I said wistfully. " 'Specially Mama's."

"I'm terribly sorry about yore mama, Miz Mudas. Terribly so. Tol' yore Daddy and now I can tell you. I jus' talked with Miz Ella a lil over a week ago at the Shucks Market. Shame." He patted my hand, blinked his welling eyes, and pulled out a handkerchief from his shirt pocket.

Seeing his eyes fill brought grief to my own.

After a moment of quiet I recovered, and said, "Thank you again for having me, Jessum. Those biscuits and sausage patties were delicious." I caught Bobby's gaze and gave a pointed look at the front door.

Catching my drift, Bobby said, "Gramps, mind if we step outside a moment and—"

"Y'all go on ahead, I need to walk ol' Cassie down the mountain an' check on the mail delivery." He reached for his cane, which was hooked over the back of his chair, and walked to the breezeway. I heard him greet Cassie and the door's soft click as it closed behind him.

I moved over to the screen door and peered out. "Bobby, I should probably scoot. If I stay, I'm putting your gramps in danger of being a target for the Klan."

"Maybe so, but you're safe here. Ain't a lot going on that begins at the bottom of this old hill that don't end up at the top real quick. Folks take care of one another here." He waved his hand dismissively.

"I should probably get going now. Ol' man Harper will have been spitting out gossip."

"I'm going with you."

I shook my head. "I'm worried, Bobby. You saw the robe. The Klan doesn't care if you're part Indian, colored, whatever," I pointed out. "They just care that you're different. And, remember, different around here puts a target square on your back." I tenderly rubbed the spot they'd branded on his back.

"I'm not gonna live my life in fear of those diddle-dicks. I want to help you. Okay?" He dragged his thumb across my lips and then kissed me, leaving a tingle on my mouth. "Let's go to Jingles first. The law really needs to be in on this."

I was relieved. Relieved he didn't hightail it far away from me and this big mess. "Okay, that's a good idea, just in case."

"It'll be safer," Bobby assured.

I thought about how warm and safe I felt in Bobby's arms—and how alone I felt when I wasn't.

Reluctantly, I stepped out of his embrace. "Let me get dressed."

A few minutes later, I came out wearing my ripped jeans and Bobby's T-shirt. I joined Bobby on the porch and saw Jessum holding a tattered Bible with a solemn look on his face.

"Bobby," he said, "if you don't mind, I'd like to show this to ya." Jessum opened the Bible and slipped out a worn folded letter and handed it to Bobby. "I gots to thinkin' how we were talkin' bout yore gramma, Miz Mudas, an' this may be 'portant for you to know, too."

Bobby unfolded the paper and Jessum put his hand over Bobby's, and said, "My gramps, 'Moss . . . Amos Crow, married a fine lady from Scotland. He was a goat herder. Uh-huh, an' he married a schoolteacher. That'd be my Grandma Catt, Bobby. Catt Crow, a fine, fine woman. My gramps had her write his story down."

"Amos Crow," Bobby studied, "you mean he was my—" We looked at each other, surprised.

"Yessir, Bobby, that'd be yore great-great gramps." Jessum flashed a proud smile. "Taught my Sara soap making an' taught me good carpentry." Jessum pointed to the porch washstand. "I may have mentioned him to ya. We called him Moss."

"Oh, yeah, so, Moss is Amos. Wow!" Bobby walked over to the cabinet and ran his hands over the skilled workmanship, admiring.

"Now, y'all two go on ahead to today's bizness, let me get on to the mail delivery truck an' see what he brings me," Jessum said.

Bobby stared at the letter in his hand.

"Go on, tuck that in yore pocket, Bobby. Don't lose it. Maybe hitch on to a quiet spell somewhere an' read it . . . visit family." Jessum gave me one of his twinkly winks.

Bewildered, Bobby folded the letter and stuck it into his pocket.

I gave Jessum a hug and he told me to come back anytime and to give his kind regards to Daddy.

Daddy. I was starting to miss him a little more. Picturing his drawn face—his grief—and last night's release from my own, I felt more than a little guilty we'd had words. But, in my defense, or call it my own mulish ways, he'd had none to offer to me. I wondered if he'd be home again today, working on his files, since he'd cleared his calendar. What would I say when I saw him?

I pushed the thoughts away and settled into the driver's side. With Bobby's directions, I steered down the hill toward Town Square, my eyes shifting back and forth between the traveled road and the rearview, checking for anybody tailing us. Bobby suggested we go around Knobmole Hill and swing back to town.

I fretted as I passed the turnoff to Summers Homestead, wondering if Daddy'd gone out looking for me last night. Couldn't have filled up his car at Harper's, that's for sure, or Harper's wagging tongue would've already led him straight to me. But I was sure Daddy would have called or stopped by Thomma-

Lyn's. I hoped she'd covered for me and kept her promise. It wouldn't be unlikely for me to run into Daddy on these roads now. It was Thursday, his busiest day of the week, and the day he liked to tie up loose ends before taking off for a long weekend, if he could. Though he'd said he cleared his calendar, I prayed he was taking a last-minute deposition or—better yet—called over to another county on legal business.

I wasn't ready to see him.

I needed answers first.

The truth.

The truth would out, as truth seemed to demand. Frannie Crow had to wait a hundred years for hers, and I wasn't feeling quite so patient. That Rooster Run ledger would exonerate Mama just as sure as Mrs. Anderson's diary had exonerated Frannie, I was sure of it. Now I just had to find it.

19

Cracker Jack Prayers

I passed Liar's Bench and parked in front of Dick's Barber Shop.

Bobby and I walked over to the jailhouse. I frowned. The WILL RETURN IN AN HOUR sign was still posted.

"Jeez." Bobby turned to the town clock. "Twelve fifteen."

"Out to lunch," we said in unison.

We walked over to the Top Hat Café and peered into the window looking for Sheriff. No Jingles. Resigning ourselves to a wait, we headed over to Liar's Bench, where Mr. Harrison, a teller from over at First Tilley State Bank, was having a smoke and reading his newspaper. We waited politely behind the bench, holding hands. Each of us lost in our own thoughts. Mr. Harrison finally stubbed out his cigarette and made his way back to the bank, leaving a cloud of smoke around us. I sliced my hand through the haze, waving the smell away as we sat down.

I looked around and then I gently poked at Bobby's jeans. "Town's pretty quiet. Amos's letter," I reminded him.

"Yeah, I wonder what this is about." Bobby stood up for a moment, fumbling. "Gramps doesn't talk much about family, only my gramma. Must've stirred him up talking about your dad and all. Never connected Amos with Moss . . ."

Carefully, Bobby dug the paper out of his pocket and then scooted close so that we could both read.

20 October 1923

After the nanny goat refused to nurse its runt, Master Anderson gave me the gray-spotted kid. It was 1859 and I was only eleven, but the Master of Hark Hill plantation always tried to do right by me, saying I was growing into a fine man. Master said, "Amos Crow, looks like you might be my only child, and though no Kentucky nigger can ever have my title, a hardworking son can surely receive a gift from his daddy if his daddy sees fit."

That made me happy. I was proud and felt two-man tall.

During the next few months I bottle-fed that goat and it became a fine one, Blinkie did. That billy sure did love me, too. Master said so himself.

Blinkie followed me to the barn each morning when I'd do chores, then back home every night, down ol' dusty Slave Row.

My mama, Frannie Crow, didn't care for Blinkie. She couldn't say as much 'cause she knew Master favored me, so she just kept fretting 'bout the broken stitches across the plantation, saying Mistress Anderson was with child again, and to watch my step.

I didn't know 'bout that. I just knew that Master was light on his feet lately. I 'spected he was just testing bourbon from his latest batch.

By the summer of 1860, Mama's worries were knotted into Slave Row. The plantation overseer had done gone and had his way with my mama, soiling her right in Big House kitchen. The shame and hurt leeched right onto my twelve-year-old Crow bones.

During it all, Mama lost the two shiny buttons Master gave her for her years of faithful toil.

Mama was busted so badly, she couldn't do chores for a whole day. Mistress Anderson ordered an account of her day's labor, and having none, Mama confessed.

Then Mistress had my mama whipped under the Osage tree, shouting out "Frannie Crow is a thief" to the yard niggers. She said Mama done stole the buttons and a day's work, cheating all of 'em. Mama never said a word while the blood ran down her length, soaking her skirts.

Two weeks later, Mama hobbled out to that ol' Osage tree and picked its fruits to make Mistress a soothing tea for the new babe she was carrying in her womb. After Mistress drank it, she claimed she got her monthly courses, and that's when Master came out to the barn and tied thirteen knots into a rope. Then he hooked the noose 'round my Blinkie's neck.

Blinkie bucked and strained his neck against the rope, trying to get away. His square eyes popped, looking fit to bust.

I tried to follow Master and plead with him. But he yelled at me and knocked me down into the dirt.

I cried when I heard Blinkie bleat for me. I begged Master to spare him. Master wouldn't listen. He just kept right on dragging my little goat over to that Osage tree.

When it was over, Master pointed to me and said to dig a hole, that I could keep the skin, but to save the meat for his supper.

Later that night, the town marshal came out to Hark Hill. Master gave him his hangman's rope, and the lawman took my mama away. I knelt down on Master's fine boots and begged.

After they hung my mama in Town Square, Master ordered me and Uncle to take down the

*gallows and store the hardware and wood back
on Hark Hill Plantation.*

*My eyes leaked buckets for two years, until one
day Master gave me my Freedom Papers, and two
hogs and the wood from my mama's gallows.
Master told me to use some of the wood to build
me a pen, but to save him the finer pieces of oak
and iron to build a sitting bench for Town Square.*

*I built Master Anderson his fancy bench,
pounding Crow sweat into its planks and
polishing the wrought iron with my blood—
Frannie's blood—and a tad of Blinkie's for good
measure.*

*Over the years, the name "Anderson Bench"
changed to Liar's Bench. And though it's 1923,
folks 'round here still like to sit a spell and spin a
tale on this ol' Liar's Bench. I know somewhere,
whether Heaven or Hell, or in between, the ghost
of Frannie Crow smiles.*

C.A.W.—For Husband Amos Crow

I picked up a hedge apple and rolled it between my hands, pressing in my pain, Amos's sorrows, and Bobby's rage until the ball split and ran sticky sap over my clean jeans.

Bobby rubbed his jaw and then lit into Liar's Bench, hammering his fist onto the empty spot between us. "Another stick for the mutt dog. I'm a damn Anderson!" he blasted. "I can't believe it. That's why Gramps never showed me," he said, disgusted.

I quickly covered the wood between us, taking Bobby's hand in mine, and said, "Most folks have kin connections if you dig deep enough.... You're still Bobby Marshall. You'll never be him." I swallowed hard. "I knew it was bad with Frannie, but I never knew it was this bad for everyone.... It's like one of those napalm bombs in Vietnam that scatters its sticky fire onto everyone in its path. Bobby, I am so sorry for your family.... My Grammy Essie must've known about Amos's letter when she recorded Frannie's history. I guess Jessum or Sara shared it with her, but she didn't get around to recording it."

"He wouldn't want it anywhere but in his Bible. . . . Let the devil be damned." Bobby set an angry jaw as he folded up the letter. He gave a flick to the paper. I held my breath, praying he wouldn't tear it up in a fit. It was important to keep Amos's history.

"Bobby, it wasn't unusual back then to . . . you know, have blood of a . . ." I let the words trickle. "You know, we have your family pieced together now," I said softly, rubbing the edge of the bench, thinking about Amos and his strong hands polishing and pounding. "You'll build your tomorrow on this." I thought about his plans for law school. "Put it back into your pocket, Bobby. It's history, everybody's history. Amos had his wife pen his words for family—for you. We have their markers now. We'll have it all recorded and clean up the cemetery and we'll—"

"Do nothing, Mudas, because ain't nobody gonna care about the graves of darkies."

I placed my hand on top of the letter. "That's not true, Bobby. I'm going to care."

Bobby breathed a weary sigh.

"Forever," I promised.

Bobby kissed the tear that had rolled down my face. "Mudas, you know what?" he whispered hoarsely. "I believe you. I believe you will."

We sat for a long while, not saying anything, just giving the bench and each other the tender needed.

After a bit, Bobby got up and paced, muttering about Jingles's whereabouts.

I kept one eye locked on the jailhouse. Growing anxious, I fished inside my pockets, withdrew the recipe card, and fanned my face. I tapped the paper on my lips, thinking about how badly I missed Mama.

I spied ThommaLyn with three of her brothers circling Town Square. She was riding shotgun in the Nova, and two of the boys were grocery'd in the back. I stood up and waved her over, excited to see her, but unsure of how to explain everything that had happened in the past twenty-four hours. Or even *if* I should explain. I'd already brought Bobby into this mess and he'd been rewarded for his trouble with whizzing gunshots and threats. Did I really want to drag anyone else I loved into my mess?

The Nova pulled up in front of Liar's Bench and ThommaLyn hopped out. Her brothers sat in the car waiting.

"Hey, you two!" she called as she made her way over. Bobby nodded and waved. "Where have you been, Muddy?" she said in a huff. She glanced at Bobby, then pulled me aside and inspected my face. "You were tight-lipped about where you were going yesterday.... And your old man stopped by the house looking for you."

"Daddy and I had a fight yesterday." I shrugged away a blush. "I'm okay." I stuffed the recipe into my back pocket and rubbed my thumb across my fingertips.

"You don't look okay. Your face is all bruised and scratched up. Your jeans are torn. And look at your knee." ThommaLyn inspected my cut and ran her eyes over the green T-shirt I was wearing. Questioning. She tugged on the hem of Bobby's oversized tee, eyebrows raised.

"I'm okay."

She reached for my runaway fingers and placed her hand over mine to still them. "You're ticking off troubles." She gave a squeeze.

I tucked my thumbs into my back pockets. ThommaLyn knew my hands were a dead giveaway that I was worrying. She knew every inch of my wardrobe, which didn't include any oversized green T-shirts. But I wasn't about to go into the steamy details of last night—not here on Liar's Bench with Bobby sitting two feet to my left and ThommaLyn's brothers over there in the car. I knew that if I tossed my romance into the daylight, my face would light up in red for all the world to see. No way. I'd wait until ThommaLyn and I were alone to spill. Better yet, alone and in the dark.

"We'll get together real soon. And I'm fine. Just fine." I stepped aside and took a seat next to Bobby. "I just went for a walk in the woods, that's all," I said, rubbing my fingers over

Liar's Bench, kneading my lie into the old wood. "Tripped over a stupid log," I fibbed.

"A log?" ThommaLyn asked, looking to Bobby for confirmation. She lifted my hand. "You and those logs."

Bobby looked from me to ThommaLyn and back again. "I should go say hi to the boys," he said, clearing his throat, "and welcome Bernie back. I haven't seen the hero since he got back from Vietnam." He walked over to the Nova to lean inside and chitchat with the brothers. Within a minute their friendly-like voices carried across Town Square.

ThommaLyn plopped down on Bobby's spot and studied me. She flipped her ponytail, a dangled bird's nest of fried curlicues that I'd given her with a home-perm last month.

"I haven't been able to talk to you." She poked my arm. "Two whole days since Ella's funeral . . . I've been fretting ever since you called yesterday. You hung up so quickly. And I could hardly sleep for worrying last night after your daddy's visit. Everyone's worried about you. Jeez, hon, I'm worried."

"Yeah, I know. I just need some time. I'm still working things out," I said flatly, looking away. A silence settled between us.

"Ya know, school's starting soon." ThommaLyn smoothed back the curls tumbling out of her ponytail. "And I know your world's crazy right now. But why don't you take a break and come over to my house? We're going boating on Mayfly Lake this weekend. And the State Fair's coming up. C'mon. It'll be good to get away. Mama and Daddy have been asking about you; they'd love to see you." She covered her worry with a floppy smile. "You sure you're okay?"

"Yeah, it's . . . well, Daddy and I had that argument. And I ran off after I gave him a heaping bucket of what-for." I shot ThommaLyn a guilty glance. "Ya know, that was liberating for all but a minute, just a minute. Until I saw how much it hurt him . . . and me." I winced. "Still, he had it coming."

ThommaLyn nodded sympathetically.

"What did you say when he came by last night?"

"I told him you were in the bath. That Mama was taking care of you, and would make sure you got supper and rest. He asked about your car, and I said that James had asked to borrow it to run an errand for Mama and was that all right? He bought it, Muddy. And, thank goodness, I was able to get him off the porch and gone before someone came along and lit truth to the tale." She crossed her fingers and traced an imaginary *X* across Liar's Bench, leaving her signature mark—a token for laying her lies down on the bench.

"Thanks for covering for me, ThommaLyn."

"Well, I owed you. You covered for me and PJ when we spent the night in Nashville." She nudged me mischievously.

I nudged her back.

"Muddy, he called again this morning. I told him you were helping Mama bring berries in from the field while I did up the breakfast dishes. Your daddy said to tell you he had to run into Nashville for the day, but that he'd be home around suppertime. Asked me to tell you to have a good day." ThommaLyn squeezed my hand. "You *sure* you're okay? I know how bad you must be missing your mama."

My soaked lashes answered for me.

"Oh, hon, I know you are."

"I'm missing her something fierce. Never dreamed she wouldn't be here for my graduating year. We would've gone shopping in the city for my school stuff this week." She'd already bought me these new Levi's. I ran my hand over the rip in my jeans.

ThommaLyn gave me a tight embrace and sniffled. "You know my mama would love to take you to buy your school supplies and new clothes, Muddy."

"Shopping?" For a second I was tempted to tell her that Bobby had asked me to the prom. To ask her about dress shopping. But if the words fell, would I risk jinxing it? Especially here on Liar's Bench . . . it just might gobble them up . . .

She patted my back. "You should come on over to supper tonight. Let Mama put some ointment on that knee 'fore it gets infected."

"Bobby gave me some. And thanks, but I can't come over tonight. I promised to hang with Bobby." I pulled away.

"I just hate to leave you like this. . . ."

"I'll be okay. Bobby's here," I insisted. "And Mayfly sounds cool for this weekend. I'll call you tonight."

"Promise?"

"Promise."

Her brother gave a short horn blast and motioned to his sister. ThommaLyn whipped her head around and glared back a warning.

We both rose. I felt better already. I thrust my hands into the pockets of my jeans and rocked lightly on the balls of my sneakers.

"Bring a swimsuit and don't forget a cute outfit," she suggested in typical ThommaLyn fashion. "That way Mama can take us to the city to shop after we're done boating. We need to get P.E. uniforms—oh, have you made up your mind about track?"

"Think I'm gonna quit," I answered, running my eyes down the length of my legs. "Like I told you, two years of dealing with Coach Grider is 'bout all I can take—him always yelling, calling me clumsy, making fun of us girls."

"Polecat." ThommaLyn's voice soured.

"Oh, I forgot to tell you, but right after you left to visit your aunt in Nashville, Grider called a meeting on the football field. He had the gall to tell us we needed to sew aprons onto our running shorts. Said it right in front of the cheerleaders and the football team."

"Peckerhead!" she puffed.

"Yeah," I sighed. "Everyone laughed, even some of the runners on our team, especially WallaceAnn and Carole. Then WallaceAnn and Carole said they were gonna ask our Home Ec teacher if we could actually sew the aprons. And put the school's letters on them in pink."

ThommaLyn frowned. "Just heard last night that Carole's not coming back to school. . . ." She cupped her hand over her belly and slid it up and down.

I thought about the pills tucked inside my dresser. "That makes three we've lost this year."

"Well," ThommaLyn said, "always knew a box of rocks is smarter than those two. Carole'll be sewing that pink onto bibs now."

I shook my head, wishing it weren't so. Carole's daddy was junk-yard-dog mean, her mama already ball 'n' chained with a litter of small kids. I reminded myself to take her a package to help with the draw checks.

"Grider's such an ornery cuss," ThommaLyn went on. "Just yesterday, I heard him bellyaching in the Top Hat Café about how teed he was when the principal told him the government passed Title Nine and—"

"Yup, President Nixon signed it, but Jesus Christ himself could lay signature across the mighty Ohio River and Grider would still find a way to drown it. He's a joke. And I'm tired of fighting Coach Grider by myself. I'm through."

"Bummer. You've won trophies for track; I always thought you'd get a scholarship, maybe have a shot at the Olympics someday."

"Coach Hall over in Mallardsburg said that, too."

"He should know, he's the best!"

"Yeah, but I dunno if I care about it anymore. And the trophies . . . well, I never said anything, and don't you either, but Daddy bought 'em for me and the other girls," I said, cheeks heating. "He picked them up in a Nashville pawnshop after Grider said no to using the athletic money on girls."

"Bastard!" ThommaLyn growled.

"Grider keeps saying he isn't gonna allow the silly-minded females to dry up the boys' funds." I shook my head. "And it's the *girls'* cake-baking sales that raise money for sports in the first place."

"Well, hon," ThommaLyn soothed, "ya know you don't need that damn track scholarship anyway. With grades like yours, I'm sure you'll get others. Everyone knows you're gonna be valedictorian."

One of ThommaLyn's brothers hung his head out the window and bleated her name. She flicked her hand over her shoulder, shushing him.

She nodded. "Okay, Mayfly Lake, we're on. Cool! I'll tell Mama. And glad to see you have Bobby around. I'll talk with you tomorrow and you can fill me in." She tugged knowingly at the sleeve of my borrowed T-shirt and turned to leave.

I couldn't keep it in any longer, my one piece of happy news. I decided to take my chances with jinxing it—I just had to tell her. I took two big steps away from Liar's Bench for insurance. "ThommaLyn, wait!" I motioned for her.

She rushed back to my side. "What?"

I cupped my hand and whispered into her ear, "Remember that prom dress I fell in love with at White's department store last year? The one you insisted that I try on?"

ThommaLyn's eyes popped wide. She bobbed her head.

"Well, I'd like to go shopping for one just like it."

ThommaLyn opened her mouth and glanced at Bobby out of the corner of her eye.

"That's right, ThommaLyn." I dropped my whisper to barely a buzz. "I'll need help on deciding which color *prom* dress would look best for the senior prom. *My* prom." I wanted to clap out the word in a cheer; instead, I lazied my speech. "Now, I'm a'thinkin', ThommaLyn, a warm honey, a peony pink, or maybe a soft jade?" Then I quickly placed my hand over her mouth and cut off what I knew would be an ear-splitting squeal. She grabbed me in a bear hug and danced us around in a circle until we were both drunk with giggles.

"I knew that boy would have a slow hand," ThommaLyn teased.

Her brothers called out, complaining of the heat. I nodded to her to go ahead.

Happy, she slipped up behind Bobby and tapped his shoulder. "We're going boating this weekend, Bobby Marshall. Maybe you'd like to come along?" Then she climbed into the Nova, leaned out the window, and yelled a very winded, "Yeeeeeee-haw!"

I laughed.

"Don't forget. Mayfly Lake," she shouted as they pulled off, her hand waving until the car disappeared around the corner of Main Street.

"What's ThommaLyn hooting about?" Bobby rested his arm over my shoulder.

"Just . . . shopping."

"Shopping?"

"Yup."

Puzzled, he shook his head. "I'm running over to Peck's for a soda. Need anything?"

"Nah, I'm good."

"Be right back." He gave me a loud smooch.

I plopped down on the bench and watched as he jaywalked across the street, then disappeared into the pool hall. Wisps of smoke and a jukebox's streaming honky-tonk seeped out.

After a few minutes, I spotted Gladydoo Mitcham, the seventy-five-year old organist over at United Methodist Church, my day brightening from seeing her and from the chat with ThommaLyn.

Mrs. Mitcham strolled out of Ginny's Bloom Up n' Dye beauty salon, her blue-rinsed hair nicely coiffed, complementing her electric-blue eyes but clashing with the long purple duster she wore. Still, her signature cherub smile made her look like the tree-top angel that Mayor McKinney put atop the store-bought pine in front of the courthouse every Christmas. She fumbled with her pocketbook, dropping her green-striped parasol.

Bobby stepped out of Peck's and stopped to pick it up for her. Mrs. Mitcham caught my eye, and I waved. She blew me back a kiss and winked, turning to chat with Bobby.

Smiling, I rested my elbows on my knees, remembering the long powdery-purple dressing gown, the one of Mama's that she'd given me to make into a play dress. I'd worn it to play in the cave with ThommaLyn. I thought about Jessum riding Daddy out to Penitentiary Hole on a tractor, and how he must have looked. I'd have to show Bobby the hole someday.

It had been years, possibly ten or more, since I'd played in that cave. An opening no bigger than six feet tall and maybe eight feet wide with a trail in about twenty-five feet, Penitentiary Hole had been declared "off-limits" by Daddy, who said it was crumbly and too dangerous. But before that, Mama had helped me bury a small time capsule inside. What and where exactly, I couldn't remember. It was so long ago. And the old cave was probably serving as a coyote den by now. Last year, while he was mending the fence row, Daddy saw a coyote carrying one of its pups out of the hole.

Bobby sprinted across the street and flopped down beside me. He pressed his hand over mine, stilling my speedy thumb, which had been sweeping across my fingertips like a cuckoo clock's hand gone cartoon crazy. I felt my cheeks take on a shine.

"That Mrs. Mitcham sure is a firecracker." Bobby laughed and shook his head. He set his Dr. Pepper between us, opened a box of Cracker Jacks, and shoveled a handful into his mouth. "Want some?"

"She could flirt the slippers right off a Gethsemani monk." I grinned, taking the Cracker Jacks. I poured a few of the molasses clusters into my hand and passed the box back to Bobby. "Thanks."

"The jail's still locked and I noticed that Jingles's car is gone," he said, munching away. "One of the guys in Peck's said he thought Jingles and his deputy ran over to Millwheat on a tip about stolen cars."

"Damn."

"Besides shopping, what'd ThommaLyn have to say?"

"Nothing much, just that Daddy had called to say he's running into Nashville today. Probably working on one of his cases. Guess we could head out to the homestead for a bit. Jingles might be a while if he's off in Millwheat," I said, crunching out my words with a mouthful of nuts and popcorn.

Bobby rattled the box of Cracker Jacks, pulled out the sticky prize, and handed it to me. He tossed back the remaining candy clusters.

I ripped open the small red-and-white-striped package and laughed at the Lucky Star wishing game—a card made into a tiny pinball game, covered with a plastic bubble. I rattled it, and watched the copper ball roll into the starred-shape YES, then bounce back and slide into the NO slot.

"Make a wish." I shoved the toy in front of him and wriggled it back and forth.

"I wish . . . I'd gotten a super-duper decoder ring instead," he pouted.

"Um, it's NO!" I chuckled. I tilted the toy sideways and studied the words: *Yes, No, Yes, No.* "Hey, when I was little, I'd always make a wish upon a star before bedtime prayers. Grammy Essie had this quote she liked: 'A prayer in its simplest definition is merely a wish turned Godward.' Phillips Brooks, I think."

I hoped that was true, because lately it seemed like my prayers for Mama were ricocheting—my wishes fading like a star's final wink before dawn. I could only pray that I would keep the one I'd made about Bobby. I traced the word *Lucky* on the card.

"What's your wish, Mudas Elizabeth Summers?"

"Hmmm . . . I wish—"

Bobby jumped up. The Dr. Pepper fell to the sidewalk and shattered apart—its toothy glass neck rolling into the street. Dropping the toy, I looked up to see a silver Mercedes crawling toward us—McGee's. Manly Carter, a man Daddy had put away for a short stint a few years back, sat shotgun, sneering out the passenger window.

"Let's book, Mudas! McGee's looking for that rooster invoice. We're not safe here, *anywhere,* until we find Sheriff or your dad. Let's go find your dad!"

Panic rooted me to the bench.

Bobby grabbed me by the wrist and dragged me toward the street. He shot McGee the bird as we hotfooted it behind his car, then slammed his fist down on the Mercedes's trunk.

We barreled past to cross to the courthouse commons, and I looked back and glimpsed my Lucky Star prize being lifted off Liar's Bench by a gust of wind, my wish tossed like litter into the street. I glared at McGee and his beefy passenger.

Bobby hopped into the Mustang while I dug inside my pockets for the key.

"C'mon, c'mon." He smacked the passenger door twice.

I fumbled with the key. Finally, I managed to grasp it and fling open the driver's side door, throwing myself into the seat. With an unsteady hand, I turned the ignition. The radio blared "American Woman." The car lurched forward twice and died. Trying again, I took a breath and eased off the clutch. The car jerked out onto Main Street.

"Knobmole Hill! Get us to Knobmole Hill!" Bobby rasped. "Then we can make it across to your homestead. He won't dare come onto your dad's land!"

"But, Bobby—"

"We have to find your dad. He's the prosecutor—he'll know what to do!"

"Okay, okay!" I tightened my hold on the steering wheel. Looking into the rearview, I spied McGee's car making a U-turn at Liar's Bench. "It'll be okay, you'll see," Bobby reassured me as I glanced back again. McGee's tires crushed my Cracker Jack prayers.

20

Powerful Pony

We rode without talking for several minutes, Bobby and I each locked in our own thoughts. Mine, occupied by attempts to bolster my courage, but getting crowded out by fear and worries.

The radio kicked off and on, alternately blaring melody and static. Bobby thumped the dash to change the station and an announcer called out Thursday's weather: "Hot and sunny." My clothes seemed to melt into my skin.

We whizzed past Gib McBride's cornfield and tobacco barn, and rounded a sharp bend. I hit a straight stretch and snuck a peek in the rearview mirror. "McGee's still behind us, Bobby."

"With a 289 under this hood, we can haul ass and leave McGee eating exhaust." Bobby's worried eyes met mine, his hands gripping the dash. "Keep it tight, Mudas, Satan's Corner is up ahead."

"Tryin'."

"Lean in a little tighter. C'mon, you can do it!"

I felt my forehead bead up with sweat. I was sure I could put some distance between us and McGee if I kept my speed on Satan's Corner. I pulled into the inside of the curve, putting all my strength in my hands and wrists. If I could just hold it and come out tight and straight, maybe we'd lose them. We were almost out of the curve, when the front left tire hit something—a rock, or a branch, maybe—and the wheel jerked, loosening my hands. Puffs of dust kicked up on the right. A hubcap flew off, hula-hooping toward the shoulder. Both of my tires squealed and the wheel wobbled uselessly in my hands. I could feel the pony slipping sideways. I turned the wheel against the slide, trying to straighten out, and the whole rear whipped back—too hard and too fast. I fought to straighten out the car's fishtail course.

Bobby yelled out, "It's Satan's Corner! Ease up on the gas!"

The car straightened, and it hit me: In our haste to get out of town, I hadn't put on my lap belt. What a fool! I reached behind me, groping for the belt, but I couldn't find it and the wheel was growing unsteady in my hand. I returned my other hand to the wheel, giving up on the belt, resigned to my stupidity. Through a haze of fright, I made my way up narrow Knobmole Hill. I could feel the car gaining speed and was almost to the top of the hill when I stole another glimpse behind us. McGee's car veered around Satan's Corner. Brakes hissed and swirls of dirt plumed from the Mercedes. Then I lost sight of their car.

"Easy, easy . . ." Bobby urged.

He looked over his shoulder. "I can't see them. Maybe they ran off the shoulder."

My thoughts were tangled, images of Mama and Daddy flitting in and out. I thought of Mama and Genevieve sitting in my car, just eight days ago. "You got yourself a powerful pony . . . always wear your lap belt, sugar," she'd cautioned.

Desperately I fumbled again for the seat belt and managed to snatch it up. I pulled it across my waist, but it failed to connect. As I struggled, the car crested a hill and the rear wheels made a different sound—not grinding, just whipping. My pony had gone airborne.

"Whoa—" Both my hands gripped the skinny steering wheel harder, my nails digging into my palms. "Hang on!"

Bobby hissed through his teeth.

"Oh—" My brain did the math right fast, but came up short on time and distance.

For a quivering second, a flash of Bobby's kiss streamed across my mind like an airplane's trailing banner.

My stomach flipped, then grabbed my throat as the Mustang dropped and bottomed out too hard on the blacktop. The car jostled me like a Tilt-A-Whirl. My head bounced off the steering wheel, hard, blinding me for a second. The sound of Bobby's head smacking the dash broke through the roaring in my ears.

Metal screeched from the pony's underside, and tires squealed and hissed. My foot took on a mind of its own, slamming hard on the brake. I felt myself being squeezed against the door, the pony going in the opposite direction, skidding sideways. The frame tilted back to the right, onto what must've been the side of the road, and kept sliding and sliding.

I leaned against the door, bracing my neck, shoulders, and legs on anything that wasn't moving. But the car kept going and going—down, sideways, and then down some more—until it finally stopped.

I heard a whimper, maybe my own. Smoke rose from the hood, obscuring my vision and stinging my eyes. I tried to think straight. . . . Out—I had to get out of the car. I fumbled for the latch, pushing and kicking until the door opened. I crawled out, whimpering for Bobby and hearing nothing in response. I scrambled farther away from the car, thinking maybe I could see Bobby if I could just get away from all this smoke. I called for him again, desperate. After a weighty pause, I heard his door crack open, followed by a thud on the far side of the car as he rolled out and hit the ground. I heard him coughing and breathed a sigh of relief. He was okay. Bobby was okay. Safe in that knowledge, I rolled over and let myself drift off into the darkness that beckoned.

Sometime later, I awoke facedown in Kentucky clay, stirred to consciousness by a loud, staticky version of Van Morrison's "Into the Mystic." I cocked my head, listening. The radio must have kicked itself on in the crash. A guitar strumming, fading into mellifluous notes, a horn laddering into Morrison's bluesy words . . . I sat up, wobbly, and spat out bloodied grit. Pieces of bluegrass and tiny shards of glass plastered my body like decorations on a cake.

I looked around, trying to get my bearings. A thicket of brush and trees obscured Knobmole Hill behind us and a steep drop beckoned a few feet ahead. The car rested upright in a deep rut beside a nearby pine. Peggy sat there, as if mocking me for not wearing my lap belt. "Uh-oh," I blinked hard. "The muffler's hanging, Daddy's gonna bust." I looked down at my body. No real blood, just a few pricks here and there from the shattered glass. My head felt like Jell-O.

I let myself fall backward and stared up at the blue summer sky. The ghostly promise of a full Sturgeon moon was already appearing, even though night was still hours away. I blinked and then rolled my head back and forth and raised my hands. "D-d-doet, dooet, doo ah ooo-O-et . . ." I slipped into Morrison's verse and sang softly. My fingers punched the air, orchestrating to the winds. "Doo . . . D-da . . . da-umn right it's to-oo late to stop now-o-o-ow . . ." I lulled myself back into darkness.

21

Too Late Now

I struggled to come fully awake, willing myself to focus on my name.

"Mudas. Mudas, wake up. C'mon now . . . wake up, Mudas!" His words drummed off me.

Two light smacks on my cheeks and my lids flew open to see Bobby's eyes full of fear. His face was blossomed with it, so full-mooned it frightened me.

I bolted upright. A deafening chorus of insects and the grating cries of squabbling blackbirds pummeled my brain. I shut my eyes and clamped my hands over my ears. The smell of burnt rubber and oil rode the breeze. A blast of radio static echoed around the hill, bass thrumming before abruptly shutting itself off.

I groaned.

Bobby embraced me. "I thought I'd lost you, Mudas. You scared the crap outta me!" His heart thundered against mine. "Here, let's take a look at you." He inspected my face.

"Ouch . . . A headache from hitting the wheel, I think." I rubbed my temples and rose to my knees.

"Can you stand?" Bobby winced as he eased me up onto my feet. A trickle of blood from his forehead slid down toward his eye.

"Uh-huh." I swayed and grabbed his arm. "You okay, Bobby? I couldn't find you. Thought I heard you once, but then everything went black."

"Yeah, I crawled out of the car after you did." He grimaced.

"Just a few scratches. Busted my forehead a bit." He wiped his blood-speckled face onto his sleeve. He clutched his side. "Ribs are a little sore from being tossed around."

"Ribs? Any of them broke?"

"Doesn't feel like they're cracked, probably bruised." Bobby took a slow breath. "It's bad that you popped that hill flying, but good that we ended up over here behind this brush. McGee probably flew right past us and is running around the county chasing a phantom car."

"I should've taken Gib's cornfield when I had the chance."

"We'd likely be in worse shape than we are now. Ol' man Gib would've skinned us alive if we so much as snapped a single stalk."

I let out a laugh, but it caught in my throat. I buried my face in my hands and sank to the grass. Bobby put his hand on my back, but it felt smothering, like he was taking up all my air.

"Please . . ." I shook my head, my face still in his hands. "Please go away, just give me a minute," I begged. Bobby moved over to the bluff in silence. Hugging my knees to my chest, I buried my face in their crook.

My body was racked with horrors, my gut hollowed. Thoughts of Bobby dead formed a grim carousal looping in my brain, squeaking: *I could have killed Bobby. I could have killed him. Killed him.* I could not stand to lose anyone else.

A spontaneous combustion lit my heart aflame, rewired my brain, and sent a singular message through my veins: I loved him. Yes, I was knee-knocking, heart-aching, scent-sense full of love for that boy. For Bobby. It was one of those clarifying moments, when life comes into focus and you see everything exactly how it is and how it ought to be. And just like that, I knew. Plain as day.

After a spell, Bobby came over and knelt down in front of me.

"Hey," he whispered, tugging gently on the hem of my bell-bottoms. "Hey, I should've driven, but there wasn't time. I'm sorry I made you do that. I just, I knew you'd driven this road a million times practicing in your dad's car. And it's a good short-cut, 'cause it's pretty much empty."

I wiped my face on my sleeve.

"Hey, look at me." Bobby lifted my chin. "At that speed, I don't know any boy who could've taken Satan's Corner any better than you—Hell's bells, Mudas, I dunno about you, but I do believe that when you tightened that curve, I saw an angel flashing a Come-to-Jesus sign." He glided his thumb across my wet cheeks.

"Yeah?"

"Sure enough," Bobby soothed.

"I could've killed you."

"I'm fine." He thumped his chest, grinning. "And you're fine. Got a bit of concrete rash going on, but hey, you're okay. I'm okay." He swept back my hair and examined my head. "How you feelin' now? Head okay?"

"Yeah," I moaned. "I only see two of you; your third just walked away."

"Good, then give us a kiss, both of us."

I raised a brow and lightly kissed the air beside each cheek. Bobby chuckled.

"Listen, Bobby, I want you to know how much it means to me, everything you're doing to help out. Putting me up at your Gramps' . . . it's—it's really cool of you."

"Aw, c'mon, Mudas. You're making me blush," he said.

"Yeah, well. I just thought . . ."

"I know. I also know I'm never going to leave you." He smiled. "Listen, the car's got a few dings, a busted side window," he said. "But I think it'll be okay. . . . It'll need to be towed back up to the road, though. And McGee'll likely realize soon enough that we didn't take the rest of the hill and retrace his steps back along this stretch to make sure we didn't pull off onto another road. So we'd best wait, maybe a half hour? Then I can climb up the embankment and try to flag somebody down."

I took a seat in the shade of a tall bush to escape the heat.

Bobby walked over to the car. He pulled out the Mason jar and stashed it inside the trunk. "Hey, Mudas"—he pointed to my jeans—"you wanna put the senator's receipt inside the diary?" He held the trunk lid open.

"Yeah, can't lose this," I said, patting my jeans, my pocket half-ripped and dangling. I gave him the paper.

Bobby put it with the journal and slammed the trunk shut, then fished out the keys from his pocket again. "Oh . . . Saw some wire in there. Maybe I can hook the muffler back on."

The trunk latch must've frozen because Bobby tried four times to unlock it, before giving up. He checked out the engine, radiator, and hoses. Hopping inside the Mustang, he turned the key. The engine cranked easily. The radio blasted Ike and Tina Turner's "Proud Mary." Inspired, he got out and unsuccessfully tried to rock the Mustang out of its rut.

Having no luck, Bobby climbed up the bank's edge. After about three minutes of alternating between standing, pacing, and crouching, he jumped up, waving both hands in the air. He hollered over his shoulder, "Someone's coming in a truck."

I dusted off my jeans and stood.

Then Bobby yelled out something I couldn't understand and slid sideways down the hill, arms raised in the air. He grabbed my hand, and muttered, "It's the ol' man!"

"Huh?" I look up at him puzzled.

"Just don't say anything," he cautioned.

"Who—"

The rumble of a loud engine on the other side of the bluff jerked us apart. A door banged shut. My body grew cold and my teeth chattered in anticipation. I took one step back and wrapped myself in a hug.

"Bobby?"

"Shh."

The sound of footsteps crunching on gravel got closer. With my heart ramming against my chest, I cupped my hands to shield against the sun's glare and looked up toward the road.

Old man Harper stood there, fists jabbed into the sides of his stained union suit, peering down over the slope. "Passed by and heard jungle music bangin' 'round the hill . . ."

"Mr. . . . Mr. Harper—" I choked, staggering a few steps back. "Radio's shorted—"

"Well, now, whatta we have here? Looks like that boy's done gone an' wrecked yore car, Miz Muddy. Tut, tut . . . now why'd ya go an' do something like that, boy?"

Bobby moved in and stepped protectively in front of me. "It's *Bobby*, my name's Bobby. And we swerved—"

Mr. Harper kicked his steel-toe boot into the ground and spit a stream of saliva out to his side. He cupped his hand to his huge cauliflowered ear. "Whassat I hear? Why, it's an Injun whoop and a nigga's whine makin' my head all bumfuzzeled."

He spit toward Bobby and pointed. "Boy, iffin' yore talkin' to me, ya best be addressin' me as Mister. Ya hear me, BOY?" Harper boomed, then turned on his heels and stomped away. "I done warned ya twice!"

I fumbled for Bobby's hand. He straightened himself upright, waiting. A door creaked open, followed by a slam.

Mr. Harper ambled back over to the ravine's perch, towering above us, a mere ten feet away, if that. He raised the ol' Slugger that he always kept fastened to his truck's gun rack, shook it at Bobby before thumping it on the ground.

"You disrespectin' me again, boy?" Harper leaned on the bat, a blob of belly flesh jiggling over the knob. He braced himself against the barrel of the Louisville Slugger, palms pressed tight, swaying like an ol' corn snake, fat with mice.

"Prick," Bobby tossed the word over my shoulder.

"Boy," Mr. Harper said, "I will take this sweet spot an' send you flyn' to Nigga Hill iffin' ya ever talks to me like that again." He cocked his head. "You thinkin' yore special coz ya lived in the big city, huh?" He picked up the bat and swung it in front of him. "Actin' all uppity to us white folks. Ruttin' after a white gal. . . . You best learn yore place in Peckinpaw, boy, or you're gonna find yoreself hanging from a Cee-garh tree one of these days."

I gasped.

Bobby squeezed my hand.

"Miz Muddy, ya let go of that Injun nigga's hand right now. An' ya get yore skinny white ass right on up here. Righ' here, righ' now!" He thumped the bat on the ground. "I'm takin' ya home to yore daddy."

"I'm seeing Mudas home," Bobby yelled.

"Boy, ya-can-jus'-kiss-my-big-red-Kentucky-Fried-Chicken-ass! Ya hear me, boy?" Ol' man Harper wrapped his meaty hand around the cloth grip of the bat, flexed his fingers, and tightened.

I took a step back.

A vein popped up on Mr. Harper's neck and his sweaty face turned a checkered, ruddy hue.

"Now git on up here, Miz Muddy, 'fore I whup that boy. That what ya want?"

I thought of the catalpa tree in Frannie's cemetery. The deep burrows of hand-carved coward notches stepladdering up the murky old bark.

I snuck a peek at Bobby. He answered back, shaking his head, and mouthing, *Run!*

My brain warned me to run, but my heart said that, if I did, I could lose Bobby.

Mr. Harper inched up to the edge of the ravine.

I shuddered.

"Ya want me to whup him?" he thundered.

I took a step toward Mr. Harper.

22

The Road Home

"Nuh-uh." Mr. Harper wagged his finger. "Ya bring me that pony's key, gal. That boy's gonna hoof it back to Nigga Hill."

Bobby reached for my shirttail. I shot him a warning look, then walked over to my car to grab the key. "Bobby," I whispered over my shoulder, "I can't watch him take a bat to you. If I don't let him take me home to Daddy, he'll find you and whup you—if not today, it'll be tomorrow or another. I can't let him do that."

We stopped in our tracks. Another car door slammed above us on the road.

"Daddy," I whispered to Bobby.

"Git on up here wid that key, girl." Harper cracked the bat against rock.

"Yessir," I said, praying I was right. Raising the key to Harper, I brushed past Bobby, sweeping a feathered touch across his hand. I climbed up the slope, leaving scree and clumps of mud tumbling down behind me.

Bobby was close behind.

When I reached the top of the gully, I found McGee's eyes pinned to mine. His jaw cut cold and a meanness climbed out. Another man stood by a faded Buick, rope in hand. McGee jerked me up by my arm and shoved me into Mr. Harper.

Ol' man Harper wrapped his arm around my neck and locked me to him. Bobby yelled out and took a step forward. Harper tossed McGee my keys and raised the bat over my head.

Bobby hesitated and McGee's man latched on to Bobby's arm and twisted it behind his back, shoving Bobby's face onto the trunk.

McGee trailed down the embankment. I heard my pony's doors open and slam, and things being tossed out. Then I heard him cursing and kicking at it.

When he came back up, McGee shook his head to Harper and whispered something in his ear. In the distance I heard an approaching car.

McGee and his men huddled in front of us, blocking, as the car drove past. Like most, the driver tooted a friendly honk, while McGee waved back.

"Let me go," I spit, struggling against Harper's grip. He dug into my flesh, pinching bone.

"Let her go!" Bobby yelled. "Bastard!" McGee's man punched him in the gut, silencing his curses.

After they were sure the car had disappeared around the bend, Harper opened his truck door and shoved me toward it. I screamed out again, and McGee whipped out his gun and pointed it at Bobby.

"You best go on home, Muddy Summers, or this boy's gonna be getting more than a whipping," McGee bit.

Bobby stretched his head off the trunk and hollered, "No."

"Boy's got to have his whipping," McGee said. "You get along, or you're gonna make it messier. You want that? Ol' Harper will take good care of you." McGee walked over to Bobby and waved his gun overhead. "Go on and get."

Harper pushed me into the cab of his truck. "Git up there." Biting back tears, I jerked off his grip and climbed in.

I stared out the rear window, my chest thumping madly. The man had the rope hooked over Bobby's neck, cinched tight while McGee tied it to the bumper. "Help him, Mr. Harper!" I demanded.

Bobby's shouts and curses rang through the knobs.

"Mr. Harper"—I shook his arm—"Mr. Harper, please don't let them hurt him!"

Harper shrugged me off and started his truck. "Boy's gonna git his whippin', learn his place in 'tucky."

"My daddy's gonna have a lot to say about this, Mr. Harper," I said with all the sternness I could muster.

Mr. Harper soured his face and scratched his stubby neck.

"Mr. Harper?"

He pulled onto the road. I twisted my head around and caught a glimpse of Bobby trailing behind the Buick running into the rope that dragged him.

"Mr. Harper, please stop!"

Harper's truck rocked into Satan's Corner with McGee's car trailing.

"Stop!" I screamed out, reaching for the latch on the door. Harper whipped out his arm and slapped me hard across the mouth. He kicked down on the gas. Star-spotted, I looked up at him for a minute and then snapped my head around.

Satan's Corner disappeared.

I couldn't see Bobby anymore.

I looked at Harper, oil droplets stitched into his upper lip, eyes hooded. I turned around again, watching.

After a few minutes, Harper clucked his tongue. "Don't know what ya could possibly be thinking, tramping all over the countryside wid that trash. Hmph." He wagged his finger in front of my face. "You'd think that after what happened to yore mama, you'd know better."

I sucked in a breath.

"Iffin' ya live wid trash, ya ends up burnin' like trash. Just. Like. Yore. Mama—"

I shot him an angry look and wiped away a hot tear barreling down my cheek. "Don't you talk about my mama—"

Harper reached over, grabbed a fistful of my hair, and yanked hard. "You watch that mouth of yors, gal," he snarled. "Lessun, ya wanna end up swinging from a rope, too, like that nigga boyfriend of yors is gonna be."

I shrieked. He gave another sharp pull to my hair, dragging my head toward his lap.

I pulled back and tried to jerk myself up.

"Ya best learn yore place in this world. Ol' Harper can teach ya. Ain't that right, gal?" He pushed my head toward his crotch, muffling my scream, and dug his knuckles into my neck.

Struggling to breathe, I reached up and clawed the air, finally marking Harper's arm.

He snatched me back up only to slam my face back into him. "Ya gonna mind me, gal?"

I stretched my cramped neck upward. "Let go of me!"

He grabbed the flesh behind my neck, pinched. "Gonna mind?"

My eyes watered from the pain, sharp and tight.

"Answer me, gal!"

I blew out a defeated, "Yes."

Harper let up on his grip. Shaking, I tried to scoot toward the door.

The truck wobbled into a curve, then Harper straightened it out and pushed down on the pedal, whizzing past the cornfield. He slowed to turn onto McBride Road.

"Why, Miz Muddy, here I am bein' all neighborly-like, takin' ya home an' yore disrespectin' me same as yore boyfriend did."

"Let me go!" I demanded. "My daddy—"

"Yore daddy," Harper snorted. He fumbled for the back of my hair, grabbed a fistful, and smashed my face back down onto his lap again, drowning out my cries. "Lil birdie done tol' me yore daddy's over in Nashville today. That birdie also tol' me you an' that no-good Injun nigga were on Mr. McGee's property a'trespassin' yesterday. Ain't that right, gal?"

I tried to lift my head. Harper's powerful hand shoved me further into his sweat-stained mechanic's suit, forcing me to gasp air through my nose.

"Same lil birdie done tol' me, you an' that boy swiped a very 'portant receipt. Ya know sumthin' about that, gal?"

I twisted my head sideways so I could see his face.

He jutted out his chin, screeched out a cock-a-doodle-doo, and laughed maniacally.

Panicked, I witched my fingers toward his face, grazing air. I kicked wildly, busting my knees on the dash.

Harper braked to a snail crawl and used his knee to steer, then yanked me up by my roots. He took his other hand off the steering wheel and backhanded me across the face, his ring cutting into flesh. He curled a fist and struck again. The truck rocked and my head whiplashed against the seat. A sharp light stabbed my eyes and haloed. Warm blood oozed out of my cheek.

"Now," he sneered, taking the wheel with one hand and grasping for strands of hair with the other, "we're gonna be passing Town Square this minute an' yore gonna keep that head down an' yore mouth where it belongs, or I'm gonna break yore neck an' dump yore body up on Nigga Hill in them woods where nobody'd find ya, understand?" He dug his nails into my scalp, scraping the skin.

I felt the pickup veer alongside the nubs of the shoulder, then jerk back to the center of the road.

Fresh pain shot through as he grabbed another clump of hair and snapped my neck back.

"Ya jus' be real still, hear me now? Ya don't want Daddy to have to buy another pine box, now, do ya?" Spit sprayed out of his mouth.

I swallowed back sobs and forced a nod, then shook my head no.

He turned his face back to the road and raked his fingers through my hair, coiling a bunch of curls into his fist. He gave a hard pull. "Lay down. I said, *down!*" He used his meaty strength, forcing me to comply.

The truck jerked to the left, then straightened.

"Now, when we git to yore house, yore gonna show Ol' Harper where that rooster receipt is, so I don't have to tear up all yore purty rooms. "'Cause iffin' ya don't . . . well, I'm a'gonna tear off all yore clothes, gal. Piece by piece." He yanked up my shirt and smacked his greased lips.

I wriggled hard, twisting my head up. "Let go . . . please, let me go, Mr. Harper."

He grabbed my neck.

"Such a delicate neck, like yore mama's. Thin an' all, like a reed . . . Wouldn't take but a lil slip to snap." He dug his nails into my flesh, pinched, then lifted his fingers and strummed them over my neck. "Ya better mind now, ya hear?"

My pulse quickened against his fingers.

"Iffin' ya give me everything I want, I might jus' keep ya around. Ol' Harper could teach ya a lot of things . . . mm-hmm."

"Mr. Harper, please, no." I begged. "Please, let me go. *Please* . . . I don't have any receipts. Bobby doesn't either. I don't know what you're talking a—"

"Now ain't that somethin', that's exactly what yore mama said, an' all purty-like, too."

"Mama?" I cried out. "You—"

His fingers tightened. "One more peep an' I'll snap that neck . . . Snap it! Ya hear?" He pressed into my skin and his voice grew tough and biting. "Jus' like I did yore mama's." He cracked a smug grin.

I whimpered.

He killed Mama. . . . He is gonna kill me, too. I held my breath as long as I could, then gulped down choppy bits of air. I tasted blood. Fighting a wave of dizziness, I tried to draw on my strength to stoke my need for revenge.

Harper slowly released his hold, then ran his calloused hand over my hair, trailing his fingertips across my neck. I felt the truck veer onto the shoulder and hit a huge rut. Harper wrestled it back onto the road.

My muscles tensed.

Choking back my sobs again, I raised my chin slightly, opened my mouth for air. "Don't . . . Don't kill me. Please! Please . . ." I pleaded. "Just let me go, Mr. Harper! I won't tell a soul!"

"That's jus' what yore mama said!"

Harper slowed the truck until it reached a snail's pace. He used his steering knee again as he reached up and unzipped his union suit, exposing himself. I screamed just as he shoved my face into his privates.

The truck hit a pothole, swerved, and settled into a tremble. Then I felt the truck swing out wide and turn left.

He ran his fingers through my hair again. Flexing his fingertips along my head, he shoved my face down farther into him, suffocating me.

"Behave yoreself."

I clamped my mouth shut and pressed my lips tightly together as I felt him harden beneath my face. I fought back a wave of nausea.

The truck turned right and then cut a sharp left. I felt the familiar mud holes of Summers Road, heard the welcoming crunch of gravel beneath the tires. Straining my neck upward, I recognized the half-broken branch of one of our ol' chinaberry trees—the one with the dangling tire swing—and the same one I'd climbed since I was knee-high.

Home! My heart pumped furiously.

He shoved me back down and relaxed his grip.

I inched my hand up alongside my face and carefully slid my fingers between my chin and Harper's ball sack.

He eased his foot off the gas pedal and moaned. The truck weaved down the road.

I thought of Bobby lowering his head to Harper, all subservient-like. Him being roped like an animal. I held my breath and made myself a promise: I was going to fight. Fight for my life—no matter what happened to me. I would not give up—no matter what.

On the silent count of three, I grabbed hold of him as hard as I could, just like ThommaLyn had shown me to do when I was five years old and horsing around with her four brothers. Never understanding that it could save my life. And never really intending it to cause harm—back then, I'd always let go. But this time I meant it. I wasn't letting go.

I latched on to his balls, scrunching hard, and twisted and pulled them, trying to rip skin. Harper screamed like a banshee and yanked me up by the hair, bending back my neck, almost breaking it. I dug in further, twisting harder than ever. I pulled and turned that awful handful for myself, for Mama, and for baby Genevieve.

Harper's body spasmed with pain. Unable to control the truck, he finally managed to slam on the brakes.

"Turn off the truck, you bastard." I spat, digging harder, squeezing tighter.

The corners of his mouth contorted and settled into a shocked O, his face drained completely of color.

I tightened my grip. "I said, turn it off!"

The engine died.

Maintaining my iron hold, I locked my eyes to his. I thought about what he'd done to Mama. His hands on her neck. On mine.

Filled with rage, I clamped down my hold on him, turned my head around to line myself up with him just so, and slammed the back of my head into his face. Surprising even myself, I connected. I heard the crunch of small bones and a puff of wilting breath. I turned to find that I'd hit my mark just right—dead center. Splat on the nose.

After a fleeting moment of shocked silence, Harper threw his head back and screamed bloody murder.

In an instant, I pulled back the door latch and tumbled out of the car, hitting rocks as I landed.

Scrambling and kicking up gravel dust, I jumped to my feet. Panting, I stole a glance at the windshield. Harper sat slumped against the wheel. His jaw was screwed tight; his eyes slits of pain. Trickles of blood ran from his nostrils. He pressed his hands to his head.

I lurched forward, shaking my fist, and screeched, "Kiss my lilywhite ass, you diddle-dick bastard!"

I raced down the long drive and up the porch steps, hollering for my daddy. Letting the screen door bang behind me, I crossed into the living room and into the kitchen. "Daddy! Help! Hello?"

I traced my steps back to the staircase landing and hollered up the steps. "Daddy, where are you? HELLO?" I turned around to the front entry, studying the door. "Why, oh, why didn't anyone ever put locks on this old house?" I groaned. I grabbed the banister and took the hall stairs two steps at a time, flying up the pine boards.

"Thank God!" Daddy had forgotten to take my door off the hinges! I crossed the hall to Daddy's room. Empty. Running over to his window, I parted the curtain and scanned the length of our drive. Harper's truck was still sitting there. Empty.

I skirted Daddy's bed to his nightstand and, with a shaky hand, picked up the ol' rotary dial phone, listening for a tone. Widow Lettie Sims was on the party line, talking.

"Who's listenin' in?" Lettie asked, accompanied by clicks, buzzes, and static.

"Miz Sims, it's—"

"Why, hello, Muddy. Me an' Peach Hobart was jus' now talkin' about you. Jus' talkin' 'bout that wonderful service Pastor Dugin gave your mama. Bless her heart. Keepin' all of you on our prayer list. Uh-huh. Ain't that right, Peach?"

A man murmured, "Yes, ma'am."

I gripped the long, curled cord attached to the phone, balled it close to my chest, and peeked over my shoulder. "Miz Sims," I scratched out a whisper, "I need to use the phone. It's an emerg—"

"How's your daddy doing, hon? Back from Nashville yet?" She sniffed loudly. "He kept me an' poor Peach off the party line all day yester—"

"*Please,* Miz Sims. Hang up! I have to call Sheriff Jingles—"

"Why, chil', everyone knows Jingles ran over to Millwheat today." She whispered into the mouthpiece, "Something 'bout—"

"Please! I have an emergency!"

". . . stolen car parts," she continued.

I brought my fingers up to my mouth and chewed on my nails. Was that the porch door I heard creaking? Or the staircase landing?

"Miz Sims!" I spooled the phone cord tight around my fingers, pressed it to my sweaty forehead. "I have to use the phone, please hang up! *Please! There's—*"

"Is there a fire?" she asked sweetly. "Always a fire with those teens, eh, Peach?" She chuckled. Peach Hobart snorted in agreement.

I slammed down the receiver, picked it up, and slammed it down again. Again. And again.

"Jesus, Jesus!" I fell to my knees, clutching the phone receiver in one hand and rubbing my temple with the other.

23

Balls 'n' Boots

The sound of wood creaking on the bottom landing of the stairs pushed away defeat and brought back function. Terror set in. I bolted upright onto my knees. Dropping the phone, I crawled over close to Daddy's door, barely breathing. I cocked my head toward the jamb. Daddy'd never had a lock on his bedroom door, but he'd put one on mine—the first and only one ever installed in the old house—after I'd begged for one as my thirteenth birthday present.

Daddy'd agreed, admitting that a teenaged girl needed her privacy and wondering if maybe it was also time to start thinking about putting some deadbolts on the entry doors. Especially since the potheads were always trespassing onto the homestead, looking for places to smoke their wacky-weed. But Grammy Essie wasn't having any of it. Daddy'd finally asked her what she'd do if one of those boys got the munchies and stole one of her famous pies. Grammy Essie'd just laughed and pooh-poohed the idea, saying, "A shotgun's the only insurance I need against pie-napping." Still, she'd agreed to give me my bedroom lock.

I put my hand over my racing heart. I was surely gonna explode with worriment. Why was I wasting time thinking about pies and the past when my life could very well be over before I ever tasted another sweet thing?

I strained to listen above the drumming of my heartbeat. The creaking seemed to have stopped. If I could just make it to my room and lock the door. Determined, I sucked in a breath and, getting on all fours, I sprang up and out the door.

I heard the *thwap* before my knees buckled. Hitting the floor, I rolled over, groaning. My back leg muscles stung from the pain.

Harper stood at the top of the stairs, the Slugger in his hands, towering over me.

Screaming, I painfully brought my knees up to my chin and kicked out as hard as I could.

He squeezed out a rush of air and fell sideways down the stairs. I scrambled quickly across the hall and into my room. As soon as I'd crossed the threshold, I shot up and slammed my door shut. I fumbled with the top lock. It didn't engage. I tried again, this time pressing my weight against the door. The lock slid into the jamb and clicked.

I took a step back, stumbled over a pile of clothes, and landed on my tail. Footsteps pounded the stairs.

Harper bellowed out a stream of curses, beating his fists on my door.

With a trembling hand, I smothered my mouth to still my cries.

"Bitch, ya better come on out 'fore ya find yourself swingin' like yore mama."

I shook my head, swimming with confusion. Panicky tears rolled down over my bloodied cheek and into the corner of my mouth, leaving a metallic taste.

The old skeleton keyhole darkened as Harper's boots dragged back and forth against the pine planked floors. He delivered a thud to the door, then another. I pulled myself up, took two careful steps back, and looked around my room, searching for something, anything that could help.

"Ya best come on outta there. This ol' wooden door ain't no match for my Slugger here." Harper whacked the door with the bat. The wood began to splinter. Flecks of paint flew off and landed like snow on the pine floor.

Bones rippled against flesh.

"Tell ya what," Harper panted behind the door, "ya jus' give me that rooster receipt ya took from McGee's an' tell me where yore mama's Rooster Run ledger is, an' I'll jus' mosey on. And if ya don't snitch, I'll tell the boys to let that boyfriend of yours off the hook. Whatcha' say? Deal?"

I didn't trust that murdering bastard for one Kentucky second. I backed up to the curtains covering the tall pane of glass and collapsed onto the window seat.

Harper grunted and swung the bat once more. Shards of peppered-white wood littered my bedroom floor. A few more hits like that and he'd be in. Grammy's doors were not meant to withstand this kind of battering brutality, just the occasional sass of a teenaged temper.

I jerked upward and scanned the room for an escape, for anything. Peering out the window, I calculated the two-story drop. I sagged against the pane, then moved the curtain aside and stared out at the persimmon tree, gauging the distance between its alligator-skin branches and the house. A good six feet, if not more—a leap I knew I could never make.

"Gots me enuff of that rope left over from yore mama. Yore messin' wid the wrong peoples here, Muddy Summers. I'm jus' tryin' to do my job an' return McGee's property to him." He banged on the door with his fists. "Yore gonna be hanging from a ceegarh tree along wid that boy tonight, iffin' ya don't give me what I want! Ya hear me? Hanging!" Harper said with a finality that pricked skin.

I gulped down air.

Harper thumped the door again, paused, and swung his bat, splitting a long crack down the center of the wood. I held my breath. He gave a hard kick to the door with the steel toe of his boot.

I whirled around, searching, feeling like a trapped rabbit quivering inside a hunter's den.

Rabbit. Rabbit. Can't catch a rabbit unless you muddy up your boots.

I bolted across the room to my bed and dropped to my knees. Reaching underneath the bed frame, I pulled out books, 8-track tapes, and a pair of flip-flops. Finding nothing to help, I ran to my closet.

Harper slammed the bat against the wood, forcing the frame to peel halfway off the door.

I groped inside the bottom of the closet, throwing clothes, track team trophies, and shoes behind me. I pressed my fingers to my temple, kneaded.

Harper kicked the door, sending more chunks flying.

Grammy's words sprang up: "A shotgun's the only insurance I need. . . ."

I glanced over at the window bench. In less than two counts, I had the wooden lid open. I dug under the pile of quilts and felt the leather sheath of Papaw's hunting knife. I pushed it aside and dug deeper, until my hand rested on cool metal. I pulled out my .410 shotgun, the one I used as a kid when I'd kicked up rabbits in fence rows. And the one I'd muddied up my boots with.

I pulled the bolt back and looked into the chamber. One cartridge sat snug-tight. I shoved the bolt forward, locking it into place. Then I plowed my hand inside the bench and rummaged through it again. Trembling, I pulled out an extra shell and tucked it inside my pocket.

One. Deep breath.

Two. Deep breath.

I turned to face the door. Raising the gun, I pressed the walnut stock to my shoulder, snugging my cheek to the side of the stock while looking down the barrel.

Can't catch a rabbit lessen you muddy up those boots. My mind burst with resolve, stoked by the courage that came from having no other option. "Muddy up," I whispered, flexing my fingers around the barrel and tightening. *I'm Muddy who catches rabbits,* I told myself. Mudas Summers, a seed rising strong from the mud to muck and rabble when others would try to bury me.

The baseball bat struck the lock. The ping of metal bounced

and scraped against wood just one second before Harper landed inside my room.

"Why, Mr. Harper . . . I do believe them boots are too clean."

I pointed the barrel at his head, then lowered it steadily to his feet and squeezed the trigger.

24

Party Lines 'n' Parting Lines

An ear-splitting explosion rattled the glass pane and rocked the walls, deafening me.

Harper dropped like a skid of bricks, the bat still clutched in his hand. Writhing and moaning between clenched teeth, he squeezed his other hand over his bloody boots.

I leaped over him, but the hurdle was too short. Harper snapped up an arm and caught me by the ankle, sending me tumbling down on the hard wood. The .410 fell out of my hands.

I screamed and jerked my ankle from his grip, then plowed my foot into his face.

He shrieked as his nose spurted fresh blood.

Crawling, I made it to the door, latched on to the frame, and pulled myself up. I stood in the shadow of the doorway for a moment, breathing hard, staring at Harper, who was half-sitting, rocking his wounds. Claret-colored puddles pooled at the bottom of his legs, his boots darkening.

I looked square into Harper's red-rimmed eyes. "Who told you to kill my mama? Was it McGee? Where's Bobby?"

He screwed up his bloody face. "Even if ya had the answers, you'd be dead 'fore ya could tell anyone 'bout it."

"You best answer me." I slipped my hand into my pocket, pulling out the shotgun shell and dangling it in the air.

"Ya ain't got the balls, bitch," he growled, bloodied spit spraying out.

"No, sir, but I do have this shell for yours."

I wiggled the cartridge and walked toward him, my eyes never leaving his, and moved catlike and quick around his body, kicking the Slugger across the floor. Then I put the shell between my teeth, picked up my shotgun, and pulled back the bolt. The spent casing ejected and fell to the floor, rolling.

Harper's glazed eyes widened and his thick Adam's apple bobbed up and down.

I wedged the cartridge into the chamber and pushed the bolt forward, locking it into place.

He shook his head, then nodded quickly, and caterwauled, "Okay, okay. Please don't shoot. I promise, I don't know where they took that boy."

"Liar! What about my mama?" I shook the barrel at him.

"Yeah, okay . . . It was me an' Manly Carter who done it. Mainly, it was Carter. McGee wanted his ledger back and—it was an accident. Promise. We just slapped her around a bit an' things got outta hand—"

I raised the gun. "Why? WHY?"

He squirmed. "Ya don't wanna kill me. Please. I gots me three kids—an' one on the way. A family—"

"I did, too!"

"It was for the Rooster Run ledger—we, we jus' went to git it back," Harper sniveled. "But when we got there, she had her suitcase packed, gettin' ready to hoof it wid that baby of hers. Couldn't let that happen an' lose the ledger. Whole lot of 'portant people's in that ledger, Muddy." He drew in ragged breaths. "Iffin' the word gets out that they's up at McGee's cockfightin' an' sleepin' wid whores, well, they'd lose their 'portant jobs right quick. . . . Now, iffin' ya jus' hand that stuff over, them 'portant peoples will give ya a reward. Uh-huh. A nice, big reward, gal, so ya can move far away from here an' meet a nice fella, no nigga trash. Live a nice life, away from all this."

I hoisted the gun higher.

"You gots to understand . . . 'Portant business. An' it ain't jus' me you's got to worry 'bout. They're gonna come lookin' for ya, too, lessun ya 'give it to 'em—" He coughed and blood sprayed, speckling the floor. "Gonna kill me, too, iffin' I don't bring it back." The reek of fear, sweat, and blood seeped from his body, filling the room with a filthy halo. "Jus' a matter of time 'fore they find the ledger."

"Not if I find it first." I straightened the barrel.

Harper tried to heave himself up. "Think! Please." He groped uselessly for my pity. "Think of my family!"

"Did you think of mine?" I aimed my shotgun at his head and slowly trailed the length of his body, setting the barrel's bead at his crotch. "My family."

I pulled the trigger.

Harper's jaw slacked and his breath flopped out of his mouth like a fish.

"Bastard!" I spat, lingering in the doorway. "I hope they soak your balls in gasoline when they slide you into Hell." I turned on my heels and walked out, hugging the gun.

Outside my bedroom, I slumped back against the wall. Sliding down, I rested my head against the barrel. Oh, dear God, how had it all come to this? My family. My broken family. Blood on my hands. Mama, gone. "Mama, Mama . . ." I wailed. "And dear God, now Bobby . . ."

After what seemed like a very long time, I gripped the barrel of the shotgun to pull myself up and walked into Daddy's room. I lifted the phone receiver up off the floor and brought it to my ear. I took a long, deep breath.

"Who's listenin' in?" Lettie Sims asked.

"Miz Sims—"

"Muddy Summers, I expect an apology this instant. That was rude banging the phone receiver while me an' poor Peach was jus' trying to have ourselves a conversation," she shamed, exaggerating a sniffle.

"Sorry, ma'am. I—"

"You forgot Peach."

"My apologies, Mr. Ho—"

"Hmph. Much better. Just don't let it happen again."

"Yes, ma'am. May I—"

"Me an' Peach Hobart was jus' now talkin'—"

"Miz Sims, when you're through talking, would you mind calling me the sheriff? There's been a shooting here—"

"O Lord a'mercy. Good heavens, what hap—"

"Thank you, Miz Sims. . . . Afternoon, Mr. Hobart."

I returned the phone to its cradle, made my way out of the room and down the stairs. Clutching the shotgun, I flung open the porch door. With my eyes welled and blurring, I blindly stumbled onto the porch and straight into a viselike grip.

25

Hanging Time

I screamed and jerked my arm away, leveling the gun at the man standing in front of me, his face ripe with puzzlement.

"Whoa there, gal." Daddy released me, dropped his briefcase, and slowly raised both hands in the air. "Muddy," he said softly, keeping his hands held high, "put down the gun."

"Daddy, oh, Daddy," I trembled.

He dropped his hands, took my gun, and laid it on the ground. "Muddy, you okay? What the hell has happened here? Why were you pointing that gun at me?"

"No, no, no, no . . . it's Har-Harper!" I spit.

"Harper? What about Harper?" He looked over his shoulder toward Harper's pickup. "What's Harper doing way out here?"

My teeth chattered, chopping off words. "He . . . Harp . . . He . . ."

Daddy reached out his hand and I grabbed hold. He wrapped his arms carefully around me, pressing his cheek to mine. I collapsed into him. After a moment, he pried my hands from his neck and stepped back to scrutinize me. "It's okay; just tell me what happened, Muddy. I won't ground you for telling the truth. Whatever it is, you can tell me."

"Harper, Harper," I blubbered over and over.

"Here, sit down, baby." He nudged and pointed at me to sit down on the grass under the chinaberry. Pushing my hair off my face, he asked, "What's going on, Muddy? Where's Thomma-Lyn? Where's your car? Did you wreck—"

"Satan . . . Satan's Corner! They took Bobby and—"

"What? Never mind. Dear God, child! Look at you, baby. . . . Your face, clothes! You're bleeding. Did you have a wreck? Did Harper tow it away? That it?"

"Bobby . . . Harper and Mc . . . Gee," I hiccupped.

"What? Look, let's get you cleaned up. Your cheeks look like a watermelon smashed on pavement. Your eye's swelling. . . . And look here, your knee is busted. It'll need some tending to. Nothing, ice, a Band-Aid, and some Mercurochrome can't fix." He dug into his pants pocket and pulled out a handkerchief for me. "I bet it hurts. Here, hold this against it. Hurt much?"

"No. Bobby . . . They hurt him . . . McGee's got him." I shook my head, taking the hankie, pressing it to my cut. "I—I shot Mr. Harper," I sputtered.

A siren's horn echoed across the fields, growing louder with each rolling howl. A second siren kicked in and piggybacked on the first.

Daddy sprang up and looked down toward our gravel lane that led to the Summers Road turnoff.

"I shot him!" I blurted out, jumping to my feet, the bloody handkerchief taking flight like a butterfly before settling on the grass. Sunspots slanted through the dark glossy leaves of the chinaberry, casting ribbons of pale ghoulish streaks across us. I cupped a hand against my brow, shadowing the prisms and squinting up at the house. I raised my hand. Daddy's eyes followed.

"Him. Mr. Harper. He's in there."

"What the hell, Muddy?" He shook my shoulders. "What's going on? Talk to me!"

The sirens grew louder and louder. Then I heard the crunch of gravel and saw puffs of dust coil around a sheriff's cruiser, with a state trooper's car trailing behind. The cars came to a halt in the driveway. A cloud of pebble dust and dirt hung in the air, dimming the bubblegum-red lights.

Daddy looked down at me, his eyes rounding.

"McGee put a rope on Bobby, and they tried to drag him . . . And Harper forced—"

A sheriff and his deputy from the nearby town of Laurelpoint got out of the car and hurried over to us.

"What about McGee? Bobby who?"

"I sh-shot Mr. Harper."

"Hush it," Daddy warned, before turning to the approaching sheriff.

"Mr. Summers. Ma'am." The sheriff nodded. "We got a call from Peach Hobart about a shooting? Thought you might have some poachers . . . Jingles is on his way back from Millwheat, but it'll be a spell 'fore he gets here. Are you okay, ma'am?" he asked, studying me, my torn clothes, and Daddy's blood-spotted handkerchief on the ground.

"Thanks for coming, Brent," Daddy said, extending his hand, giving a brisk shake.

Sheriff Brent nodded. "Ma'am?" he asked again, tilting the brim of his uniform hat upward, hooking his thumbs behind his gun belt, waiting. "Do you need medical assistance?"

I took a deep breath and crossed my arms. I stood there a second, feeling heat rise on my face. What he was really asking me was, if I'd been violated. The question lingered in the sheriff's eyes, prying.

I looked down at my ripped shirt and scratched arms, then brought my hand up to my cheek to wipe away drips of blood. I thought of Melissa James, a shy but pretty fourteen-year-old girl, who'd been violated by two of the Murphy clan a few years back. When it got out around town that she'd been soiled, she was labeled a slut and a troublemaker. The shame changed her life, driving her to that lonely stretch of two a.m. railroad track. After her funeral, some of the menfolk, and even a few of the women, had scoffed before they'd whispered, "She'd asked for it." She hadn't. No more than I'd asked Harper to force me into his crotch. But, to this day, no one had ever come forward to defend Melissa's honor, nor any of the other Melissa-likes whose honor had been stained around these parts.

"Miz Summers"—he peered down at me—"do you require medical attention?"

Daddy's hand slipped into mine. I felt it twitch, then he squeezed. Once. Twice.

My breath quickened.

And a third time to drive home the urgency.

I let my gaze drop to the sheriff's scuffed chlorofram shoes. "No . . . no, sir. I'm just fine." I hitched a thumb over my shoulder. "Upstairs," I puffed out. "He's the one who needs a doctor."

Daddy slowly released his hand, leaving his approval glistening on mine. I rubbed my palm across my dirty sleeve.

The men looked at Daddy and then back to me. Daddy cleared his throat and nodded an affirmation. The sheriff and his deputy bobbed their heads and scurried across the drive toward the house.

I searched Daddy's face, full of confusion. I tried to collect all of my thoughts, to make sense of them, but I couldn't scrape the words off my tongue. Exhausted by the effort, I fell silent.

Daddy gripped my shoulders. "Wait here and don't say a word," he ordered, before turning to follow Sheriff Brent and the deputy.

Car doors slammed and I turned toward the driveway.

Trooper Herb ambled up the long, gravelly road, trailing two shadows.

26

Cameo

My breath caught when I saw his eyes spark in the evening light. Eyes locked, we ran to each other. Bobby spread his arms and I swayed forward, falling right into them.

"Mudas," he murmured over and over, kissing my face and rubbing my arms. "I was so worried. Are you hurt?" He stepped back. "Here, let me see."

"Bobby, you're safe—"

"What'd that bastard do to you?" he growled, wheeling around me, fists clenched.

I rubbed my swollen face. "I . . . I'm fine now."

"I'm gonna jack his jaw!"

Trooper Herb blocked him with a firm hand on his shoulder. "Stay put, son."

"Where is he?" Bobby rioted, brushing aside the state trooper's hand. "So help me, I'll kick his teeth in."

The trooper jerked Bobby's arm back and planted his feet in front of him. "Don't make me whup you, son. Now, you best stay put or I'll have to 'cuff you." He raised a warning brow.

I touched Bobby's shoulder. "It's okay. I'm good. Really." I inspected his torn shirt. "But, you—"

"I'll rip his balls off—"

"I don't think that's gonna be necessary. I'm okay, Bobby. But you don't look so good. Let me see you—your neck." I traced my finger above the blistering line that circled his neck. "What happened back there? Where's McGee?" I rushed. "How'd you find the trooper?"

Bobby patted his jeans pocket and pulled out his knife. "Remember this?" He kissed the bone handle on his pocketknife. "I carry this everywhere, and always keep it sharpened. Mudas, I wished you could've seen their faces when the cut rope went flying and slapped their back window. Here I'm hurtling over the side of the road and them driving off into Satan's Corner." Bobby grinned big. "After I cut myself lose, I ended up down the embankment toward Gib's cornfield." He rubbed his shoulder. "Damn rock nearly took my shoulder off."

"Oh, Bobby . . ."

"It's only banged up a little." He rotated his arm. "I ran to McBride's. His wife let me in and called the trooper. Trooper picked me up. Don't know where that bastard McGee is."

"Thank God, Bobby!"

"You sure you're okay, Mudas?" His eyes scanned the length of me and then bore into mine. He clasped me in a tender hug. "You're sure?"

"Yeah." I pulled away, growing anxious, and forced a half-hearted smile. "I'm just relieved to see you."

"Miz Summers?" State trooper Herb tipped his Smokey the Bear hat with one hand and held Mrs. Anderson's old journal in the other. "You okay, ma'am?"

I nodded vigorously. "Mrs. Anderson's journal. How did you get to it? It was locked in the trunk."

Bobby skated his fingers through his hair. "Trooper here drove us by your car and, well, I was afraid to leave it there in case McGee came back. I figured he'd tear up your car looking for that rooster receipt and might find it, so . . . sorry, Mudas . . . but I busted the lock open with my knife and gave the diary stuff to the trooper here."

"I don't care. It's only metal."

"Stay put, kids," the trooper warned, "I'm going inside to have a word with the sheriff."

Bobby hugged me, murmuring soothing words in between the biting ones he pitched to an out-of-sight Harper.

The trooper returned a few minutes later. "Do you need me to call you a doctor, Miz Summers?" the state trooper asked, taking a quick inventory of my appearance.

"No. No, I don't think so, Trooper, just some scratches and bumps. No, sir." I squared my shoulders, trying to steal a bit of poise, as much as I could right then.

"Miz Summers, can we go inside? I'd like to talk to you about what happened today—here."

I looked to Bobby and then back to the trooper.

"I told him everything, Mudas," Bobby explained. "Everything. 'Bout McGee, the rooster receipt—everything." He touched the ribbon on my wrist.

The trooper tucked a clipboard and the old journal into the crook of his arm. "Bobby, you can wait up on the porch," he said, taking my elbow and leading me up to the house.

Bobby hesitated, eyes swamped in worry.

I spent over an hour at the kitchen table telling him everything I knew about McGee and Harper, everything else that had happened in the past two days, except for the private bits about me and Bobby, and the slippery bits about Harper's advance. We were interrupted twice: First, when Daddy came bursting in, his face gone Casper-white, his gray eyes watered with anger. Trooper Herb quickly escorted him out to the porch, despite Daddy's arguments, threats, and pleas. The second interruption came when the wail of the Laurelpoint sheriff's siren kicked up in the driveway, then drifted away off into the dusk of the day.

"Miz Summers," the trooper spoke softly, "they've taken Harper away. You're safe now. Please go ahead with your statement. You left off where you and Bobby were sitting on Liar's Bench today. Then McGee pulled up? Do you know what time this happened?"

"Yessir . . ." When I'd finished, the trooper shut his clipboard and excused himself, asking me to wait there. He ushered Daddy and Bobby into the kitchen, telling us to stay put.

Daddy grabbed me tight, choking back a cry. Bobby shuffled over to the window, giving us the moment.

"I owe you, Bobby. Thanks for getting hold of the law." Daddy extended his hand. "Muddy"—he turned to me—"Bobby told me everything on the porch. Thank God you're okay. Might have Doc Lawrence come out and check y'all over."

We stood in silence and waited for the trooper to return. Daddy, trying to wrap his brain around everything. Me, just trying to think, blink, and breathe. Bobby looking like he wanted to punch his own shadow.

Trooper Herb stepped back into the kitchen holding a plastic bag filled with Mama's ribbon that I'd given him, the Anderson diary, and McGee and Senator Yinsey's rooster receipt. He set them down on the table. Resting his elbow on his holster, he cocked his head toward Daddy, and asked flatly, "Mr. Summers, can you tell me how you came to have this ribbon in your possession?" He pointed to the bag.

With shaky hands, I grabbed the edge of the table and eased myself down onto the chair, waiting for Daddy's answer. The answer that'd been dogging me, the puzzle I couldn't finish. Couldn't even find an edge piece, which had left me bitter. So bitter that I'd tasted sourball green every time I thought of it.

Daddy looked confused for a minute. I sucked in a worried breath. Then he patted his trousers' pockets, slipped a hand inside one, and fished out a teensy white box. Flipping back the hinge, he pulled out a cameo ring, the one I'd seen with Mama's ribbon looped through it, and the one I'd accused him of buying for one of his women.

"Muddy, I hope you can forgive me. Your mama stopped by the house about two weeks before your birthday. She'd gone to First Tilley State Bank and unlocked her safety deposit box to get out your gramma Mudas's ring. Your great-great gramma Mudas Tilley's ring before that. See the inscription here on the Band, *M.E.T.* Mudas Ella Tilley." Daddy tilted the cameo ring toward me and pointed to the inside of the gold band.

"Yes . . ."

"Ella and baby Genevieve met me directly after she came from the bank that day." He frowned and his eyes glazed over with dampness. "She said she was afraid that if Tommy saw the ring, he'd take it from her." His face hardened.

"He would," I murmured. "Would've sold it for pill money."

Daddy nodded a "yes." "Ella asked if I would take the ring to a jeweler in Nashville to get it resized to fit your finger, so it would be ready for your birthday." He paused, studying the ring. "I promised Ella I would do that for her. Muddy, your mama wanted you to have it on your birthday, no matter what. So she dug into Genevieve's diaper bag and pulled out a packet of hair ribbons that she said Mrs. Whitlock had bought for the baby. Then your mama knotted one to fashion a chain to hang the cameo from. 'Just in case,' Ella said, 'Mudas can wear it around her neck if you can't make it over to Nashville in time and, when you finally do, she'll have a pretty new ribbon for her hair.'"

I felt my eyes grow milk-saucer wide. That was just like Mama.

Trooper Herb's pen glided over paper, soaking up our conversation and recording it on his clipboard.

"I got buried with my work, Muddy." He sighed heavily. "Picking out your car. I—I plumb forgot. And then everything . . ." He trailed off. "Then everything went to hell in a handbasket last Friday, baby. I had a meeting in Nashville today with the Assistant U.S. Attorney. I dropped it off at the jeweler's and picked it up on my way back. I couldn't think clear when you found it and I was beside myself with grief."

Trooper Herb looked up at Daddy and shook his head as if to say sorry.

"Muddy, I hadn't kept my last promise to your mama. But you were so distraught, I was afraid to give it to you, fearing you might throw it away in anger."

I probably would've, thinking what I was thinking about his secretary and all.

"Well, Muddy, I was upset, too, about our . . . our spat."

I nodded, grateful that he was too polite to go into the details of the argument in front of company. Still, the hurt I'd caused made me feel ashamed.

"Baby, I hope you'll understand—it just didn't feel like the proper time to give you this beautiful thing from your mother. I wanted it to be special for you, a happier time. After the funeral, ThommaLyn's folks called. They planned to have a birthday party for you at Mayfly Lake this weekend. Nothing big, just something nice, and give you back your birthday. I was going to give the cameo to you at the party."

Bobby said, "ThommaLyn's brothers told me about the surprise."

"She did ask us to Mayfly Lake."

Daddy held the ring out to me. I took it, closed my eyes, and pressed the ring to my lips. "Thank you, Mama," I whispered, slipping it onto my finger. Sweet an' snugged-tight. A perfect fit. I peered closely at the raised silhouette, carved in what appeared to be ivory, its color a soft blush. "It's beautiful." It felt special. Like someone had just given me back a tiny part of Mama and my family.

"Your mama got it on her seventeenth birthday, same as her mama. Sorry I didn't give it to you on yours." Daddy ran a finger over the ring, pleased with the fit.

The trooper closed his clipboard. "Anything else, Mr. Summers?"

Daddy took a deep breath, held up a finger, signaling the trooper to wait. "Ella was just getting ready to turn over more information about McGee. But we'll never know it. McGee's ledger has been lost."

"What—Mama and you? She was part of an investigation?" I felt my whole body blink into darkness, then sling back into light.

He shoved his hands deep into his trousers and cocked his head toward me. "Muddy, it's something neither your mama nor I could ever talk about to you, for your own safety—everyone's safety. Not even to Jingles. We worked together with a close-knit group of officials . . . Your Mama was very brave, and had offered her assistance to help put away some very bad men."

The trooper reached into his bag and pulled out my ribbon. "I'm sorry for your loss, Miz Summers," he said, handing it to me.

I thanked him and knotted it carefully around my wrist.

"Mr. Summers." He looked to Daddy. "I'll file my report. I expect Jingles to be here shortly for his. And I suspect Mr. Harper will be indisposed . . . for a while at least. But McGee hasn't been arrested yet. In the meantime, you might want to think about getting some locks on these doors." He looked to Bobby. "Son, I'll take you home to your parents so you can get those wounds cleaned up."

Worry lines set teeth across Daddy's brow and nipped into mine.

27

A Good Man's Scent

A week later, I sat on my window-seat bench seeking the quiet to reflect about everything and the last loose end—the ledger. Outside the window, a tree branch banged the pane, casting a fork across my arm like a water witch. I peered down at the ribbon and wished Mama had left more helpful clues. Maybe she had nothing more to tell me. Maybe someone else had scooped up that ledger. Without that ledger, the threat of retaliation from McGee and his good ol' boys hung over all of us like a leaky gray cloud.

Harper was still in the hospital and had lawyered up, though he would be facing a trial down the road on kidnapping and possible murder charges, Jingles had said. "But that could be a year or more from now, and if anyone wanted to bail him out, they certainly could," Jingles added. I wondered if the senator would. I had no idea about the others, or if McGee was even in Kentucky, lurking, maybe waiting to spring out from behind the next cigar tree.

The screen door slapped me out of my thoughts. I jumped, something I was doing a lot of lately.

"Muddy," Daddy called up the stairs, "Bobby's here to take you running."

Coach Grider still wouldn't let us girls work out, but I knew the school track stayed open for the football players, and the boys' track team, and they didn't seem to mind if I used it.

Bobby had been sticking to me like glue ever since Harper. And Daddy let him—in fact, he encouraged it. Daddy had been so troubled, he'd taken to sleeping with his shotgun not a few feet from his bed, and keeping his Louisville Slugger kickstand'd against our kitchen door.

Jingles took away my .410 and said he would need to hold it a bit. Daddy protested, saying the .410 was only evidence against me, so why did he have to take it? I'd overheard Jingles funnin' to Daddy about my aim, "Harper will make it, but he'll be recouping for a long while. Meantime, I suggest you tell Muddy that when she gets her .410 back, to sight it in at least once in a while." He'd winked at Daddy.

The next day, Daddy got a deadbolt for our front door, and for some reason that made me sad, like something else had been ripped away.

I tied my sneakers and hurried down the stairs. Bobby greeted me with a smile. "Ready, Mudas?"

"I am," I said, wanting to kiss him, but not with Daddy hovering.

Daddy fussed over us, warning us not to dally too long afterward and to keep to busier town roads.

When I got to the bottom of the porch steps, I turned around. For a second I was shocked by what I saw. The last week's worries had road-mapped Daddy's normally smooth face and climbed right up around his eyes, making them gaunt and dull.

"Did you forget something, Muddy?"

"Uh . . . Yeah, I put the cabbage casserole in the oven and set the timer. Be sure and take it out when it goes off."

"Can't wait," he said. "It's been years since I've had that dish."

I jumped into the passenger's side of Bobby's truck. He cranked the motor three times and couldn't get it going. "Sorry, the starter's going out," he said sheepishly. He got out, looked under the hood, and shook his head.

"That's okay. You've been driving me 'round enough. My car won't be fixed 'til next week, but we can ask to borrow Daddy's."

Under Daddy's watchful eye, I drove his Mustang slowly down the gravel drive, waiting until we reached the end of Summers Road before giving Bobby a kiss.

We pulled up to the side of the field and the track around it. Only a few cars and trucks were parked in the big lot. We'd been going late, when the birds took to the nest and the breezes lifted.

Bobby ran one lap with me and then moseyed over to the bleachers to chat with a boy from his shop class.

As my soles pounded out their rhythm, my mind went to places I could not control. Mostly back to Mama, the missing Rooster Run ledger, and other hard thoughts. But after I was done, it felt like the track had chewed them up until the next time.

On this fifth time out to the track, I saw him. He wore sunglasses and a ball cap, and field glasses hung from his neck. I couldn't make out his features. But I saw enough to know he was a stranger, not on his evening stroll. He just stood there looking out over the field and track, mostly at me. He always left when I did. His truck must've been the white one, because it was the only one that didn't look familiar.

I wish they'd find McGee and that ledger . . . I wish I could find it and put an end to this. I did two more laps, striding past Tim Jackson, Peckinpaw High's number-one running back, before Bobby signaled me it was time to go.

When we reached the lot, Bobby cursed. Running up to the flat tire, he kicked it. "Slashed . . . damn."

"At least they only got one," I said, and looked over my shoulder and all around, but no one was there. The white truck was missing. My thumb lit into my fingers and swept across while Bobby got out the jack and spare.

When he finished changing out the tire, we climbed inside the car. "Guess they got startled and couldn't slash the others," Bobby said.

We drove off in a worried silence. After a spell, Bobby said, "Want to grab a burger?"

"I was hoping you'd have supper with us," I said, anxious to get home. "I made Mama's red cabbage casserole. It's really good."

"That sounds better than a greasy plate from the Top Hat."

When we got home, I found Daddy in the side yard grilling on the ol' charcoal.

"Burgers and dogs tonight." He frowned as he handed me a plate of cooked meat.

"What? But I made red cabbage casserole."

"You *almost* made cabbage casserole." He raised a brow and followed me inside.

"I can't believe it." I set the plate on the table and opened the oven door and saw raw cabbage and apples.

Daddy chuckled. "You turned on the timer, not the oven. Seems like I remember someone doing that before," he teased. He laughed fully, something I hadn't heard in a while.

Giggling, I opened the recipe box and dug out Mama's index card. "Yeah, she even reminded me. See?" I tapped the words Mama had written: *RED CABBAGE—HEAT. Don't forget the oven.* I pushed it under his nose. "Right there."

Daddy grinned. "We'll enjoy it for breakfast, Muddy. Sit down and eat your burger."

I lingered over Mama's words, smiling. Then I saw it. In the slant of the setting sun streaming through the windows, faint words came to life. I walked over to the kitchen window and raised the recipe up. Sure enough, brown words leaped from the page and thunder rolled through me. *Rooster Run Ledger— Penitentiary Hole.*

"Daddy." I motioned over to the table where he'd taken a seat beside Bobby. Mama's words slipped around my mind. "I think I hear Genevieve squirming around. Why don't you go get her up and put a change of clothes on her?" she'd said.

"Daddy." I turned to him with my eyes filling. I held out the recipe.

"What is it?" He walked over to me.

I pointed to the words bolded in the waning light from out-side.

Daddy rubbed his whiskers as he studied the recipe. "That'd

be the ol' Penitentiary Hole out back, used in the Underground Railroad," he said softly.

I found my voice, barely. "My time capsule's out there," I whispered. "No one but Mama knew where we hid it. I wonder if she could've—"

"I suppose it's possible."

"It's her message," I breathed.

He studied the recipe again. "With the investigation coming to a head real fast, Ella probably realized she needed to hide the ledger and send me a message in a hurry, without Whitlock or anyone taking note."

"The Tilley Bank pouch, Daddy! I put my things in the bank pouch. The one Mama used to bury my time capsule in long ago, right before you said the hole was off-limits."

His eyes widened. "Well, what are we waiting for?" Daddy reached for the flashlights tucked inside a drawer and handed one to Bobby. "Muddy, show us where."

We filed out the door, with me leading the way across the field.

Bobby caught up and grabbed my hand as we made our way around the pond.

"Whoa, y'all need to be careful. Watch your step," Daddy hollered from behind, shining his flashlight toward the bank. A water moccasin slithered across the grass, slipping into black water, the trace of ripples dispersing into darkness.

"It'll be pitch-black soon," Daddy announced. "Muddy, y'all best follow close behind me."

Across the hills the maddening cry of coyotes bounced in short bursts, rattling my bones. Involuntarily, I shivered and we stopped to listen. After a moment, the noise faded and the last light of the day slipped behind the oaks. Daddy pressed on.

I nudged Bobby and we fell behind him, letting his flashlight lead the way. In the quiet country night, we weaved our way through a thicket of branches and brush. We stopped about ten feet from Penitentiary Hole. Daddy motioned for me to wait while he stepped up to the mouth of the cave.

"Hell's bells!" Daddy's shout filled the quiet.

Bobby jumped in front of me.

"What is it?" I asked.

"Coyotes."

I peered over Bobby's shoulder and captured the shadowy blur of a coyote streaking its way across the meadow. "Oh, yeah, there it goes."

"Well," Daddy said, "looks like those damn coyotes have set up their den in here again. I chase 'em over to Luke's property, and he chases them right back."

Daddy and Bobby turned their flashlights to the cave. "All clear," Daddy said with relief.

I ducked inside before he could snatch me back, stumbling across the rocks to the end of a jagged wall. As soon as I touched the cool rock, the memories of us burying my childhood time capsule flooded back.

Bobby and Daddy crowded behind me as I ran my hands along the stone wall, searching.

"Mama slipped my time capsule into one of these crevices, then wedged a big ol' rock in front of it," I said.

They raised their lights. I clawed feverishly at the cracks, sending chunks of rubble flying at my feet. "Here, it should be here." Lifting my foot as high as I could, I kicked hard, loosening a dark, weather-aged rock. Another kick and the stone sprang free, tumbling to the ground.

Daddy let out a low whistle.

"The bank pouch . . . It's still here!" I eased it out of the tight hole and unzipped it. My hands turned to butter as I tried to pull out the journal. I handed over the thick red book to Daddy and peeped inside the bag of childhood memories: coins, scrap paper, two pieces of Bazooka bubblegum, a turkey's wishbone, and pieces of fool's gold that my papaw had given me.

Daddy whistled again, softly this time. "Damn. Ella always told me if anything should happen, if she couldn't get me the information directly, she'd find another way. Never dreamed it'd be this way."

Gold lettering on the front of the journal read, *Rooster Run*.

We hurried back to the house. Daddy called the authorities,

and within an hour the ol' screen door clapped greetings to all kinds of officials.

Close to midnight, the last lawman, an FBI Special Agent, left the homestead with the Rooster Run ledger in his grip. He told Daddy, "We talked to Harper again. When Harper was told we had the ledger and that we could work something out, maybe reduce his time in the pen for his testimony against McGee an' his cronies, he got a bad case of the loose lips. Said he'd lost some big cockfighting bets with McGee a while back and was still working them off. Harper's been his strong-armed flunky. Claimed he was just trying to erase his debts—needed to bring in extra cash for his growing family. It was almost 'a relief' to be outed, he said, because he knew McGee would hunt him down and kill him anyway." The federal agent paused.

I breathed a sigh of relief.

"Well, with that and the ledger here"—the agent slapped McGee's journal—"McGee, his thugs, and Harper won't see the light of day for a long, long time. We've picked up McGee in Nashville, and we've got him nailed tight for racketeering, gambling, prostitution, and accessory to murder."

Daddy turned to me and winked with tired eyes. "That girl has sure made me proud, Daniel. A fine daughter for any father."

His words thawed my heart.

Special Agent Daniel bobbed his head, and said, "There's at least one murder here we know about, maybe more." He paused and looked at Daddy, as if he had maybe more to say. Then he said, "Ella's work's going to save a lot of lives. She had the back pages almost all deciphered. Got us some big names, even. They'll be going down river to the big hooscal." Special Agent tossed me a reassuring smile.

Daniel nudged Daddy toward the door, leaned in close. I strained to hear them.

"Rainey Jefferson's been missing over by Wellsburg for a long spell," the agent was telling Daddy. "And if that don't stripe the socks pink, the kid's name is on the Rooster Run list. Poor Jefferson, just a colored boy fishin' for catfish in a pond where he wasn't s'posed to."

The lawman paused a moment. "They hung him, Adam, along with his pup. Out there in the Anderson slave cemetery, and McGee's Rooster Run ledger even tells us where they buried the boy. McGee had the Cooper brothers do it, says so right here. The Cooper twins . . . Who would've thought? Sons of bitches."

Bobby turned and our wide eyes met, both of us thinking about the freshly notched tree we'd seen, and about how close we'd come to the same end like poor Rainey.

"Scum. I can't wait to see McGee fry." Daddy cut switchblade eyes. "Punk's been a thorn in my side ever since our first scrape in high school. Remember that, Daniel?" Daddy bent over and rubbed his knee. "I had to settle our score in the school parking lot one day after a couple of friends caught him keying my new car. And again when he bullied John Jukes."

"That's right . . . Ol' JJ . . . the moonshiner's son," Daniel mused. "You were quite the runner back then, before you tore up the knee with that scrape . . . Yeah, I remember all that, too." The agent gave Daddy a friendly whack on his back. "I'll never forget the time we got a'hold of his daddy's 'shine and used Mrs. Jukes's canning funnel to drink it. Chased the hooch down with her pickle brine! Damn, that was a long time ago. Wonder whatever happened to that scrawny kid?"

"Well, Daniel," Daddy said, returning a friendly slap to the agent's back, "that scrawny kid grew a few more inches, went to the city, and became a kickass police captain on the Louisville Police Department."

The men laughed softly, easing the tension in the room.

I went over to the sink to splash some water on my face, then reached for two mugs and filled them. I handed one to Bobby, and said, "So Daddy ran . . . I never knew." We both sat down, sipping more on the men's conversation than the drink.

Daddy glanced over at me. He looked so tired—hollowed— but he managed a ghost of a smile. I felt all the hurt and anger that had hugged stubbornly to my shoulders melt away. Though

I knew bitter words that branded the heart could not be easily cooled by the tongue, I made myself a promise right then. He was family. Every bit a part of my being, from my grit-colored eyes to the sturdy spirit that hammered at my soles. He was there, just like Mama was. I figured it was going to take a while and some more learning on my part to reckon with our heartbreaks and the past that hounded us in the present. But one thing was for certain: I needed him, and I would do whatever life called for to keep him close.

Before Special Agent Daniel left, he shook mine and Bobby's hands. "Nice work, kids. You've broken a case we've been working on for years. And because of this, a lot of folks are gonna be mighty appreciative." He turned to leave, but stopped, flipped open his briefcase, and pulled out the journal of the mistress of Hark Hill. The agent thumbed through its delicate cotton pages, then wagged it in front of Bobby. "Son, the trooper put this in the file, but I don't think we'll need it. I've cleared it with the assigned prosecutor. Maybe you'd like to have it as a keepsake for your kin?"

"Thanks, sir," Bobby said, taking the diary and holding it tight.

After another exchange of handshakes, Daddy pushed open the screen. I heard the agent's murmurs piggyback onto the screen door's clap. "Sorry about your loss, buddy. I know how much Ella meant to you." They moved onto the darkened porch. I shifted to a nearby window, leaning into their words with Bobby behind me.

Daddy grunted. "I worried like hell 'bout her being involved. Too dangerous." Grief hung in his throat. "Damn, if only I had protected her—gotten her out in time."

"Adam, we all thought Ella would be safe. You couldn't have known how bad and deep it ran. Hell, no one did. She agreed to keep McGee's books, to help make ends meet. Had no clue about his illegal dealings. Once she found out, she came straight to us. And, damn, I sure felt bad asking her to sign up as one of McGee's escorts for that upcoming party, just so we could get more witness on him. Guess I thought she could get us enough one last time and then get out quick and safe."

I let out a low breath, relieved, and let those words cycle around. My mama wasn't a whore. I'd felt it all along. Known it couldn't be true.

"Yeah," Daddy murmured, "I worried about how that would turn out, what with McGee's wandering eye and all those big shots looking for a good time. But she didn't listen to me. And here, I'd been blind drunk with guilt 'til I met with the Assistant U.S. Attorney today and compared notes. Turns out, Ella had already given them enough on McGee to move on the indictments, even without that ledger." He laughed, low and bitter.

"Sorry, buddy," Daniel said. "Seems like only yesterday when I'd stood at the wedding, toasting you two. *Damn.*"

I turned to Bobby, my eyes wide. "I can hardly believe it," I marveled.

Bobby smiled and draped his arm across my shoulder. "That's real cool, Mudas. Guess they really did love each other after all." I nodded, a wistful grin spreading across my face.

"I had big hopes," Daddy mourned. "Wanted to start over for real. Had this big plan: I was gonna take her to Liar's Bench and beg for her hand—do a headstand on an Osage ball, if that's what it took to get back to where we started. She'd gone to counseling, given up her bottle, same as me. I was real proud. Hopeful, Daniel . . . That gal had a rough life, losing her three sisters, her parents . . . and then what I'd put her through."

Bobby said, "Your mama sure was gutsy taking on all those powerful assholes. Brave like you."

"Brave . . ." I tasted the word and let the surety idle in my heart.

The two men stepped down from the porch and walked up the drive to the agent's car, the conversation fading as they went.

Alone, I clasped Bobby's hand. "You know what? Holding this diary makes me feel like I'm holding the truth—and shedding all those lies about Frannie and this town. Just like the Rooster Run ledger erases the stain on Mama and shines light on her truth. I'd like to show this to Ginny Meade, so she can set things right."

Bobby grew silent for a moment. "It's like Liar's Bench," he whispered, and touched the leather journal. "Your mama and my great-great-great gramma—bounded together by rope and by wood that soaked up the poison of all those lies—lies spun up on Hark Hill Plantation." He shook his head. "And both unbound by the plantation's books . . . there's blood in them books."

Daddy offered to take Bobby home since his truck wouldn't start, but he declined, asking if he could place a call to his parents for a ride instead. I knew Bobby did that for the two of us, so we could have a few more moments together.

After Daddy gave us permission to wait on the porch, he took a seat next to us. Bobby and I waited for him to leave. When he didn't, I fixed him with one of Grammy Essie's horned looks. He slipped quickly inside and let the squeak of the screen door smother his chuckle.

Bobby took my hand. We sat on the porch swing, fully charged, winding and rewinding everything that had happened, both tuckered out, but higher than two kites sailing on the gust of an April wind.

The air stirred. A warm breeze of jasmine and neighboring tobacco crops comforted us like a welcome-home hug. I rested my head on Bobby's shoulder and watched as the moon cast bluish slivers of light across our joined hands, disappearing into the wooden slats along the length of the porch.

We stood when a car's headlights bounced off the trees and watched as its beams illuminated the bottom of the drive.

"That's my folks."

"Guess you better go."

"Yeah."

"Yeah." I shifted.

"Yeah," he whispered, and slid his hand into his pocket and jiggled coins.

" 'Night, Bobby."

"Good night, Mudas." Halfway across the porch, he glanced back. "Girl, are you gonna kiss me good night or not?"

I lit across the boards. "I am." I laughed, pressing my lips to his—a lingering kiss that became a deep embrace. He lifted my hand, studying the cameo ring on my finger. "Tomorrow, I'm going down to Peck's and buying up all their Cracker Jacks. When I get my super-duper decoder ring, will you go steady with me?" He grinned a little sheepishly, waiting.

I felt my heart burst with happiness. "My Lucky Star wish comes true."

Bobby pulled me to him. I rested my head against his chest and snuggled in closer, inhaling his scent, savoring. The "good" scent, the one Grammy Essie had told me about. The one I'd been searching for. The one that curled toes and brought a dance to the eyes. The one that squeezed the heart, sweetened the tongue, and Tilt-A-Whirled the brain in sweet rays of warm sunshine.

In Bobby's arms, the world and all her cruelty slipped away, and the heaviness of my recent days disappeared on the night breeze.

28

To Each Is Given

It could've easily been left unnamed, but unlike most small towns carved out from the back roads of Anywhere, USA, that had their staples of folklore and history, Peckinpaw, Kentucky, had its Crow's Perch—a bench commemorating the benevolence of one of its most honorable daughters, Frannie Crow.

Used for both the telling of tales and for courting, the bench sat nestled between two pansy-filled copper pots that rested on the curb in front of the town's diner and leather goods store. And in western Kentucky, a good epilogue is the happily ever after of any tale, just as sure as the bench's weathered planks of oak and wrought-iron arms were the support.

Less than four weeks after we found Mrs. Anderson's diary, and a little more than a century after the hanging of Frannie Crow, I stood beside Daddy in Peckinpaw's packed, smoke-filled courtroom, with Genevieve cozied tight to my hip.

Daddy petitioned the judge to posthumously exonerate Frannie of her crimes, presenting Evelyn Amaris Anderson's journal as evidence—his only evidence—and two teens as the only eye-witnesses to its discovery. In closing, Daddy argued that the ruin of truth through cruelty only serves to weaken the very marrow of a town.

Three weeks later, the mayor delivered a proclamation to the townsfolk, dedicating the old Liar's Bench to Frannie Crow.

The summer after our senior year, Bobby headed to Boston, and I stretched my runner's legs to Louisville. I'd gotten my full track scholarship. Even Coach Grider smiled and congratulated me. I reckon Southern minds can bend with time, though not enough of them, or fast enough.

After the pleas and sentencing of McGee and the others, and after the deeper investigations and media reports had all died down, and folks' talk turned church-mouse-quiet when I happened upon them, I began to understand the part that would never leave me—that would never go away: two hangings more than a hundred years apart, as different from each other as the standing oak is from the sunflower in the field. But connected, too—connected by the fertile Kentucky soil and the evils they foretold.

Sometimes still, if I sit on Crow's Perch and cock my head just so, I can hear Grammy Essie quoting old St. Jerome, her words blowing through the Osage leaves like pieces of paper rattling around in a Dixie cup: "The scars of others should teach us caution," she whispers.

And somewhere, whether in Heaven or Hell or in between, the ghosts of Frannie Crow and Ella Mudas Tilley are smiling.

Below are old family recipes from mother-in-law Gladys Richardson's recipe box that you may want to try.

Red Cabbage Apple Casserole

5 or 6 slices bacon
3 tablespoons melted bacon fat
2 tablespoons apple jelly
2 tablespoons sugar
1 medium onion, chopped fine
2 tablespoons red wine vinegar
Dash of nutmeg
Sprinkle of cayenne pepper
1 teaspoon caraway seeds
1 large head of thinly sliced red or green cabbage
2 to 3 apples (use River Wolf for sweetness
    or Jonathan for tartness), peeled and thinly sliced
½ cup water
Salt (to taste)
Pepper (to taste)

Cook a few slices of bacon in skillet, set aside, save the bacon fat, and mix it with the sugar and jelly. Stir. Add onion and sauté. Stir in vinegar, nutmeg, and caraway seeds; then heat five minutes and set aside skillet mixture. Layer the thinly sliced cabbage and sliced apples in a lightly greased casserole dish. Pour on skillet mixture. Mix in crumbled cooked bacon. Add salt and pepper to taste. Pour in ½ cup water. Cover dish. Bake at 350 degrees for 75 minutes or until cabbage is tender.

Potato Candy

1 potato (size of egg)
1 pound powdered sugar
½ to 1 cup peanut butter
2 teaspoons Kentucky bourbon (optional)

Boil potato with peel on. When done, remove skin and mash.
Mix in powdered sugar while potato is hot, adding sugar a little
at a time. Sprinkle a biscuit board with powdered sugar and
knead mixture like dough. Roll out and spread the dough with
peanut butter like you would a slice of bread. (If using bourbon,
mix in with peanut butter before spreading.) Then roll up like a
jelly roll. Let the roll rest for 5 minutes before slicing.

LIAR'S BENCH

Kim Michele Richardson

ABOUT THIS GUIDE

The suggested questions are included
to enhance your group's reading of
Kim Michele Richardson's
Liar's Bench.

DISCUSSION QUESTIONS

1. The South of 1972 was not far removed from Freedom Riders, police dogs, and water blasts attacking peaceful protesters. How does the Civil Rights Movement influence Mudas? How does it affect her actions, her fears, and her relationship with Bobby?

2. Kentucky straddles the "deep" South and the Midwest's industrial heartland. Mama was torn between those two worlds. Bobby also feels the pull of the big city and dreams of "getting out" of Peckinpaw. Muddy also has high hopes for herself, but she feels a deep connection with her hometown. Do you think she will live out her days in Peckinpaw? Or will her aspirations take her elsewhere?

3. In the large majority of divorces, mothers retain primary custody of the children. In *Liar's Bench,* Muddy remains in her father's care, which would have been particularly unusual in the '70s. Is Adam a good father? Does his gender make him ill-equipped to parent a teenage girl? How might have Mudas's life turned out differently if she had continued to live with her mother?

4. *Liar's Bench* is infused with descriptions of the plants, the sky, the soil, the birds, and their songs. Have we, today, lost the ability to see, feel, and appreciate our natural surroundings? Have we become disconnected from nature?

5. In relation to Frannie and Amos, it is difficult to live with the specters of our past. Is it possible to move forward? Does history ever allow a clean slate?

6. Today, we live in the age of information. Everything is accessible, right at our fingertips. With that in mind, consider how Muddy's story would be different if it happened today. Would it be easier for her to find out the truth about her mama's death? Or would the wealth of information be a smoke screen, making it harder than ever to distinguish fact from fiction?

7. Imagine being a seventeen-year-old. That scary twilight-gray area of youth. Close to freedom, but still so far away. The constant undercurrent of *Liar's Bench* is Muddy's desire to shed the skin of her childhood and take on the shiny new coat of an adult. Has that process changed for young women since then? How? Is it easier or more difficult?

8. Grammy Essie explained "true love" to Muddy through scent. Our sense of smell plays a powerful part in our lives. How does the sense of smell affect your life, and how does it influence us, either romantically or in our culture? How does smell trigger emotional responses? Are there any particular scents that evoke childhood memories for you? What are they?

9. Title IX is a portion of the Education Amendments of 1972 that states (in part): "No person in the United States shall, on the basis of sex, be excluded from participation in, be denied the benefits of, or be subjected to discrimination under any education program or activity receiving Federal financial assistance . . ." Today, it's hard to imagine there was a time when girls couldn't participate in school sports because of gender. Are there any current policies that we will look back on, fifty years from now, and find unfathomable? Is this how we define progress?

10. "Most all of us kids were still riding on the coattails of the peace and love movement, trying to find ourselves, to let loose the flower child hidden in our barn-wide bell-bottoms," Mudas tells us. Meanwhile, hundreds of thousands of boys, including Bobby's older brother, are fighting overseas in Vietnam, brought there by choice or by the Draft. How does a war overseas affect life back home?

11. Do you have any family recipes that you treasure? Will you pass them on to the next generation in the same way that Mama gives Muddy the cabbage casserole recipe card and Grammy Essie makes potato candy? How are food and family linked?